Water
Burn

Christina J. Reyenga

Published by **Voventure** 2798 Bay Court , New Lenox, IL 60451

ISBN:
ISBN-13: **978-0615575902**
ISBN-10: 0615575900

First Edition

DEDICATION

To Dad and Mom

What Readers Have Said…

"Christina moves the story along, she doesn't drag. She grabs you in the beginning…"

"This story could be made into a movie, I felt like I was seeing it in my head."

"This is a gripping story in the romance-paranormal genre."

"I liked 'Beastly', I loved 'Water Burn'."

"Right from the prologue I could not put Water Burn down."

Facebook Fan page:
http://www.facebook.com/christina.reyenga

Twitter:
https://twitter.com/#!/search/realtime/cjreyenga

Author's Webpage: www.reyenga.net

ACKNOWLEDGMENTS

I'd like to acknowledge first of all my dad and mom here as this is my first published novel. They've encouraged me in my dream of writing "stories" since I was too little to write real sentences. Thank you for your time, effort, and love.

Ron, Cheri, Michael, Michelle, Jon, and Jenny, you were the whole reason I even started writing Water Burn. The numerous times Michelle, Jenny, my sisters, and I spent on Teal Lake growing up, planted the seeds of this story in my head. Your friendship over the years is greatly appreciated.

A big "Thank-You" to Dawn, Bill, Lauren and Angela! The week Ryley (the little black city poodle who didn't understand why we were in the middle of nowhere for a week) and I spent up in the north woods with you was incredible and a learning experience I will never forget. Your hospitality and ability to answer my questions and get me out and about in Hayward were beyond valuable. Without you, Water Burn would not have been possible.

Laurie, Donya, Brianna, Ann, Abigail, Rachel, Sarah, Stephanie and Rowena, thanks for taking interest, talking, and listening!

Jaclyn, thanks for attending writers' conferences, movies, and spending hours of "author" talk with me. Our similar interest in fantasy and the "unusual" is a part of our friendship I'll always love.

Finally, I'd like to mention my husband, who despite his teasing and amusement out of making me watch scary movies is a full support to my writing and creativity. You make my life a romance, Joshua. Thank you for your love.

Prologue

Water.

Rain pattered on the window panes of my cabin. Most would find it soothing, but my breath stuck in my throat as I glared at the tantalizing droplets on the glass. Each glittering splotch tempted me. "We want you," they seemed to call, "and you *know* you want us."

As I gripped the arms of my chair, I pondered my life up to this point, and why I wanted to experience the liquid running down my skin.

Hush. Drop. Drip.

The sound of the rain reminded me of seductive whispering, and I longed to close my other senses as well as I could close my eyes. I was cursed.

Splash.

The sound of a disturbance on the lake took away all reflections—I wanted it now! Water. The feeling of it against my skin, so cold and smooth. I lunged out the door, and my heart fluttered with excitement as the rain soaked through my clothes. The taste, smell, and touch of it melded together in a delicious combination of the senses. I stripped my shirt and jeans off and dove into the lake. Water embraced every inch of me, bubbling underneath, tickling my stomach, legs, and tail. Regret set in as I bobbed above the depths of the lake, and I realized what I'd done. The blood in my face grew hot, and I clenched my fists under the light waves. I knew I'd never be returning to shore again.

1

- Five months earlier -

I'd chosen my green dress—the same color as my eyes—which gathered at my trim waist. Taking off my glasses and putting in contacts, I studied myself in the mirror to make sure everything was correct. Flicking a couple of strawberry blonde curls away from my eyes and fixing my bra so it wouldn't show in the low neckline of my dress, I allowed myself to indulge in a little vanity.

"Jeanine, get down here!" Mom called up the stairs.

"I'm coming!" I shouted back, and with one last glance in the mirror I hurried down the stairs to see Mom standing on the bottom, her hair in its usual tight bun.

"Go into the basement and get some wine."

"'Mom, most everyone coming to the party is underage," I said, hoping to avoid a trip to the basement. I was bound to get dust on my dress, as the basement was being remodeled.

Mom crossed her arms. "I know, dear, but there are also going to be adults there. And don't think we're going to let you graduate without a toast." She smiled.

Giving in, I hurried down the hall toward the basement door. The scent of cut wood and welding struck my nostrils as I walked down the stairs. Everything about the basement seemed different. The plaster from the first remodeling had been removed to reveal that our basement's walls originally had been made completely of stone, like a dungeon's.

The wine was stored in a large room in the left corner of our basement. The Chardonnay was my mom and dad's favorite. No need to bother with turning on the lights; I'd memorized our wine cellar room. I reached out in front of me where I knew the Chardonnay was stored, but instead of the smooth glass of a bottle, my hand touched something sharp. Reaching up for the light, I flicked it on so I could see what had pricked me.

A small blade glinted in the light; it reminded me of a dagger you'd see in a movie set in medieval times. Picking the dagger up to examine it, I noticed that the silver-tinted hilt was shaped like some sort of lizard or snake, but looked almost human at the same time. Its long, silver tail curled partway up the blade. Creepy. What was it doing in our basement? Numerous times had I been sent down to get wine, and I'd never seen it before. The dagger had been lying on the shelf below the Chardonnay. I knelt down for a closer look but fell backward. Landing in an open space was not what I expected to happen, but I fell flat on my back instead of leaning on the wall that had always been there before.

Thick dust flew everywhere, getting into my eyes and nose. Great. My dress probably didn't look so hot on me anymore. Blinking my stinging eyes and snuffling out the irritating dust specks in my nostrils, my eyes finally focused to see an entrance to another room inside the wine cellar, a room that was revealed after the plaster had been removed. Bringing myself to my feet, I stared into the darkness of it. I hadn't noticed it, because I hadn't turned on the lights before now. It was a gaping black hole in the wall. The thought of a secret room in my own house intrigued me. After all, historically significant stuff was what I lived for now, since I was going to be a history major. It'd be a great story to tell everyone in my history classes. I'd have to come back with a flashlight.

"Jeanine." Dad's voice made me jump, and I whirled around, the dagger still in my hand. Dad's gaze went down to its sharp point. "What are you doing?"

"I was getting the wine for Mom," I said.

"Well, you took long enough," Dad snorted. His gray hair and mustache were well-groomed for the party tonight.

"What is this room?" I took a step into the black hole.

"They found it after tearing off the plaster, along with that." Dad pointed at the dagger. "Not sure what the room was used for, nor why that was in there. There's also a basin in the center of the room filled with water."

This last bit sparked my interest. Who had made this room? Why had they made it? And why had they plastered it over when they first remodeled?

For once in a long time, I felt excited about something. My graduation party could wait, not this amazing mystery right here in my own basement. Then a thought struck me, "Is Grandpa Stafford coming tonight?"

"Yes." Dad's face turned to a scowl at the mention of Grandpa. He grabbed the bottle of Chardonnay from me. "No more about this room. You've got guests already arriving." He turned to head up the stairs.

I followed him, but my hopes grew as I thought about Grandpa coming. He knew more and cared more about our family history than anyone else.

Arriving up the stairs threw me into a whole world of party guests. I must have spent longer in the basement than I'd thought.

"Jeanine, that green on you looks beautiful." Diana's familiar ivory-toned face came into view as I turned the corner in my house.

"Thanks," I said, giving her a quick hug with my free hand. So my dress hadn't been ruined.

"What are you holding?" Diana's dark eyes were focused on the dagger I'd taken up with me.

Feeling heat rush to my face, I lowered it. "I found it in the basement; I was going to put it away."

"Greg is here." She waved off my oddity as usual and began talking about boys..

"Oh, goodie," I muttered, giving her a frown.

"The date didn't go well, I take it?" Diana's lips curled upward.

"You could say that." I paused before adding, "I sort of left before anything happened."

"You'll never end up having any fun," Diana said frowning. "I really don't understand you."

"Hey, I gave it a try, okay?" Upon seeing her frown remain, I added, "I can't wait to date college boys."

Diana's face brightened. "You're right. Me either. It'll be so much better than these immature guys we have to deal with now." She put her arm in mine. "Come on, I'm going to introduce you to my boyfriend, Sean."

"Wait, you have a boyfriend?"

"I do now." Diana grinned. "That's why I was hoping you and Greg were together. You at least should have given him a try," she whispered with a giggle.

I wanted to ask, Since he wasn't good enough for her, why would he be good enough for me? But I just rolled my eyes.

A macho guy stood by the lemonade table. Diana had probably met him while modeling. He appeared to be about as boring as any guy could get. He smiled when he saw Diana, but then his eyes traveled to me, or at least traveled down my neckline. Yuck.

I scanned the room. Everyone looked the same. They all were here for my graduation, they all were dressed up, and they all were rich people that I'd known my entire life. But a tall gentleman with white hair caught my eye. A long hooked nose with spectacles on the end of it was probably his most prominent feature. Grandpa Stafford.

Pulling free from Diana's arm, I gave her boyfriend a little wave. "It's nice to meet you."

"I'm Sean." He extended a hand. His eyes flickered to the dagger and widened.

Switching the dagger to my other hand, I took his hand. "Jeanine," I told him, like a polite debutante. I turned to Diana. "I've got to get back to my guests, Diana. I'll talk to you in a little bit."

Hurrying toward Grandpa, I put my free arm around him. "Grandpa, I'm so glad you could come!"

"Congratulations, Jeanine!" Grandpa said, smiling at me. Besides his white hair and wrinkled skin, he didn't seem very old. Standing a good 10 inches taller than my 5'6" height, he was an intimidating sight. He gave me a squeeze in return for my embrace.

Holding the dagger in front of him, I took a step back. "What do you think?"

Grandpa's face grew serious, and he narrowed his gray eyes. His withered hand took the dagger from me. He turned it over and scanned the blade and hilt, running his rough fingers across the tail of the intricately carved creature with reverence. Grandpa's many stories over the years of historical findings had always fascinated me. I could hardly wait for his explanation to my discovery. Finally, he spoke. "Where did you get this?"

"In the basement."

"Where in the basement?" His deep voice turned to a whisper.

"In the wine cellar. There's more though," I said.

His eyes met mine. "What?"

"They found a room after the plaster had been pulled away."

Grandpa's gaze went over the dagger again. "Show me."

Taking his arm, I led him toward the door of the basement. Someone's hand touched my shoulder before we could go down the stairs, and before actually seeing whose it was, I knew: Greg's.

"Jeanine, we need to talk."

"Go ahead without me. I'll join you in a second," I told Grandpa.

Grandpa raised his bushy white brows at both of us before nodding and continuing down the stairs.

"Yes?" I asked Greg, crossing my arms over my chest.

"You just left me last night." Greg frowned.

My eyes left his face and stared at the ceiling. "And?"

"And, Jeanine, I know you don't think we could work out, but I think you're my true love," he whined, his words sounding so cliché I almost gagged.

"Sure you do," I said. Focusing my gaze again on the basement door, my pulse pumped with impatience. By now, Grandpa had already found the room and was looking through it without me. Turning from Greg, I began down the stairs. "I'll talk to you later; right now, I really don't have time." Shutting the door behind me to give a clear message that he'd better not follow, I hurried down the steps and into the wine cellar.

Grandpa stood staring at the expanse of darkness the secret room's entrance created. He held the dagger up into the wine cellar's light. Taking his spectacles off, he squinted his eyes, studying the dagger again.

"Why did they cover this room, you think?"

"I'm not sure, but I've heard stories about this. I never believed they were true."

"Huh?"

Grandpa's voice had again dropped to a whisper. "They say that our ancestors originally immigrated to America to escape religious persecution. Most of them were part of a strange sect." Grandpa produced a lighter from his pocket and directed it into the darkness of the room. "My grandfather used to tell me about a room he'd sealed up because it was cursed."

"Cursed?" The flicker of the lighter's fire cast dancing shadows across the inscribed walls. The room was rounded, and as my dad had claimed, a huge basin was in the center, filled with water. A constant drip from the ceiling plunked inside the basin.

"He said the room had been used for rituals and blood sacrifices," said Grandpa.

Curiosity sparked, and my adrenaline pumped harder. I took a step into the room. "Was that what the dagger was used for, then?" I asked, narrowing my eyes.

"Perhaps," Grandpa said, giving me a mysterious smile. "Come on, let's take a closer look." He held the lighter up to the walls. "See these paintings and writings on the walls? It describes what they needed to do."

"Needed to do?" My spine prickled when I caught sight of the floor; a smeared handprint-like stain of a rusty color stood out against the dark stones next to the basin. "Dried blood?" I pointed to it.

Grandpa nodded. "It would seem."

"Weird, but interesting," I murmured.

"You'd think so…" Grandpa's voice trailed off as he kept staring at the marked-up walls. Weird symbols and pictures were among the etchings.

"I knew you'd like to come down here and see this," I said, pride swelling within me.

"I'm glad you told me about it, because your father should seal up this room again," Grandpa said, his voice almost too deep to hear.

My gaze shifted to him, and I noticed he no longer seemed amused by the room. His gray eyes darted about the walls, and worry lines formed on his brow. Without warning, he let go of the switch on the lighter. Except for the faint glimmer of light shining in from the wine cellar, we were encased in darkness.

All the excitement I'd had about going in the room now vanished like the glow from Grandpa's lighter. "Seal it up again? Are you crazy?"

"There must have been a reason before." Grandpa shrugged and stepped out of the room. "I think it'd be best to put the dry wall over this when they finish remodeling."

"What? Why?" Then I realized Grandpa was joking and trying to freak me out. Letting out a laugh, I stepped out of the room to join him and patted his shoulder. "Grandpa, I should go get a flashlight. Maybe we can figure out what they used to do in there."

"Jean, listen to me when I say I don't think that would be a good idea."

"How could you seriously believe in stupid mumbo jumbo like that? This room is harmless. Our ancestors were superstitious."

"Jean, please promise me that you won't go back in this room." His face seemed made of stone.

Just like that, the one man whom I thought had understood me, betrayed me. Trying not to show the disappointment on my face, I took the dagger from the shelf and hurried out of the room in the wine cellar. I didn't want to talk about it anymore.

2

Digging in my drawer for the flashlight I kept in case of power outages, I thought about what I needed to do. Whether or not Grandpa wanted me to, I was going to investigate that room further. Grandpa didn't see this as a chance for us to learn more about our family history. Well, I'd prove him wrong. Noise from below my bedroom told me that the party was still going on and that no one was missing me.

No one missed me.

That thought hit like an arrow to the heart. Maybe I'd discover something amazing in that room downstairs, something that would change history! They'd have to notice me then. I was a boring stick in the mud. Jeanine. But soon, that'd be different. Imagine the stories I'd be able to tell my roommates and classmates at college. Famous people would want to meet me.

My hand struck something hard between the clothes in my drawer, and I brought it out to reveal the flashlight. I grasped a book about ancient symbols from my shelf. Maybe it would help me decode what the walls in the room said. Slipping all of this into my backpack, along with the dagger, I hurried down the stairs and crept past the party guests into the basement again.

Feeling rather giddy, with my pulse quickening, I entered the secret room. Flicking my flashlight on, I scanned the walls, searching for an answer to the purpose of this room. The word "thy" and a picture of the dagger Dad had found were in the first block, then the words "shall draw." There was a symbol on the wall, then the words "into thy basin." I opened the symbol book and scanned through its many pages. The symbol meant blood, so I assumed my ancestors had placed blood into the basin using the dagger to cut themselves.

I wanted to relive what they had done, but hesitated. Here I was where possibly hundreds of years ago, my ancestors had done what this writing said. Didn't all the great historians reenact things to better understand what people did long ago? Curiosity overwhelmed me. Taking the dagger, I glanced around. There was no blood except my own in this room. Trying not to close my eyes, I brought the dagger to my palm and made a quick slice. Red appeared in the wound, and I held my hand over the basin. Blood dripped into the water, the sound of it echoing against the walls. A chill of excitement rushed through me. What did they do next? I shone the flashlight on the wall again: "Wet," symbol, "with basin," and symbol.

I scanned through the book and found that the missing words were "body" and "water." Translation: wet body with basin water. Yuck. That seemed a little disgusting. My blood polluted this water, and who knows how long the water had been standing here. Whatever, I could take a shower afterwards. Dipping my hands in the water, I splashed myself with it, but I realized I had gotten it on my fancy dress as well. *I can always get my parents to buy me a new one,* I assured myself.

Shining the flashlight on the wall again, I read the symbols and words. "Wet body with basin water five more times, and take thy dagger to bleed into thy basin once more." Finishing the ritual, I felt proud of myself. The water in the basin seemed so attractive now, like what I had been doing was a game at a water park. Besides the letting of blood, of course. I turned to the last part of the writing, but it was made entirely of symbols -- symbols that were not in my book.

"I told you not to come back here!" Grandpa's voice boomed.

Turning around, I laughed. "Grandpa, come on, I—"

"What were you doing?" Grandpa stepped in the room; his tall frame seemed more frightening than usual. Then his eyes noticed how wet I was. "You did what the writing said?" His eyes widened.

"I—"

"How could you be so stupid?" Grandpa growled. "Do you know what you just did?"

"I couldn't read the rest of the symbols, so I didn't finish—"

"Oh, you finished, all right; you just brought a curse on yourself!"

At the mention of a curse, my breath caught in my throat for a moment. "What do you mean? This was a ritual."

"Look, I will tell you what those symbols say!" Grandpa pointed at the wall, so I shone my flashlight on them.

"Now this be thy fate, a serpentine monster of lakes.

Driven away from man, may for water thou burn instead of land.

Only truest love shall unbind, this curse to which thou shall be tied."

The words gave me goose bumps, but I remained calm. Grandpa had to know that was a bunch of garbage. "Come on, Grandpa, stop it." The words were said to calm me, more than anything.

"That ritual was done to enemies. They didn't do it to themselves, and now you've just—"

"Grandpa, relax, nothing happened to me." I stood and held out my hand. "See? I got a little cut. That's the worst that's happened." After a long pause, I added in a firm and logical-sounding voice, "There is no reality or truth in this. It's just something people did long ago." Although, I had to admit, our ancestors were pretty screwed up if they had tried to put hexes on people.

Grandpa stared at me, studying my soaked clothing and my face. His expression grew calm. "Maybe you're right."

"Good. Now why did you come down here?"

"Everyone was wondering where the graduate went," Grandpa said, his face beginning to brighten. "I guess, you're right, Jean; I was just being superstitious."

"I'll join you in a second. Let me put a new dress on and clean up." Disappointment set in. All I'd learned from this experience, was that my ancestors were crazy enough to think they could curse their enemies with stupid rituals. Still, it'd make an interesting story to tell people when I got to college.

Grandpa turned to leave. "Okay, I'll let them know you'll be a minute or so."

"Thanks," I said. After packing my flashlight, book, and the dagger inside my backpack, I walked away from the secret room and tip-toed up the stairs. Slipping past the party guests again so no one would notice how horrible my dress and water-smeared makeup were, I arrived in my room in record time. Having my own bathroom comes in handy sometimes. Turning on the faucet, I dunked my face under the water.

As I cleaned up, an extreme cramp went through my shoulders. Giving a small gasp, I staggered backwards. My head grew dizzy, and a prickling sensation, like the kind that one gets when their limbs fall asleep, spread throughout my entire body, creeping its way into my limbs. I grasped at my arms to make sure my circulation wasn't cut off. My breath left me when almost unbearable pain seared through my spine. Something strong was pinching the back of my neck. Putting both hands on the sides of the sink's counter to support myself, my gaze caught on one of the most ghastly sights ever beheld: A monster stared back at me. Its pupils were slits instead of round. The entire body of the creature was covered in smooth gold, green, and brown scales that formed diamond patterns in its skin, much like a lizard's. Realization dawned. My fears were confirmed when I raised my own hand, only to see that the monster's webbed and clawed fingers moved with mine.

R-r-rip

Fabric in my dress tore to accommodate a painful addition of sharp spines running down my back. It stopped, but soreness remained as a shadow of the intense pain I'd experienced seconds before. Minutes seemed to pass as I stared into the mirror, my serpentine eyes blinking back at me. My ears had turned pointed and long.

At that moment, I came to the conclusion that I must have never woken up this morning; this entire event was a dream. Our house didn't have a secret room in its basement that our ancestors had used to curse people. Any second now, I'd wake up and find myself getting ready for the party guests. My nice green dress would be in one piece, hung up in my closet, instead of in tatters swinging from the sharp spikes that ridged my vertebrae.

"Jeanine!" Mom's voice called up the stairs.

Wake up.

"Jeanine, we're all waiting for you! We're going to make a toast!" Dad joined in, sounding more than irritated.

"I'm coming!" I shouted back, my voice sounded scratchy and out of tune. It hissed and had lost much of its sweetness.

"Hurry up!" Mom yelled.

"Be down in a few minutes!" I answered back, trying to correct my voice without success.

Wake up.

Someone's footsteps sounded on the stairs. To become a monster was one thing. But to be discovered by my family and everyone I knew -- at my own graduation party -- would be beyond humiliating.

Wake up!

Why couldn't I awaken from this nightmare? Scrambling out of the bathroom, I tripped over something. Craning my neck, I realized with further dismay that, not only was I covered in scales and spines, but I also had a very long and snaky tail. To make matters worse, walking upright with it seemed almost impossible. I crawled toward my bed, wishing to hide under the covers. Once I reached the bed, a new sensation occurred that felt refreshing, like water poured over me. Catching sight of my hands, I realized my skin had once again returned to its natural creamy, smooth appearance.

The door swung open at that moment.

3

Mom stood in my doorway, her hands on her hips, hair tied in its usual style, and irritation etched in the lines on her face. "And just what do you think you're—" Her words stopped, and she stood with her mouth hanging open, staring at my tatters of clothes.

I tried to use what was left to cover me more, but it was pointless.

"What the hell have you done to your dress, Jeanine?" At last her voice returned.

"Ripped it?" Unable to think of anything else to say, I felt my cheeks burn. Should I tell her about what had just happened? No. Not yet, at least. Maybe it had been a hallucination and I'd imagined it happening because Grandpa had freaked me out in the basement. But no, my clothes were torn.

"Never mind. I don't want to know," Mom said, putting her hand to her forehead and closing her eyes. Letting out a long breath, she added, "Just get something decent on and come downstairs." Turning around in a flourish of skirts, Mom shut the door behind her with a bang.

I stood there, holding the clothing pieces up to cover myself. Shock set in. My body began to shake. My limbs wouldn't work, even though I willed them to walk toward my closet. Inhaling deeply, I tried once again to move. My steps were shaky. "It didn't happen," I said aloud. "It didn't happen, because you're not still a monster." The curse said that I'd become a monster, but that would be a full-time thing if it had placed itself on me. Besides, who believed that sort of crap? If curses like this could happen, then why aren't there lots of monsters discovered every day?

Tap. Tap.

Someone was knocking on my door. "Wh-who is there?" I stuttered.

"Grandpa," his deep voice answered.

Oh, great, I thought. Holding the torn fabric closer to myself, my limbs began functioning again. I dug in my closet for a dress, but realized that my bra and underwear weren't doing their proper job anymore. "Give me a minute," I said, hurrying to my dresser.

"Don't rush," Grandpa said.

After my Mom's tirade, I was beginning to wonder what my party guests must think of me. Slipping into a simple blue dress, I opened the door.

Grandpa stood there, and his gaze traveled to my face. "What's going on?"

A shiver went up my spine. He knew that something strange had happened. I hoped he wasn't thinking about the curse I'd supposedly brought on myself. Words wouldn't form on my tongue, despite the fact that I wanted to explain myself.

"What happened to your other dress?" Grandpa arched his brows inward, forming a V on his forehead. He pointed toward the discarded heap by my dresser.

"Didn't like it anymore."

"Jeanine, what *really* happened?" Grandpa crossed his arms.

"Nothing," I answered, but I could feel my pulse in my neck and face. My world was spinning. "I need to get downstairs." Without another word, I brushed past him, but I could sense his eyes following me.

Once I appeared back at the party, Diana rushed to my side. "Where did you go? I've been looking everywhere for you." She grabbed my arm. "Come on, they're going to make a toast to you."

"Uh, okay." My mind felt over-stimulated. A glass was shoved in my hand.

Dad stepped forward from the crowd, holding his glass in front of him. "Jeanine Stafford, I am very proud of you. You've shown devotion to your schoolwork, and from a very young age you've been interested in history." Dad paused for emotional effect. "I still remember you in pigtails asking Grandpa all sorts of questions." This was the part where I was supposed to cry, but I felt nothing. The speech sounded practiced, probably created by Dad's secretary even. "Your mother and I love you and wish you the best in these next defining years of your life." Raising his glass, Dad said, "So cheers to my beautiful and talented daughter, Jeanine!"

Out of the corner of my eye, I noticed Corrine holding a glass of water up and giggling with her friend over how grownup they were to be toasting along with everyone else. For a moment, my eyes focused on the water as she lifted the glass to her mouth. Something strange happened in that moment: It was as if the only two things in this large room were the water glass and I. But Corrine downed the water, breaking the spell, and everyone returned. They were staring at me, waiting for me to drink to my dad's toast.

I raised my glass and took a sip. The Chardonnay stung my taste buds. I didn't like wine very much. I preferred water. Setting down the glass on a table, my mind remained muddled, but I tried to smile. The longer I felt normal, the more I began to doubt that anything strange had happened. A growing sense of unease plagued me, but I walked toward Diana and her boyfriend, not knowing what else to do. I sure didn't want to see Greg right now.

"So why did you change your dress?" Diana asked.

"It was getting uncomfortable," I lied.

"That's a pity; it was so pretty on you." Diana smiled. "So what are you going to do this summer? Got any plans?"

"Um, I was thinking of visiting Washington D.C.," I answered, beginning to feel like my old self. "Figure it'd be great to visit some historical sights and get ready for college."

A rough, worn hand touched my arm. "Jeanine," Grandpa's voice said. He held pieces of my dress in his hands.

"Yes?"

Grandpa smiled at Diana and Sean. "If you'll excuse me, I'm going to steal my granddaughter from you just a moment."

After we were away from the party guests, my plastered-on smile disappeared. "What is it?"

"Tell me what happened upstairs," Grandpa said. "Tell me why this dress is torn up. And don't lie to me, because I promise you, I will figure it out."

"I, uh, don't remember exactly how it got torn."

Grandpa raised to my view something that sparkled. It was a glass of water. "Are you sure you don't remember?"

My eyes stared at the glass for a moment. I'd never noticed how water swirled around when in a cylinder. It was beautiful.

"Why are you so enthralled with this water?" Grandpa asked, snapping my mind away from it.

"I'm not," I defended, but my eyes darted again to its transparent surface.

"The curse did take effect," Grandpa said. His gaze went to the glass. "You got water on yourself while upstairs—"

"What does that have to do with anything?"

"—and you transformed into a monster."

"Grandpa!" I shushed. "Please, don't say that out loud." Seeing the look of sadness on his face made me want to slap him. "And you're wrong."

"Then you wouldn't mind me pouring this water on you?" Grandpa lifted the glass. Its contents swirled.

How could he? Did he think this was a joke? Here, right in front of the party guests? They were still in visual range of me. Maybe it wouldn't be a bad idea to take him to a private room where he could pour water on me and see nothing happen. In fact, I wanted to test his theory. Plus, the sensation of water on my skin would feel good. Grandpa walked toward the bathroom next door to Dad's office.

"Just don't get any water on the floor," I joked. Somehow I just couldn't believe that what had happened before would happen again.

Grandpa splashed a tiny drop on me, and for a moment it felt welcome as it dripped down my arm. Then pain in my spine occurred much like before. Groaning as the spines and scales began appearing, a sense of dread fell like a heavy weight upon me. Grandpa pulled his handkerchief from his pocket and rubbed dry the spot where the water had contacted me. The pain subsided, and the spines and scales sucked themselves back before another one of my dresses was ruined. Phew.

"Horrible," Grandpa murmured. "Don't tell anyone about this."

As if that wasn't obvious? I wouldn't tell anyone about this even if my life depended on it, but the only words I could squeak out were, "I won't."

Silence after saying this made me even more nervous. What was Grandpa thinking? Part of me was disappointed he'd seen the transformation, because now I couldn't deny that it had happened. Even now, I denied it from settling in my mind, despite what I'd just gone through.

"We're going to have to figure out how to keep this a secret until you can break the curse," Grandpa said, killing the silence.

"Break it?" Something loud happened outside of the office; the party was getting crazier.

"You have to have true love shown."

"Huh?"

"Remember the writing on the wall in the room? It's the one way this curse can be broken." Grandpa dumped the rest of the glass of water in the sink. "Shown truest love."

I watched the water slither down the drain until I realized what I was doing. Scrunching my eyes shut for a second, I visualized my monster form again. Water is a bad thing now. "Shown truest love?" I questioned. Everything I knew about life previously, I'd begun to doubt. Do I even know what true love is? "How do I find that?" I asked aloud.

"I'm not sure." Grandpa sighed. "Maybe it's even more complicated than it sounds."

"Or simpler than it sounds." Growing hope began to sprout. "Maybe all I have to do is find someone to love."

"Find someone to love...." Grandpa's voice trailed off.

Just thinking about what this curse–if it remained–would do to my future made me shudder. Forget going to Yale; forget escaping my family and stagnant friends. Who could rid me of this curse quick enough that I could be free this summer and go to school this fall without anyone finding out about it?

4

"Enjoying the party, Greg?" I asked.

Grandpa stood a good distance away. I knew he was watching, but I didn't care.

Greg raised a brow. "Changed your mind about me?"

"You said that you thought I was your true love. Those are powerful words, you know," I remarked, putting my arm in his.

Greg's face lit up. "I guess they are."

I dipped my voice into a sweet whisper. "And you look really handsome tonight, I might add."

"Yeah, I guess I do." Greg laughed, his egotistic personality so apparent I wanted to puke. "Maybe it's because I knew I'd be seeing you." He winked.

Oh gosh, did I have to put up with this? So many things about him turned me off, but then an image of my monster face staring back at me in the mirror made me grip his arm tighter. Think about true love. True love. I love him. Love is a choice. Right? That's what they always say. I choose to truly love this guy, and I need to show him. "I'm thinking of giving you a second chance. Maybe tomorrow?" I asked. Giving him a huge smile, I turned. "I'd better say goodnight to everyone now, but don't worry. I think we're going to have a wonderful time tomorrow night. Don't you?"

"Yeah," Greg said. Something about the way Greg smiled back caused me sudden irritation. He thought he held me in his hand now. But it didn't matter because, like it or not, I needed him.

*

"Last night was not the time to be antisocial," Mom scolded me at breakfast. "It was just plain rude of you to abandon your party guests."

A sleepless night had left my eyelids feeling like they were made of iron. Grandpa sat across from me, and Corrine sat beside me at the table. Dad had already gone to work for the day. I hoped Mom had forgotten about the dress because I had no explanation. All I needed to do was avoid water until night. Then the curse would be broken, and the entire mess would be over.

Sounds of rushing water brought my head up. Where was the noise coming from? Patty stood at the kitchen sink washing dishes. The water ran down the plate she was scrubbing like an avalanche. How would it be if I stepped over there and let the water sweep over me like that, too? Realization of my thoughts occurred, and my face heated up.

Ignore it, I told myself, clenching my fists. Ignore it and go upstairs. Right now. Standing and taking a step away from the table, I was interrupted in my escape by Corrine.

"Where are you going, Jeanine? Mom said you had to help clean up the house."

"C-clean the house?" My mind had to work fast. "That's not going to work because—"

Grandpa stood and cut me off. "Because I am going to take her to New York City today."

"You are?" Corrine stuck out her bottom lip in a pout. "But I had wanted to go with next time you went."

"That will have to wait till next time, baby." Grandpa patted Corrine's head. "This is a special graduation present."

"How come you didn't tell me about this before you came, Dad?" Mom asked.

"We just decided last night while we were in the wine cellar,"

Grandpa said, grinning at me.

"Okay, well, don't be back too late; I heard that Jeanine is going on a date with Greg tonight." Mom laughed. She'd taken the bait.

*

We had traveled around the buildings of New York City without once getting out of the car. I guess Grandpa had wanted to make sure no one else saw me as a monster. He dropped me off for my date with Greg.

"So you're going to break the curse with that boy?" Grandpa asked.

"Yep." I chewed on my lip.

"Are you sure he's your true love?"

"Of course, Grandpa. He even said it himself."

"Then why haven't I heard you say it?"

His cynicism got to me. "Because I wasn't going out with him before."

"I sometimes act more like your father than my son does." Grandpa said.

"Dad's busy." I don't know why I'm defended Dad. He's never been there for me at all. I don't even know what to say to him when I see him. His speech had been like the inside of a balloon: filled with air.

"I feel responsible for what's happened." Grandpa sighed.

Thoughts that had haunted me during my restless night returned. "What will my parents do if they find out?"

"It's hard to say. They don't believe in that sort of stuff, do they?"

"What do you mean?"

"Like supernatural stuff."

His words sounded pretty absurd. I laughed. "Um....I don't either."

Grandpa cocked a brow. "You don't?"

It was like a smack to the face. I didn't believe in the supernatural, and yet I'd believed that I was cursed. "Maybe I do...." My voice lost itself in my thoughts. Would my parents believe that, scientifically, something was wrong with me? They might take me to a bunch of doctors and specialists before they sent me to a lab to be experimented on. Grandpa had a point. He'd been the only person who'd witnessed me performing the curse and who knew about the history of our house.

"Grandpa, did your father tell you anything more about that room? Like why he sealed it up?"

"He said it was cursed, and it had nothing to do with our family anymore." Grandpa shrugged. "I never believed him, but I got this strange feeling going in there. Then I read the walls and thought it best that we leave the place alone like my parents did." Grandpa paused. We had pulled up to Greg's parents' nice-sized house. "My father was always a smart man, but he had a lot of belief in the supernatural too."

"Which is what I lacked," I said, sighing. Even now I felt rather stupid for having performed a ritual like I had, especially one involving my own blood being shed. Glancing down at my hand, I noticed the small cut still there as a reminder of what I'd done. "This whole thing will be over tonight."

"Yes," Grandpa whispered, unbelief crinkling his old brow.

Thanks, Grandpa.

"Pick me up at eleven," I told him. "I'll call you if I need you earlier." I shut the door behind me before he could say any more "encouraging" words.

Taking a deep breath, I rang the doorbell. Greg answered it, his features too smug. It was as if he knew I needed him. "I think you have the wrong house," Greg said, chuckling at his own joke.

I tried to laugh with him. "Very funny. Are your parents home?"

"No," Greg said, winking. "Come on in."

Feeling like a robot controlled by someone else, I placed my arms around his neck and smashed my lips against his.

Greg responded by pulling me in closer and kissing me back.

He wasn't a bad kisser per se, but I felt repulsed all the same. My tongue curled back, as if not wishing to come in contact with his as it began exploring my mouth. Pulling back, I forced a smile at him. "I think this night is going to be pretty spectacular." Sheesh, I was beginning to get as bad as him with my insinuations.

"I'll have to agree. I didn't know you could kiss."

Forget about his annoying habits. Focus on breaking the curse. The sound of rushing water reached my ears and I froze. I'd forgotten all the fountains his family had in their house. In the foyer, there was a fountain of a stone girl pouring water out of a jug.

Sh-sh-sh.

Its sound was soothing, and the water fell with graceful, smooth beauty.

"Jeanine?"

Closing my eyes, I turned toward Greg. "Yes?"

"Come on, we can go outside by the pool if you want." Greg took my hand.

"Okay," I answered, following him.

"Why this sudden change?" Greg asked.

I shifted my gaze down at his hand holding mine. "What do you mean?"

"Well…." Greg grinned at me while saying this, "I'm not an idiot. You used to be so uptight. After all this time, why are you letting go?"

"Maybe something happened to me yesterday that changed my mind," I said, winking at him. "You did say that I was your true love."

"Well, I didn't propose marriage or anything." Greg snorted out a laugh.

"Did you mean it when you said I was your true love?"

Greg's smile disappeared, and I could feel his hand tense. "I guess."

"Well, I think that you're my true love, too," I said, smiling at him and squeezing his hand.

"That's good," Greg mumbled.

We reached the back patio and the glistening water of his pool.

To my surprise, Greg scooped me up in his arms. "Come on, let's go in the pool!"

"What!" I screamed. We neared the water's edge, and I beat him with my fists. "Please! No!" I'd never screamed like that before in my life; it hurt even my ears, not to mention my vocal chords. "Don't let that water touch me!"

Greg dropped me. "Wow, Jeanine," he said, frowning. "I thought you liked swimming."

"I do. I promise, I do. I just figure we've got all night. Why rush to that part when there are so many other wonderful things we could be doing?" Now to show my true love. I didn't even know what that was, but I figured it had to do with giving myself to him somehow. Standing, I began unbuttoning my shirt.

Greg took a step nearer to me. "Oh, I see," he said, his voice low.

I shrugged my shirt to the ground.

"Wow, I always knew you were hot," Greg said, grinning. After pulling off his own shirt, he placed one of his hands inside my bra, while his free hand pulled me closer to him. Laying his mouth against mine, but giving too much fervor in his kiss, Greg smothered me with his lips. My body didn't want to reciprocate.

He pulled me tighter and in his urgency, knocked something in the water. Something cold and wet splattered my legs. Alarm filled me. Water. I opened my eyes during the kiss. Maybe he wouldn't notice the transformation if I kept kissing him. After all, I would dry off pretty fast; it was only a little water. But it would be impossible for him not to feel my soft skin turn to scales. Maybe I was cured of it now and nothing would happen.

Just as that thought had passed through my mind, my back snapped, and I jerked away from him. My muscles cramped up, pain sliced down my spine. It was happening again.

5

Greg's eyes were wide, and his expression filled with confusion and horror. Mainly horror. I didn't blame him. "What the hell are you?"

The pool of water seemed even more tempting now that I was fully a monster. But still I managed to speak. "Don't be afraid of me; I'm still Jeanine. I just need you to love me, and then this curse will be broken."

"Oh shit!" Greg closed his eyes and curled up into a ball at my feet like a little kid. "Stay away from me! Don't talk."

I gripped his shoulders and shook him. He needed to snap out of it.

Greg swore, jerking away from me and scrambling to his feet, which intensified my hold on him. He wasn't going to run away. He needed to break my curse.

"But you said that Jeanine was your true love," I hissed. My words came out reptilian sounding. In reality, I could barely understand them myself. Even then I could see that my words weren't processing in Greg's brain.

He shook his head. "I don't know what you are, but I never loved Jeanine."

Somehow, I knew right then that the curse would never be lifted. No one could get past this. And here I had been, loving Greg, but nothing happened! The curse had stuck. "No," I said. The word was more to myself than to him. Releasing my hold on his shoulder, I noticed angry red scratches had appeared. Raising a hand to my vision, I saw parts of his flesh hooked in the curve of my cruel claws.

"Please, don't eat me!" Greg whimpered.

"I'm not going to eat you," I told him, taking a step toward the pool. My clothing was ripped. If I transformed back to normal, I'd be naked. What time was it? Grandpa had said he'd pick me up at eleven, but it was not even close. Eight thirty at the latest.

During my time of distraction, I heard Greg bolt for it; he slammed the door of his patio behind him and locked it. I needed to get home right away, before the police showed up, or animal control, or whomever Greg was going to call to come to his rescue. He was pathetic. Maybe I should leap in the pool, so I'd stay wet enough to reach home without having to run naked through the streets. Of course, there was the fact that people might see me as a monster. Would it be better for people to see a monster or a streaker? There had to be something to wrap myself in here. My gaze went to my shredded clothing and my shirt that I had discarded earlier, and I bent to pick them up. Seeing my monster hands stained with Greg's blood as they picked up the clothing whipped me into a harsh reality.

Greg hadn't broken the curse.

I was stuck. Stuck as a monster forever. Untamable fear caught in my heart at that moment, spreading like a virus to the rest of me. I began shaking. My eyes darted to Greg's house. He watched me from the window, his eyes huge and a phone held to his ear. I needed to make my escape.

Trying to run, but tripping over my tail, I began scrambling for the six-foot fence surrounding Greg's yard. I wondered how I was going to jump it, but my legs seemed enhanced for springing and climbing, and my tail helped with balance. I was over the fence within seconds; I'd hardly had time to think about climbing it. Something about my reptilian attributes made me quiet and fast as a snake slithering through grass. Once out of his yard, I realized I was near the street where any passing car could notice me. But Greg's home was only two short miles from my house. Digging my monster hands in my torn pants pockets, I tried to find my cell phone. I finally had success and brought it out, holding it between my claws gingerly, trying not to break it. It was hard to dial, but I got

Grandpa's number. I held the phone to my elongated ear and closed my eyes as it rang.

"Hello?" Grandpa's voice sounded concerned.

"I'm headed home," I said.

"What?"

"Greg saw," I mumbled.

"I'm coming," Grandpa said, "and stopping him before he gets you killed."

"Killed?"

"Just get home and stay there," Grandpa commanded. "I'll take care of things, Jean." His tone sounded serious, as if he had made up his mind about something.

"Okay," I managed to say before hanging up.

The deep sound of thunder hit my ears at that moment. "Get home," Grandpa had said. The first raindrop fell like an ointment on my burning skin. The headlights of a car shone at me, and I ducked low against the fence. Maybe they wouldn't see me, or just not pay attention. Closing my eyes to hide the whites in them from the car light, I waited until I felt the car's turbulence swish past me. I let out a sigh of relief and began slithering, crawling, or hopping my way back home, not able to really verify which of the three I was doing. Never had my house seemed like such a welcoming place. But I knew my family waiting inside would not be thrilled to see a monster enter their house. The rain hit harder, soothing every scale on my body. Tapping against the door, I almost hoped no one would answer. How else could I get inside? Footsteps approaching the door were disappointing to hear.

"Yes?" Patty opened the door for a second, but when her eyes settled on my face, she babbled something in her own tongue and slammed the door.

That went relatively well, I thought to myself. At least I

couldn't understand what her choice of swear words was. An idea struck me, and I shifted my gaze upward. My room window was usually open. Maybe I could crawl up there and dry off before anyone else saw me. All I needed was to go around the back and climb up the side of the house. There were plenty of vines draping our antique house. It would be simple. Especially with my newly acquired abilities, I thought.

I jumped our fence, much like I had at the Peterson's house, and scanned the side of our home up to my open window. I grasped hold of one slippery vine after another as the rain continued to pour. My prehensile tail found a good use as a fifth way of gripping. Before I could worry about heights, I was climbing in my window, dripping water on the floor of my clean room. The sound of people talking downstairs made me realize that Patty had probably caused quite a commotion about the creature at the door. Time to dry off before someone believed her. My eyes caught in the mirror situated above my bed. I wanted — but had forgotten how — to cry.

*

I had completely dried off and returned to my "normal" self. Changing into new clothes and fixing my hair and makeup, I felt brave enough to face my family. I hoped Grandpa would be back soon. The commotion persisted as I walked down the stairs.

"Patty, I bet it was just some kid dressed in a costume or something. They were trying to scare you," I heard Dad say. He stood with his arms crossed and wore a frown.

"But sir, you not see this creature. It real! Very real!" Patty would chatter in her own language every few seconds. "No hoax."

"What's going on?" I asked.

All heads turned to me. Corrine rushed to my side and grabbed my hand. "Jeanine, there was a monster at the door! Patty saw it."

"It stood like people, but it had claws, long tail….and its face…." Patty shuddered. "Its face was covered in scales."

"Patty, I'm sure it was a kid pranking you," I said with guilt on my conscience since I knew she wasn't making anything up.

The door opened, and Patty jumped with a little yelp. Grandpa stood with Greg in the doorway. They both were soaked from the rain. Grandpa had a gruff expression on his face, and when Greg caught sight of me, his face grew pale as if he were seeing a ghost — or a monster. However, Grandpa seemed surprised to see me looking myself. He didn't know of my new abilities that had allowed me a way into my room through the window.

"Patty, if you'll give us a minute as a family…." Grandpa whispered toward her.

Patty kept chattering in her language but disappeared down the hall.

"Corrine, I think you should go with Patty," Grandpa said.

Corrine hung her head. "Oh, why do I always have to—" she began, but Grandpa gave her a stern look that would have frightened any kid, and she shut up and walked down the hall after Patty.

Not able to stop the sudden onslaught of shaking that overcame me, I stared at Grandpa, clutching my hands against my sides to stabilize myself. Would he tell them? In our discussion in the car, I thought he'd advised me not to say anything about this to them.

"What is it, Dad?" my father asked, crossing his arms over his chest. His gaze went to Greg then, and he raised a brow. Maybe he was wondering if I was pregnant or something.

"This is something that needs to stay in this group…" Grandpa's voice trailed off.

Worry lines formed on Mom's brow, and Dad uncrossed his arms. "Yes?" Dad said.

He was going to tell them. Most of me wanted to go back to my room and hide under the bed, but part of me was curious as to how my family would take it. The outcome wouldn't be good. My stomach and head began to ache. The nightmare would never end now.

"I want Jeanine to tell you, though," Grandpa said.

How generous of him, I thought. "I've been cursed," I said. My insides wanted to spill out.

"Huh?" Dad asked.

Grandpa gripped Greg's shirt as he fidgeted.

Too prideful to tell them that I had brought it on myself, I said, "The room in the basement cursed me."

"Why—" Mom began.

Dad interrupted her by giving a short laugh. So much for sympathy. "That is the most ridiculous thing I've ever heard!" he said.

"It's true." Grandpa nodded at me. "I've told Greg that you'll pay him to keep his mouth shut."

"Well, I don't know where your mental state is at, Dad, but what sort of curse are we talking about?" Dad asked.

"She's a monster," Greg said, finding a voice.

I had an impulse to hiss at him, make him piss his pants, but realized that perhaps there would be another time for that. Not in front of my parents, at least.

"She doesn't look like a monster to me," Mom said, her voice rising in pitch. "Greg, I'm shocked that—"

"I'll have to agree with Helen on this," Dad said, narrowing his eyes at Grandpa and Greg. "How dare you call my daughter a monster?"

"I know that she doesn't look like one now, but she became one a little bit ago," Greg said. The smoothness in his speech had vanished. "How much are you gonna pay me? If you don't believe me, look what your daughter — that thing — did." The way he had said that made me shudder, like he thought my humanity no longer existed. Greg pulled on the neck of his button-down shirt to reveal the scratches I had given him with my claws.

6

"That doesn't prove a thing," Mom said.

"Please, pay the kid, and make him sign a waiver, Derek," Grandpa ordered. I'd never heard him so serious.

Dad frowned but motioned for Greg and Grandpa to follow him. They traveled toward his office. Mom's hand grasping my wrist made me gasp.

"What is this about?" Mom asked, her face livid.

"It's true," I said, half of my mind somewhere else. Both of my parents, Greg, and Grandpa knew. I'd never tell another soul, I vowed to myself. "It happens when I get wet," I explained.

"I don't believe you," Mom said, giving a little laugh, as if she were taking this as a joke.

"I'm serious. Have I ever been one to make up stuff like that?" Grandpa had been right. Everyone believed what they knew, what they could see. Why couldn't Mom just believe me at my word? I was her daughter after all.

The sound of a door opening stopped Mom from answering me. Greg and Dad came from the office. Grandpa followed them, his eyes set upon me for a second. If only he would give me a glimmer of a smile, let me know that all hope was not lost.

"Goodbye, Jeanie." Greg waved a handful of cold cash in front of my face, grinned, and said to me in a low voice, "freak," before slamming the door behind him.

"I can't believe—" Dad growled, but Grandpa shook his head, and Dad shut up.

"I hope this is just some huge practical joke, Jeanine," Mom said.

"It's true, Helen," Grandpa said. "I'll show you how it is true." Grandpa disappeared for a moment and came back with a glass of water. Again my eyes couldn't help but follow the sloshing of the water in the cylinder. I knew what he was going to do. "See how she's looking at it?"

Dad furrowed his brows, but didn't say anything. Mom crossed her arms and rolled her eyes.

"And then if this happens…."

Before I could stop him, Grandpa splashed the water on me. It smacked against my dry dress and dribbled down my skin as the transformation began to take place. Oh great, another set of clothes ruined. Pretty soon I'm going to have none left, I thought, before the pain became too intense to even think straight. I could hear Mom scream, and Dad yelled something. The strain of my spine sprouting spikes and a tail emerging from my normal human tailbone impaired my ability to see the looks on their faces.

"See what I mean?" Grandpa said after the transformation had completed.

Mom was grasping Dad's hand, and Dad had his arm around her in a protective hold. I hadn't seen my parents that close to one another in a long time. It was sort of encouraging, in a weird way.

All I could manage to say was, "I'm sorry."

Dad spoke first, even though he was shaking just as much as Mom. "So Greg was telling the truth? Thank God I made him sign that waiver."

Mom closed her eyes. "This can't be real!"

"I'm afraid it is," I said. Every time I talked, they both flinched.

"Maybe it's a disease," Dad said, but his voice trailed at the end of the sentence. He didn't believe this to be the case, and I knew it.

"As you can see, it is not a disease." I lifted my hand for him to view. Curling my fingers in an aggressive gesture, I thought of Greg's now-scarred shoulders. "And it's true that I did accidently hurt Greg."

"We can't let anyone else find out about this," Dad announced.

"How can that happen? Every time she gets wet she becomes a monster! How can that be avoided?" Mom's voice had turned to shrieks. My monster ears were more sensitive, and the shrieks irked them. I winced.

"Please, don't say that, Mom." I realized that soon my normal appearance would return, and I wanted to be very much alone now. Turning from them, I slithered or crawled up the stairs and into my room. The rain continued to pound. Blobs of water formed on my window and blurred the lights from the lamppost outside. I could still hear Grandpa and my parents talking. An idea struck me, and I went to the sink and moistened my skin. Curiosity as to what they were going to do with me came upon me. And although my human ears had never been able to hear through the walls, my monster ears could.

"Jeanine will never be happy now unless she is near water," Grandpa said.

"What do you mean?" Mom asked. I could hear her pacing the floor.

"Her mind and body crave water, much like a drug." This statement Grandpa made caught me off guard but made complete sense. The spell had said something about the victim yearning for water to burn, or something like that.

"We can't let anyone see her anymore. Something could happen," Dad announced. "First, we should have a doctor look at her."

"A doctor?" Mom shrieked. "That wouldn't do any good, and you know it. The more people who know about this, the more our entire family reputation could be ruined. Why is she cursed?" I knew this question was directed to Grandpa.

"Remember how I told you that the first Staffords in America followed a sect, Derek?" Grandpa paused, and Dad didn't answer him, so Grandpa continued. "Jeanine brought upon herself a curse from the room that you uncovered."

"But how? I went in that room, and I'm all right," Dad said.

"There was a ritual on the walls, which she followed," Grandpa said.

My face grew hot at the mention of this. I'm so stupid. Stupid. Stupid.

"That is silly. I've never heard of anything so absurd," Mom announced. I could picture her fluttering her hands by her face.

"It's beside the point," Dad barked. "We just need to figure out what to do with her now."

"Is there no way of curing her?" Of course Mom would ask that.

"The writing on the wall said that truest love shown would break the curse. But it didn't work with Greg," Grandpa said. Did I detect a sigh after that?

"Then it's hopeless?" Dad asked.

Hopeless. I crouched low on the floor of my room. I didn't want to hear any more.

Crash!

Jumping up with a start, I turned to see what had fallen behind me. Ugh, my tail had knocked a lamp down. Glass shards scattered everywhere. A few sprinkled across my tail. I raised it up, and the shards fell off. It was an interesting sensation to have a tail. It degraded my sense of humanity but was still quite interesting. My backbone now seemed a limb.

They would be coming up to see the cause of the breaking glass noise. I heard their footsteps even now approaching.

Raising myself to my feet, I locked the door. Tears welled up in my eyes without invitation. I rushed to my bathroom and gripped the sink, staring into the mirror. "I hate you!" I yelled at my reflection. "I hate everything about you! You are stupid, pathetic, and boring!" The image glaring back at me was frightening when it grew angry — nose wrinkled, teeth bared, eyes flashing — but I continued my tirade. "You made a mistake that you'll never be able to fix! How do you feel now? Huh, Jeanine?" I roared. Panting and staring at the monster as if waiting for the reflection to answer me, I cried out, "A stupid waste, that's what you are!" Collapsing to the floor, I held my knees to my chest; my tail curled around my feet and hugged me in. I'm a disgusting freak, and I will be one forever, I thought.

Knock! Knock!

"Go away, and leave me alone!" I hissed through my sobs.

There was whispering going on behind the door. They were trying to figure out what to do with me. One of them tried the door.

Bang! Bang!

"Jeanine, come on, let us in!" Dad's voice boomed. He must have been the one who'd hit the door.

"I said, go away!" I shouted back in a roar. Never had I grown this passionate when talking with my parents. In fact, my obedience and non-rebellious spirit was a trait that Mom had bragged about to her friends numerous times.

"Jeanine, we understand you're upset, but think how we feel...."

Those words made my eyes tear up even more. Of course I was

upset! Who wouldn't be upset? You try being a monster, Mom. It's pretty easy to become one, I thought.

"I have a proposal to make that I think will make you very....happy," Grandpa's voice called.

"Happy?" Standing to my feet, I walked to the door. "How could anything make me happy anymore?" I asked, a bitter laugh escaping my throat.

"Your parents have agreed to let you stay in my cabin," Grandpa said.

Grandpa's cabin! The small log home had been a Stafford family-of-long-ago purchase. There was just one small thing about it that made me staying there ideal: It was located in the remote Northwoods of Wisconsin. Opening the door a crack, I made direct eye contact with Dad, then Mom. I wanted them to grow uncomfortable underneath my hypnotic serpent gaze.

"We'll get you a plane ticket this week, in fact," Dad said, giving me a very false smile.

Mom reached out her hand but jerked it back before touching me. "It's for the best, honey. You'll get some time alone to figure this thing out."

"You're sending me away then?"

"Oh no, pumpkin," Dad said, looking hurt. "Think of it as a vacation."

Out of the corner of my eye, I could see Grandpa roll his eyes and sigh. They were sending me away. "Goodnight," I said, before closing the door.

*

"Where are you going, Jeanine?" Corrine asked. She had come into my room uninvited as I packed my suitcase.

"To Grandpa's cabin," I said in a monotone voice. I didn't care that she was in my room. Sorry….*ex*-room.

"How long will you be gone?" Corrine asked, her eyes huge. They made me uncomfortable. Why did I feel like I'd miss her? She's just my annoying little sister.

"I don't know," I said. My eyes began watering again. They'd done a lot of that lately. Something that used to be so foreign, sophisticated, and intelligent Jeanine Stafford, was now plagued, frightened, freakish, and cursed.

"I'm going to miss you," Corrine said, putting a chubby hand in mine.

"What?" I asked, glancing down at her. Surprise filled me. Had she just said she would miss me, after my bad attitude and ignoring her all the time? "Um….okay. I'm going to miss you too." I squeezed her hand and then dropped it, so I could place the last pair of jeans into the suitcase. The sound of my door opening filled my ears, and I turned to see Grandpa standing there.

"Come on, Jean. It's time to go."

The words made me feel as if an execution were awaiting me.

Corrine followed me out of the room, and Mom and Dad were waiting in the foyer. Mom bent to give me a hug. I wanted to hug her back but couldn't. Instead, I felt like a wooden dolls without joints. Dad wrapped his arms around me, too, but he was worse than Mom at faking his sorrow over me leaving. So much for his toast about me. I didn't know what made me want to cry more: the fact that I was a monster, or the fact that my parents loved me conditionally.

Grandpa took my hand and squeezed. It didn't help, though.

He led me out the door to a limo with shaded windows. Why was I not surprised? The sound of little footsteps chasing after me brought me to a halt. I turned to see Corrine standing behind me, her hands on her hips.

"You didn't give me a hug yet," she said.

"Oh, I'm sorry," I mumbled, kneeling down to allow her to be the same height as me.

"Send me pictures," Corrine said, swinging her arms around my neck.

"Okay," I choked, unable to say anything more. Why did I think that, out of my entire family, she was the one who would miss me?

Grandpa stood holding the door open behind us. "We don't want to be late for your flight," he said.

I stood, forcing my shoulders back, my chin raised a little, and nodded. "Let's go now."

I let out a long sigh.

"I'm sorry that this happened, Jeanine," Grandpa said.

"I know," I murmured, my mind far away. Nothing made sense anymore; life had come to an end. I was dead.

"I'll have everything you need sent to you," Grandpa said, squeezing my hand.

"Yeah."

"And make sure that you get all the movies you want. You'll have your own computer and Internet access. I'll make sure it's set up special for you." Grandpa continued, "It doesn't matter what it costs."

"Great," I said, closing my eyes. The jets of a plane overhead burst into my hearing. We were at the airport.

"I love you, Jean," Grandpa said, putting his arms around me. "Remember that. I always knew you were going to do great things." He paused for a moment as if he had just realized how terrible that had sounded. He added, "I mean, you are still going to do great things with that knack for history you have."

"Yep," I said, barely hugging him back. "Goodbye, and thanks for all this." Deep down, I'd come to a realization that even if I'd stayed home, I'd be no worse off. My parents shunned me. My "friends" would never understand, even Diana. Goodbye forever, normal life.

7

Upon entering the plane, I sat down next to a heavily made-up woman with a fake tan. She leaned over toward me. "I'm so glad I'm sitting next to you," she said, interrupting my wish for solitude. "I always end up next to some 300 pound guy. He always takes up more than his share of our seats."

My numb mind hardly understood what she had said, but I comprehended that she was making a joke, so I tried to chuckle. Inside I thought, Lady, you don't realize it, but you're sitting next to a monster. I'm sure you'd much rather sit next to a fat guy.

A heavyset man came lumbering down the aisle. He stopped in front of our seats. "Excuse me, but my ticket says I'm supposed to sit here."

"Huh?" I glanced up, and the tanned woman began digging through her purse to check her ticket. Heat rose in my cheeks as the realization dawned on me that, in my depressed state, I'd forgotten to check my ticket. "It's me," I said, stopping the woman from searching her purse anymore. "I'm sorry," I remarked, feeling a little flustered and embarrassed.

The poor woman laughed despite herself, and I thought it noble of her. I hoped the overweight gentleman didn't take up too much of her seat. How ironic was my life?

My *real* seat was 8B. I'd get a window seat. Oh, goodie.

A tall, slender young man approached my row. Nodding me a greeting and giving me a vague smile, he sat down next to me. Sadness in his features kept me from speculating further. I had someone with whom I could share misery with at least.

After the plane was off the ground, the flight attendant came by. "Would you like something to drink?"

The mentions of liquid made my senses come to life. Please, don't order water, I thought toward the young man. Please. Please.

"I'll just have water," the young man said in a deep voice.

The flight attended glanced at me. "You want something?"

"N-no," I found myself stuttering. I was so stupid. I could've banged my head against the window, except that would've cracked my glasses.

"Okay." He looked back to the flight attendant. "I guess just one water then."

He chuckled, flirting with the attendant. I crossed my arms over my chest before I realized I was already judging the guy. Greg kept floating through my mind whenever I saw any young man.

"Hey, I'm Mark."

I turned to see his hand extended out to mine. "Jeanine," I said, taking his hand. His handshake was firm, and his skin was thick in texture. He must have done hands-on work in the past.

"What's bringing you all the way up to Hayward?" Mark asked. He gave me direct eye contact, and I studied him. He had thick eyebrows the same shade as his dark, almost-black hair, which waved across his forehead in a roguish sort of way. I realized his eyes were a foggy blue, contrasting with his dark hair. He probably could play the villain in any movie and do a good job of it, for there was an intimidating seriousness to his face.

Realizing I still hadn't answered him and had just been staring at him, I tried to think of something to say. "Uh, well, I'm—" He must think I'm clueless. "I'm sort of running away from the busy life. It's a vacation." Finally, I'd said something sound.

"Running away?" Mark's face seemed to be stone; I couldn't read it. "Huh. You and me both."

"Where are you from?" I asked.

"I'm sort of going home. I live near Hayward, Wisconsin." Mark answered, his tone wistful. "I left the backwoods for some big city adventure."

"So you came to New York?"

"Yep." Mark's eye contact left mine and looked ahead.

The flight attendant was returning. She handed Mark the cup of water. It swirled temptingly in his cup. Every time he moved, the water in the cup moved in circles.

"Jeanine?" Mark's voice interrupted my obsessive thoughts.

Blinking, I realized that he was holding his cup over his lap, and my wide eyes were staring at his groin. Blood pumped into my cheeks, and I forced myself to look out the window instead of allowing the water to continue its captivation. "Sorry, I just realized I am thirsty." I made a pathetic attempt at a cover for my oddness.

"Uh, okay. Hey!" he called up the aisle to the flight attendant. "She changed her mind. Can you bring another water?"

Wishing I could melt into my seat, I closed my eyes and leaned as far back into the cushioning of the hard airline chair as possible.

"Here," Mark said.

When I opened my eyes, a cup of water swished in front of me. I took it as if picking up a venomous snake and placed it in my cup holder.

"Thanks," I mumbled.

"Are you going to be staying in Wisconsin long?"

"I'm not sure." This conversation wasn't going to a place I wanted it to. "Why did you come to New York?"

"Um, like I said, I wanted some different experiences," he said, not giving me eye contact.

Did I detect something defensive in his voice? For some odd reason, my curiosity was sparked about this guy. "Sorry, I didn't mean to pry," I told him, glancing out the window.

"It's no problem," Mark laughed. "Do you have relatives out here — I mean, in Wisconsin — that you're staying with?"

I realized that I was talking to a complete stranger who could be a con man or murderer for all I knew. "Um....yeah," I lied. Bending down, I dug in my backpack and took out a book so as to appear like the conversation was done.

"Have you read *Pride and Prejudice* before?"

I glanced at the cover to find the book I'd pulled was indeed *Pride and Prejudice*. Still he continued to disturb me. What was wrong with the guy? "No, I haven't. Have you?" I tried not to sound annoyed.

"It was my sister's favorite book, so I wondered—" Mark said.

"Maybe I'll like it, then," I said, interrupting him. I glared into the book as if interested. In reality, I was waiting for him to stop talking. It worked, and the rest of the flight continued, to my delight, without event. After a casual goodbye and wish of good luck from Mark, we landed, and I left the plane, feeling prepared for the pointless existence I now would partake of.

*

"What do you mean you don't have any more cars?" I asked, my voice somewhere between a shout and a sob.

"Sorry, ma'am," the rather porcine-looking man answered. The gum in his mouth bugged me. "It's the musky tournament, and we don't have any vehicles available."

Not even a bike, right? I thought bitterly. Someone tapped my shoulder, causing me to jump.

Mark stood behind me. "You left this in your seat." The book *Pride and Prejudice* was held out toward me.

Heat burned in my cheeks as I took it from him. "Thanks," I said.

"Maybe I'll see you around," Mark said, giving me a vague smile and a wave. He could tell his showing up had disgruntled me.

I watched as he walked away in a young, long-legged, guyish stride. An idea hit me out of nowhere. "Wait!" I called out after him.

He turned, a dark eyebrow raised. "What is it?"

"Um....I was wondering if you could maybe drive me somewhere. Do you have a car?"

"You mean to say you don't have a ride?" Mark crossed his arms. He must've been thinking about how dense I was.

"I don't." Admitting this was easy. I just hoped that I was making the right choice, but in the end, I had nothing to lose anymore.

"I guess I could drive you to where you need to go. Where do you live?"

"Off of Teal Lake."

"You live off of Teal Lake?" Mark smiled. "I live off of Teal, too. Come on, I'll take you there."

I didn't want to think this through anymore. Sometimes one just needs to take a leap of faith. Besides, so far this guy seemed pretty decent. "Okay," I said.

I followed him, carrying my few belongings with me. It looked like he had a rental waiting for him.

"Here, let me help you with those," Mark said, taking my luggage and placing it in the trunk.

Wind picked up, and my nostrils were assailed with various pine and forest scents. The wildness of this place frightened me, but it touched a part of me not yet explored. The part that wanted to be free and wild. Perhaps it was the monster inside of me wanting out.

"You coming?" Mark asked.

"Yes," I said, giving him another glance; this time I smiled. "Yes, I'm coming." Why I almost felt giddy puzzled me. I got inside Mark's rental and buckled myself in.

"Do you like the book?" Mark said, trying to make conversation.

"It's quite interesting. I've never read it before, but when I watched the movies, I found the historic accuracy — since the author is from the time that she wrote — much to my benefit." Here I was already going back into history geekdom.

"Really?" Mark asked. "My sister, Jessie, made me see it," he murmured.

"Made you?" I laughed, much to my surprise. "Did you like the story then?"

"It was sort of slow-paced, you know?" Mark's hand reached for the radio. "What do you like to listen to?"

"Um." I'd never listened to music much in the past because I had never seen much practicality in it. But now I wasn't sure. "What do you like?"

"Pretty much anything." Mark began flipping through the stations. "This is pretty cool. My car doesn't have a radio this nice."

I realized he was commenting on the rental's system and nodded. "So are you staying long in Wisconsin?"

Mark stopping flicking through the stations and brought both hands back to the wheel. "I'm not sure, actually."

"Why?" I asked.

"Because I'm here for a funeral."

My gaze went to his face. It was serious and controlled, but I could see the sadness in his eyes become heavier. "A funeral? I'm sorry. Was this someone you were close to?"

Mark nodded.

"Thank you for driving me," I said. Something inside of me wanted to comfort him, regardless of the fact that I didn't know him.

"No problem."

We took a turn down an even more remote road, passing a sign for a Native American reservation. "How far away is Teal Lake?" I asked, breaking the ambience that seemed to choke both of us.

"It's not far. About half an hour away," Mark said. "In New York that seems like a long distance, but not when you live in the Northwoods."

"Are you going to be staying with your sister then?" I asked.

There was a silence that followed this question, making me worry. Were he and his sister not on good terms? Then Mark's face turned to me, his eyes filled with pain. "She's dead."

8

"I'm so sorry, Mark," I said, after words returned to me.

"But I will be at our parents' house during my stay," Mark said.

I sucked in a breath. "What happened to her?"

"She was murdered."

The word rang over and over in my mind. "Murdered?" Knowing my voice must have raised in pitch, I cleared my throat. "That's horrible!"

"Well, everyone but me thinks that she was mauled by a bear." Mark's quiet tone held an iciness that made me want to shiver. I held my breath without meaning to as I waited for him to continue. "But I am almost positive it wasn't a bear."

Shifting in my seat, I wished to change the subject, but curiosity as to whether my new home was safe ruled that option out. "Mark, I am truly sorry that happened. Are there a lot of murders in this area?"

"Um....no." He paused for a moment. "Why do you ask?"

"I just was wondering because you suspected that a person killed her."

"I just don't think it was a bear." Mark's voice was almost a growl, "I know it couldn't have been. Like I said, Jessie is too smart Or was...." His voice trailed off. "What about you? Do you got family?" His question startled me, but I figured he no longer wished to talk about his sister.

"I have a little sister, and my parents live in New York with her."

"Are they okay with you moving all the way out here?"

Yes, Mark, they are relieved, I thought. But instead I said, "Yeah."

My tone must have sounded depressed, because Mark shot me a quizzical glance. "They don't want you around I take it?"

"Why would you assume that?" I snapped at him, forgetting for a moment that I was talking to a complete stranger. Well, not so much anymore. I guess you could say he was a new acquaintance.

Mark kept looking ahead at the road. "Why don't they want you?"

"They were fine with me!" I defended. "I mean, that's like me asking whether your parents cared if you went to New York."

"Touché," Mark said. "Forget that I asked."

A distant sound of thunder rumbled, and I took a quick breath. "Is it supposed to storm?"

"Huh?" Mark glanced out the window toward the sky. He wasn't at all like Greg, but there was something about his strange features that intrigued me more than Greg's boyish good looks. His build was slim, yet there was nothing fragile about it. "Are you afraid of a little thunderstorm, Jean?"

Surprised at his familiar way of addressing me, I wanted to slap him across the face for a second. Then I realized that I had been ogling him, so I shouldn't blame him for anything. "Yeah, I'm terrified," I said with a laugh. "Who likes them anyway?"

"I do," Mark said.

"You would," I flirted, but bit my tongue. Why was I flirting with him? The first raindrop splashed onto the windshield of our car, reminding me of why friendship with anyone was out of the question. It trickled down slowly and ran into another drop that landed beneath it I turned my attention back to Mark. "Why do you like them?"

"Thunderstorms?" Mark gave me a vague smile. "They're untamable."

Mark turned down another more remote road, which caused the car to bump up and down in protest to the gravel that didn't do a very good job of filling the potholes.

"When is the funeral?"

Mark's face clouded over again, and I felt sorry for asking. "Saturday."

"Were you two very close?" I asked.

"Yeah," Mark said. The rain fell harder, hitting the windshield like tiny bullets. "Looks like we're going into a downpour."

Oh great. If this wasn't ironic, I didn't know what was. I reached for the radio and turned the dial up on the sound. There was some blaring rock music on, to my relief. It drowned out the sound of the assaulting rain.

"Like this song?" Mark asked.

"Yes!" I yelled, turning it even louder as the rain grew harsher. The smell of the rain floated into the car, making me wish I had a nose plug on. Then I realized the song was about some guy and how he wanted his girlfriend because she had, as he put it, "a sexy rack." Nice. But I continued to bob my head to the song as if I was into the music. "It's not so much the lyrics," I announced over the music. "It's the rhythm, you know?"

"I see," Mark said, his voice so quiet in volume that I could barely hear him. Or was the music so loud that everything else sounded quiet?

The siren song of the rain was still driving me insane. Just one little drop — that was all I wanted. Closing my eyes to keep the image of the water out, I kept rocking my head to the beat.

"We're almost to Teal," Mark announced, bringing me a little hope and also some fright. I'd have to get out of the car in this rain and Mark, unless he was blind, would definitely be able to see what happened when water touched my skin.

"I'm glad we're almost there," I said, trying to get my mind focused away from the water. I had a headache from the blaring music. "So, do you have any other siblings?"

"Nope," Mark said. "Hey, we're here. At least, we're at my house. Now where is your place? Did your relatives give you an address?"

Crap. I'd forgotten how I had lied to Mark on the plane. Placing my hands to my cheeks to cover up the redness, I said, "Mark, I'm not staying with relatives."

Mark's ghostlike eyes stared at me for a moment. They were disturbing to look into for long periods of time. Shifting my gaze to my lap, I watched my hands shuffle.

"Why did you tell me you were, then?"

"Because I didn't know you. I didn't want you knowing that I was living alone."

"You're living alone, way out here?" His gaze was so intense, I could feel it.

"Yes," I said sheepishly.

"Why are you doing that to yourself?" Mark stopped the car and put it in park. The rain kept spattering against the windshield, but it had slowed to a sleepy patter.

"Why am I doing what?" And why was Mark concerned? He didn't even know me.

"Living alone like that. My sister did the same thing."

A chill pumped through my veins.

"My parents live in Florida half the year, so she had the place all to herself during the time that it happened." Mark ran his hand through his hair.

"Where did they find her?"

"By the lake," Mark said, his voice lowered. "She was pretty torn up." He looked out his side window, trying not to let me see his face.

"Oh god," I said under my breath. "She was alone."

He turned the radio down so we wouldn't have to shout at each other anymore. "I don't like knowing that you're alone."

"What?" Even though what he had said made my stomach turn, I didn't expect him to be so concerned about me.

"It just seems wrong to let someone like you, an inexperienced city girl, live in a cabin by yourself after a young woman around your age was murdered in this area."

"Maybe it *was* a bear," I said, feeling my heart beat in my head. So much about this place seemed unknown, even to the locals, and it was unknown to me. This was the perfect place for me to hide.

He started the car again, not answering my question, his face set in a grim expression. "Let's get to your cabin. Which one is it?"

"It's the fifth on this street. The address is—"

"Well, ours is the sixth, so I guess we just drove past it." Mark had closed the conversation about his sister as quickly as he had opened up to it, and I wondered why. He maneuvered the car around.

"Are your parents back from Florida yet?" I asked.

"They came as soon as they heard about Jessie," Mark answered.

The rain had slowed to a drizzle. By the time I got out of the car it would be over, I hoped, and I wouldn't have to look like an idiot who didn't want to get out of the car.

"We're here." Mark brought the car to a stop.

I needed to think fast. "Wait!"

Mark's gaze went to my face. "What is it?"

"I should pay you."

"Pay me?"

"Yes."

"You really are something, aren't you?" He shook his head.

Surprised at his sudden flirting, I tried to clear my head enough to come up with a way to make the conversation last a little longer. "I really have to insist on paying you," I said. "How much do you want?"

"Nothing. I'd have to drive out here anyway." He smiled. "Just think of it as a 'welcome to the neighborhood' present."

As far as I could tell with my acute sensitivity, the rain had now stopped, making my escape safe. "Okay," I said, opening the car door and stepping carefully onto the soggy ground. The wet scent of the rain hung in the air, making my nostrils tingle. Drops of water hugged to the leaves and needles of every tree, dripping periodically from their branches. Sounds of birds singing in praise of the rainstorm's departure and the waves lapping on the shore of the lake enchanted my mind. The forest. It was such an alien world to me. How would I survive out here alone? The solitude of this place was enough to make me shake uncontrollably. There wasn't a single siren, rush of cars, or chatter of people anywhere as there had been in busy New York.

"You look a little freaked out," Mark said, interrupting my thoughts.

"Um....I am." For some reason my eyes were watering.

"Who are you, anyway?" he asked, his eyes narrowed.

"Excuse me?"

He chuckled. "Well, you're sort of....weird. I've never met someone who wanted to live alone in the middle of nowhere. I know you said on the plane that you were running away, but....I didn't take it seriously, until now."

"Why do you say that?" I snapped, feeling agitated that he was able to pick up on my emotions without knowing me at all.

"I don't know....sorry," Mark grasped my luggage in his hands. "Here, I'll help you get these into the cabin."

"Thanks," I mumbled.

The path up the cabin consisted of sparse rocks over mud. How nice. Good thing I'd come prepared and worn hiking shoes. I'd never again get to wear my fashionable high heels I'd bought with Diana. The cabin looked rustic. I knew that it was almost as old as my house back in New York.

"Nice place," Mark said once we reached the front door. "I thought an old guy lived here, though."

"That's my grandpa. My family has owned this place for generations." For a moment, a rush of Stafford pride displayed itself. But then it hit me: I wasn't very proud of my ancestry anymore. They had been into cursing people, after all.

"Well, I guess this is goodbye, then," Mark said. He put out his hand. "Good luck."

Shaking his hand I replied, "Yeah, thanks."

"And remember, if you need anything, I'm right next door."

"Okay," I said, smiling at him. "Goodbye."

Our eyes connected for a moment, but then Mark turned his gaze from me and took a step backward. "All right," he said, turning toward his car.

Part of me wished that he'd stay just a little longer so I wouldn't have to feel alone yet. The sound of his car door slamming shut and his engine starting made my eyes water once again. I watched as his car drove away, and once it disappeared from view behind the trees, I entered the cabin. Compared to the mansion I'd lived in before, I felt claustrophobic here. There was a living room about the same size as my room in the New York house; a kitchen off of that, about half the size of the living room; and a door, which I presumed led to the bedroom. Mark had placed my suitcases inside the door, and I lifted them up. Besides how small the cabin felt, the quietness was suffocating.

Opening the bedroom door, I was not surprised to see that the room was equal to the size of my closet back at home. With a queen-size bed situated in the right corner and a tiny closet and drawers to the left, there was hardly enough space for me to walk between the two. I unzipped my suitcase. Grandpa had left two notes inside it. One was on how everything ran at the cabin, so I left it open on the bed. Unfolding the other note, I tried to read his chicken scratch handwriting.

Jeanine,

I will be visiting you in a week's time at the request of your parents. (Why my mom and dad couldn't make a personal journey, I don't know.) *Please know that everything at the cabin should be in order, seeing as I just stayed there. Enjoy your time, and I will continue to search for a way to rid you of the curse.*

Love,

Grandpa Stafford

Taking in a deep breath, I sat on the bed and looked out the window. I could tell from how clean the place looked that Grandpa hadn't lied about staying here recently. He must have left the lake house to go directly to my graduation party. The windows were clean, and the room didn't seem dusty in the least. Reaching into my pocket I dug out my cell phone and turned it on. I noticed in my missed calls that Diana had tried to reach me. The knowledge that I'd probably never see her again struck me. I hadn't even said a goodbye to her. Making up my mind to call her, I began dialing, but realized that there wasn't any service in my cabin.

Perfect, I thought, with a roll of my eyes.

Traveling into the living room, I found a back door leading down to the lake. I stepped outside and held up my phone to see if I could achieve any bars anywhere. The wind had picked up, and the water lapped in waves against the shore. Without thinking I followed the sound until I stood near the shore. Grandpa's pier had a rowboat tied to it. The boat moved with the water.

Up, down, up, down.

The nature around me smelled fresh with just a hint of fish, wet earth, and weeds. Tiny fish swarmed around the pier's metal legs. A raindrop fell on my glass lens, dripped off, and slid down my cheek. The familiar burning started.

9

"I am not losing any more clothes over this," I said, gritting my teeth to prepare for the painful ordeal that would follow.

After I'd removed my blouse and jeans, another raindrop hit my bare shoulders. It felt nice at first, but sure enough, within a second, my spine snapped as I began metamorphosing. Each transformation took about five minutes at the most, but it was five agonizing minutes, worse than any pain I'd ever suffered. I blamed it on my skeletal structure changing as well as my skin. After it was finished, I stood panting on the pier, the raindrops beating harder against me, soothing the scales from burning, much like they had the other night at my home. Looking down, I realized that my cell phone had dropped onto one of the wooden boards of the dock. Crouching low on the dock, I grasped the phone in my hands — or claws, as it were — and wrapped it in my discarded clothing. The water in the lake was too inviting to pass up, and since no one was around to see, I decided to swim.

Taking another step toward the end of the dock, I stared over the edge. The waves still hit, rocking the pier lightly. Without another thought, I jumped in and ducked beneath the surface. Never in my life had I felt so free. Not only did I have a body that seemed designed for swimming — it propelled itself in the low-gravity water — but the full emersion in water ended the burning in my scales. Opening my eyes, I found that although the water was murky from being a fresh water lake, it didn't sting my eyes like it had in the past when I'd opened them as a human. My tail acted as a rudder, giving me the ability to maneuver as easily as a crocodile could. Glancing behind myself, I could make out the metal poles of the dock's support and the small fish darting underneath to the shadows it offered. The sound of disrupted water filled my hearing, as it did in the past when I'd swim underwater in a pool, but now I could hear more than that; it was as if I could map out the riverbed with my hearing. Rising to the surface, I found that the water was chest deep. I lifted a clawed hand out of the water and examined it. The webbing between my fingers fascinated me: They were a thick brown-green in color, much like the rest of my scaly skin. I'd marvel more at it if it wasn't *me* who had the webbed fingers. The monster form felt graceful and sleek in the water compared to the clumsy, ugly feeling of being on land. I dunked my face once again underwater and propelled myself forward with my webbed feet, heading farther out from the shore and diving deeper into the water. Water weeds brushed against my bare skin and minutes ticked by. I remained submerged; my lungs were not asking for air, or even tiring. The sound of something in the water to my left shot adrenaline into my system, and I whirled to face whatever it was, claws ready to defend. A large fish, about the same length as my leg, swam lazily nearby. When it caught sight of me, it turned itself away and became lost in the greenish-brown oblivion of the lake water. Glancing upward, I realized that I was floating in the deep, unable to touch the ground and nowhere near the surface. It sent my brain into panic. How long ago was it that I had last breathed? The sun's image overhead blurred under the water; it looked more like a glowing ball with ripples passing through it, scattering the light, than a solid sphere. It must have stopped raining. Even under the water, the sun hurt the eyes, so I couldn't look at it for more than a second. Kicking my legs hard and quick, it seemed minutes until I broke through the thin sheet of water into oxygen-filled air. At the surface, land looked far away. I realized my body floated prone, so any cabin house with a good pair of binoculars could get a glimpse of my frightening, unnatural face. I submerged once more, turning back to the cabin. Although this experience had felt quite enthralling, it left me depressed and disgusted with myself, especially regarding the fact that there was no one else to blame but me for this strange, inhuman experience. When the poles of the dock again came to view, I surfaced and stood near the shore, looking up at the cabin. The mud near the shore stuck to my toes and squished as I walked toward land. I halted when reality hit: I knew there was no one waiting for me in that cabin. Feeling overcome by this, I sunk once more under the water and lay on the muddy sand and weeds. I realized, as a human I'd feel gross doing this, but for some reason my reptilian humanoid body enjoyed the softness and shifting of it. I belonged here more than I did lying on the bed of that cabin.

*

I laid staring at the ceiling of the cabin's bedroom, trying not to shake with fear. There was nothing left in life for me. Dreams, ambitions, and friends had been whisked away because of one stupid mistake I'd made. Water was unavoidable. Every time I heard the waves lapping or smelled the lake from the fresh breeze carried into the cabin, images of me swimming invaded my mind. Water flowed in a dance with the wind. I closed my eyes and still could see the large fish swimming nearby. My cell phone lay next to my bed, still not receiving a signal. For some odd reason, I'd begun to not care if I ever reached Diana again. Let her think the worst of me or even think me dead, because I now am dead. Quite dead. Resurrection was impossible.

*

I opened my eyes the next morning, wishing that they'd stayed shut. Feeling suicidal upon awakening was never a good sign. My dreams last night had held memories of my past life and things that would have happened in the future — college and studying history being the main theme of them. But then, in my dream, water had been poured on me and I'd turned into a monster that everyone wanted to kill.

Swinging my legs over the side of the bed, I stretched and blinked my eyes to get them to focus, trying to remember where I'd put my glasses. They lay on the kitchen table. At least, that's where I'd last seen them. Not having anyone to remind me, like Patty or Mom, was becoming a problem. I'd always been a little forgetful, but now living on my own made that a terrible curse. I prepared breakfast from the meager supplies Grandpa had left me. They would last a week. And since I didn't have any vehicle, I'd starve if Grandpa didn't keep to his word and come. Of course, I knew that Mark guy lived next door now, so maybe I could get a ride from him to go into town. In my suitcase, my parents had given me a credit card that I could spend on anything I wanted; very kind of them to leave the exiled child some money. A bird chirped outside and I heard a sudden splash on the lake. It awoke the part of me I now loathed.

"Don't think about it," I ordered myself aloud. My voice echoed in the empty cabin, disrupting its stillness. Oh great, I thought, I've started talking to myself. Now I'm not only a monster but also going crazy.

After eating breakfast, I decided to watch some movies, since Grandpa didn't have satellite or cable for his TV. I put in a movie — a romantic comedy, one of my favorites — but hated it now 'cause everything ended up happy. I wound up throwing my paper cereal bowl at the screen while screaming.

*

"You look horrible! What have you done to yourself?" Grandpa stood in the doorway of the cabin holding bags of groceries. The wrinkles on his brow increased.

To tell the truth, I wasn't surprised at his words. "It's what happens when one is decaying from the inside out," I said dramatically, with a dry tone.

"Well please, don't decay while I'm here," he said wryly. "I've brought you some food, and I'm going to make sure you get a car or something." Grandpa's gaze scanned my living condition. He could see the mess on the kitchen table, the dishes sitting by the sink, and the laundry lying on the floor.

"A car? That would be nice; then I can drive around boring Hayward."

"It's not boring. You'd be surprised what you find in little towns like these."

"Yeah, Grandpa, the cute little town thing isn't working for me," I said, taking the groceries from him. "Come on in. Are you going to stay the night?" After a week of solitude, seeing another human being made me feel needy.

"I was hoping to stay a couple of days, if that's all right with you," Grandpa said, smiling. "What have you been up to?"

"I have no life," I said, and then added with a sarcastic note, "Oh yeah....I swam in the lake yesterday — and the day before that, and the day before that—"

"I get the picture." Grandpa frowned. "And it doesn't look like your attitude has improved since last I've seen you."

"Yeah, you try being a monster for a while. I'm sure your attitude would be one of bliss." I rolled my eyes.

"Jeanine," Grandpa said in a stern tone. Could anyone blame me for sounding cynical, though? He set the groceries on the counter and then began cleaning up my table without asking.

I felt defensive: This was my home, and I didn't want him messing around with it or judging its mess.

"Stop!" I shouted. "I'll clean it up!" I yanked the dishes from his hands and rushed them to the sink, placing them down with a loud clatter.

"Jeanine, I'm sorry. I've been trying to find a way to break the curse—" Grandpa began.

My temper continued to rise. I couldn't stop it. "I'm in hell here! Do you hear me? This is a horrible, slow death!" I turned on the sink, not caring that the water splashed me. I was so used to the change now. The pain tore through me, but I had grown fond of it because I had begun to like punishing myself. I'd even learned to talk while transforming. Grandpa's eyes widened a little; he must have forgotten how horrifying it looked. "Just stare at me. I'm sure that'll make you feel better. Your granddaughter is cursed."

"Please, Jeanine, you need to calm down." Grandpa put up his hands, and for a moment it looked like he was about to start crying.

Seeing his hurt made me break down. I began crying. My anger turned to sadness and guilt. I'd just tried to shove away the only person who cared about me. "I'm sorry, Grandpa. I'm sorry."

Grandpa took a step toward me and placed a hand on my shoulder.

I flinched. I didn't want anyone to touch me anymore. There couldn't be any physical contact when I was a monster. It was too humiliating. "Don't touch me," I said between sobs, and Grandpa let go and stepped back.

"You need to get out of this cabin," Grandpa said, interrupting my pity party, but I didn't hate him for it.

"I'd love to, Grandpa, but I'm afraid." I continued to cry and feel pathetic.

"What are you afraid of?"

"I'm afraid that someone will see me as a monster."

"Yes, I know that, but just avoid water." Grandpa crossed his arms. "You're made of tough stuff, Jeanine; I've always known that. Don't give up."

I sniffed. "There's another thing that worries me."

"And what is that?"

"On my first day here, I met this guy, Mark — I don't know his last name — but he said his sister was murdered next door."

"I do know what you're talking about. But I wouldn't have sent you if I had thought you were in danger." Grandpa paused. "I was in the area when it happened. She was found down by the lake. They think she was mauled by a bear or cougar or something," he said, stroking his chin. "I knew that girl, and she wasn't very smart when it came to wild animals. I don't think you have anything to worry about, though. You won't go out and about if you see either of those, will you?" I realized that Grandpa was talking to me as if I were a baby instead of eighteen. It was the 'you're a big girl' kind of talk.

"Of course not, Grandpa. What do you think I am, a five-year-old?"

Grandpa chuckled. "Once you have a car you can go wherever you want around here. I think it'll be good for you to start making friends."

"I still don't know," I said. "Just thinking about talking with people and trying to be normal....any moment someone could spill a glass of water on me."

"Jeanine, look at it like this: Any minute you could be struck by lightning."

"I don't understand what you mean—"

"I mean that you can't let a what-if control your life."

"Still, Grandpa….lightning? I wouldn't go out into a thunderstorm thinking I'll be safe." I laughed; my tears had left, and now bitterness remained behind, resonating in my laugh.

"I'm going to get you a car tomorrow. Let's say we have some dinner now and then get some sleep." Grandpa didn't wish to debate with me any longer. I couldn't blame him. I was pathetic.

10

Greg stood by his pool, staring at me. I was in monster form. "You're so ugly!" He sneered. Then he stepped forward and began shaking me. Wait, someone was actually shaking me! I had been dreaming. My eyes flew open; the rough hands that grasped my upper arms let go.

"Haven't you ever heard the phrase, 'Let sleeping monsters lie'?" I growled.

"Very funny, Jean," Grandpa said. "It's good to see your sense of humor coming back."

I groaned and rolled to my side to face him; his face was contorted with urgency. "Why are you waking me up?"

"We're going to get you a vehicle."

I glanced at the bedside clock. "At five in the morning?"

"Yes. An old friend of mine, Tom Jeffers, has a truck he's selling. I told him we'd pick it up." Grandpa opened the shades to reveal that the sun was just making its appearance in the sky.

"A truck?"

"Yes; you'll like it, though. I saw it on my way in here. He said that we had to come early because he'd be out fishing most of the day." Grandpa pulled my covers off, exposing me to the cold northern-Wisconsin morning air.

"Hey!"

"Hurry up," Grandpa ordered. "He said he'd be leaving at

5:30."

*

"What did Mom and Dad tell my friends?" I asked, as we drove toward Tom whatshisname's house to get the truck.

Grandpa didn't answer me. He narrowed his eyes and shifted his spectacles. Something was up — something that he didn't want me to hear.

"Grandpa, what happened?" My tone was cold, but not at him; I was beginning to feel hatred toward my parents.

"You committed suicide, and they've asked me to tell you not to call any of your friends, even if you get cell phone service. They held a funeral for you....bought a gravestone."

"How come no one told me about this?" My eyes were watering up. I'd never talk to Diana or any of the people I'd known there again. Why was I sad about that? I'd always thought them boring and predictable. But still, I should have had a right to say how I'd died. And it hurt beyond anything that my parents were hopeless when it came to curing me. "How did I do it?" I swallowed.

"You jumped off a bridge."

"Nice. So no body was found, I take it?"

"Yep."

"Well, isn't that great; my parents would rather see me dead than expose me as a monster to the world." I'd said that aloud, when I had meant to keep it in my thoughts.

"I guess so. They said they did it for you." Grandpa's voice had dropped low. "We're here. Remember to be on your best behavior. And whatever you do, don't get wet."

We got out of Grandpa's rental. Tom's place was a dump. There was a little trailer, with car parts strewn about in his yard. A black beater truck that would make any of my New York friends laugh was parked in the tall grass. Grandpa knocked on the door of the trailer, and a scruffy guy with a beer belly overhanging his belt answered the door. He scratched his greasy hair. If the truck even worked, would it be sanitary to touch?

"Hey, Fred. You here for the truck?" Tom asked.

"Tom, I'd like to introduce you to my granddaughter, Jeanine Stafford."

"Nice to meet ya." He put out a hand. There was no way I was touching it after it'd been through that hair.

I smiled instead and gave a little wave. "Nice to meet you too, Mister...."

"Please, call me Tom." Tom raised his bushy brows but then chuckled and took back his hand, much to my relief. "So you're the one who is gonna take the truck off my hands?"

"I guess so," I muttered, and followed him and Grandpa toward the junky vehicle.

"She's been through a lot but got a new engine, so she should last you awhile now." Tom rubbed his hands on his distended stomach before digging in his trousers pocket to bring out keys. He handed them to me.

I took them as if I were picking up a piece of garbage. The guy probably *never* washed his hands. Grandpa shook his head at me and gave me a frown. My face must have given away my emotions. Of course, I realized; who was I to judge anyway? I mean, every time I stepped in the shower I sprouted a tail and claws.

"Thanks, Tom," I said to cover up for my rudeness.

"No problem. You're a city girl, aren't you?" He squinted one eye at me. Creepy.

"Yeah—"

"You'll get used to the Northwoods soon. It doesn't take that long." Tom patted me on the shoulder and gave a glance at Grandpa. "Well, I gotta get going. I'll see ya all later. Fred, why don't you show her how to operate this thing?"

"I'll make sure to do that." Grandpa smiled. "Take care."

Tom had another truck, which looked a tiny bit better than his last, and took off in that. I stepped up to the driver's side and hopped onto the seat. Sinking into the seat about an inch wasn't a reassuring first impression of the interior of the truck, but I turned the keys in the ignition and could hear that the engine was newer than the truck itself. "Why did Tom sell me a truck with a new engine?"

"I don't know. Tom's a character." Grandpa shook his head and chuckled. "Just be thankful you have this."

Placing my hands on the steering wheel and checking to make sure everything was familiar enough that I could drive the truck on my own, I nodded. "I think I can handle it."

"Good," Grandpa said, turning from me and toward his rental. "I'll meet you back at the cabin."

Following Grandpa's car back to the cabin, I found the classical station on the radio. Turning on the radio made me think of Mark almost immediately. Had he gone back to New York after the funeral? Or was he still convinced his sister was murdered? We drove past Mark's house, and I almost turned into his driveway to see what had happened.

Contrary to my first thoughts on the truck, it wasn't bad. Not as nice as our sporty newer cars at home, but it did its job. I parked next to the cabin and hopped out of the truck, my spirits lifted a little.

*

"Did you know Mark's family well?" I asked Grandpa as we sat for lunch at the table. The question had run in my mind the entire morning.

"Who's Mark?" Grandpa raised a brow, and a smile played on his lips. He must be thinking I'd already found someone to crush on.

I laughed. "He's just this guy I met on the airplane, the guy whose sister died next door."

"Oh." Grandpa's face transformed from playful to solemn. "I don't know them that well; just know a day before I left she got mauled by a bear."

"Mark thought that she was murdered."

"Of course he'd think that. He was always a bitter young man."

"I thought you said you didn't know them."

"Yes, I didn't know them well, but they were my neighbors. That musician kid seems to be one confused soul." Grandpa shook his head. "I'd stay away from him."

This knowledge made me want to get to know him better. There was a mystery about him now.

"Anyway, I think I'll be leaving tomorrow; summer classes are starting next week at the university," Grandpa said. "Did you make yourself some swimming clothes yet?"

"Swimming clothes? Grandpa, I'm a monster."

"Well, I hate to tell you this, Jean: You have the same body, just it's covered in scales, and you've added a tail." Grandpa shrugged. "I just don't want anyone ogling my granddaughter."

"Grandpa!" My eyes felt like they'd pop from my head, and my face went cold in mortification. "No one is ever going to see me anyway." I bit my lip. I didn't want to have to wear clothes while swimming; it'd get in the way of how fast I could travel. "And anyway, I don't plan on going in the water too much," I added, knowing that was a lie.

"I thought you said you'd been swimming every day?"

"I have....but that's not my choice."

"Interesting...."

"What do you mean?"

"I mean that you've become addicted, just like the curse said you would." Grandpa's face looked sympathetic.

"Thanks for bringing it up," I snarled, and stomped out of the kitchen to my room, slamming the door behind me and locking it. When Grandpa left tomorrow, I wouldn't be mourning him. Maybe I liked living alone more than I'd first thought.

*

Rain tapped against the roof of the cabin that night. Each drop felt like a bullet to my brain. It hadn't taken me long to realize that rainstorms were the worst temptation. Water was close and everywhere. Removing my nightgown, I opened the window of my cabin. The rain smelled so good to me, and the hurt of transforming welcoming, like atonement for being stupid enough to bring a curse on myself. Crawling out the window and through the grass, I reached the end of the dock and stared at the now black water. Was I brave enough to submerge myself this late at night? There wasn't a choice. I'd succumbed. I dove under.

*

Blinking into a bright light, I awoke groggily. Where was I? The sound of birds singing and water lapping against me indicated that somehow I'd slept outside. But where had I slept outside? My eyes were adjusting to the light, and I could make out a cabin in the distance; it wasn't mine. The back door of it swung open, and a male figure stepped out. Since I wasn't wearing my glasses, and my eyes were still bleary from sleeping, I couldn't make out any details of him. My tail flopped to the side and curled itself as I stretched. My tail! Oh I was a monster! Where the heck was I? Whoever the person was, he was headed right toward me! I found that I had been lying on a large rock, half submerged in the lake.

"What the—?" the man said. He'd seen me, and I recognized his voice. Mark.

Oh great. I ducked under the water and swam away from the shore as quickly as possible. Surfacing when I was a safe distance away and gripping hold of a log that stuck from the water, I could see Mark standing on the dock staring after me, a look of complete shock on his face. Our eyes connected for a fleeting moment, and I opened my mouth to say something but decided against it and dove under. Heading out into the open water, I didn't want to risk him seeing me return home. I'd learned that I could hold my breath for over twenty minutes. If I stayed under and out of sight, maybe he'd leave. What had possessed me to fall asleep on his shore? Trying to remember what I'd done last night was difficult. I'd gone down to the water to swim in the middle of the night. I remember it had been no different than swimming in the day because of my ability to map out things through hearing, much like a dolphin or bat, using echolocation. At the bottom of the lake, I rested and thought about how Grandpa had left this morning, and I'd missed saying goodbye. I was dead in his world, anyway. I rose to the surface a few feet away from my dock and checked to see if any boats were out. It was a quiet day on the lake; one far out boat was in the distance, but even with binoculars it wouldn't notice me.

*

Grandpa had left a note on my kitchen table, which I got as soon as I'd recovered my human form and dressed. "Jeanine, I figure that you're out swimming. My plane is leaving soon, so I guess I have no other choice but to leave you without a goodbye. Use the truck when necessary, and be cautious about showing yourself to anyone. Your Loving Grandpa Stafford."

How nice, I thought, as I collapsed on the couch. Well, so much for not letting anyone see me. I needed to pay a visit to Mark.

*

Not knowing why I felt so nervous knocking on the door of

Mark's house, I kept fingering my hair in my hands. I'd worn makeup, something I hadn't done since the plane trip over.

Mark answered the door. "Hey."

"I suppose you don't remember me," I said, giving a stupid little laugh.

"Yeah, I do," Mark said. "What brings you here, Jeanine?"

"Um, I just wanted to see how you were, and—"

"You're checking on me?" Mark chuckled and took a step back to allow me inside the house. "Do I look all right?"

"Well, yes." An awkward silence followed.

"Okay, why don't you come in and tell me why you're really here." Mark said with a laugh.

He couldn't be like Greg. Did he really mean that? "I'm not that kind of girl," I muttered.

"What do you mean?" Mark raised a brow.

"You know what I mean," I said, turning from him. Why had I even bothered visiting? And why did all the guys I meet turn out to be losers?

"Are you serious? You actually thought I was—" Mark laughed. "Jean, I wasn't meaning it that way. I guess it did sound kind of bad." Mark rolled his eyes. "But there has to be a reason you came here other than to check on me. Do you want to talk or something?"

His face was sincere, and I had to confess, despite my cynical attitude, I did believe that he'd been perfectly innocent. "Okay." I smiled at him and then laughed. "Wow, I can't believe how I assumed the worst of you right away."

"It makes me wonder if you've had guys pull stuff like that on you before," Mark said, giving me a grin. But upon seeing my face, his grin disappeared. "You have, haven't you?"

"Yeah, my last boyfriend was a douche."

"Man, I'm sorry." His cabin was more like a lodge. It was quite roomy, and there was a fireplace blazing in the living room. "We can sit here." He motioned toward a couch and a recliner. He plopped down in the recliner, and I sat very neatly on the couch. "So, I never learned your last name."

"Stafford. And what is yours?"

"Calvin."

"Well, I guess we've officially met now." I rubbed my upper arms. The warmth from the fire made this place feel cozy. "How are you doing? Like it must be hard, with your sister and everything."

Mark's playful attitude seemed to vanish completely. "I think I know what killed her."

"Oh, so it was an animal," I said, breathing a sigh of relief.

"Not really an animal that I've seen before. There was this creature on our shore this morning. I know you're going to think me crazy for saying this. It was shaped like a person, sort of, but it had this long tail, like a lizard, and spikes going down its back, and scales covering its entire body."

It was great to hear someone describe me so warmly. "Wow," I said, trying to hide the shock. Oh great, now he thought *I'd* killed his sister.

"Go ahead and laugh at me, but I'm serious. I even took a picture."

"A picture?" My voice raised a pitch, and my eyes widened and mouth dropped before I could control myself.

"Yeah, on my iPhone." Mark dug in his pocket and got up to sit by me on the couch. "See?" A blurry picture showing my face, one of my clawed hands gripping a log, my tail curling out of the water, my mouth open, and my eyes staring glared back at me from his iPhone's glossy screen. He'd taken it from the second time I'd surfaced. I could shoot myself. Why had I resurfaced so close to him? I could write a how-to manual for stupidity.

"Ew," I said, wrinkling my nose, deciding to act as if I'd never seen the creature.

"Nasty looking, huh?"

Why thank you, Mark, I thought. "Yeah," I answered.

"You should have seen its claws: they were so sharp-looking," Mark said. "I am almost positive this is what killed Jessie."

"Why would you say that? I mean, you could have Photoshopped this." I'd better play it cool, like a normal person. "Some people are really good at Photoshopping."

"So you think I'm lying?"

"No, but I'm just saying, that's sort of....silly. Like a monster in a lake...."

"Loch Ness has one." Mark seemed bemused by my unbelief. "You don't have to believe me. But I'm going to bring its head—"

"What!" I interrupted him, and I felt my face grow cold.

"I'm just saying, it's dangerous. It killed my sister."

"How do you know that?"

"It tore her apart. One of her arms was found in the lake."

If I didn't feel like throwing up now…."Oh my—"

"Yeah." Mark shook his head. "I'm going to kill whoever or whatever killed her." His face was filled with vengeance, and I couldn't blame him.

"It ripped her apart?" My voice was squeaky.

"Yeah." Mark got up from the couch and fell back into the recliner.

"I still don't understand why you're so convinced that....whatever it was that you took a picture of, was what did it." I said, trying to regain my composure.

"I'm positive," Mark said defiantly. "You just don't believe it's real, but you will when I bring its body out of that lake."

"And how are you planning to do that?" I asked, crossing my arms.

"I don't know." Mark leaned back in his recliner and tucked his iPhone back in his pocket. "I just want retribution."

That was a pretty big word for some backwoods guy. What was his day job, anyway? "What did you major in?"

Mark's eyes gave me direct contact, and I was caught in their spell. They were so strange. His dark features were so opposite them. I realized that if I'd met him in high school in New York, Diana and I would have gossiped about him as being just plain freaky. But his strangeness attracted me. There was something mysterious about it, as if he were unpredictable and exciting. It was silly, really, to think that if your appearance was strange you had to be interesting. And yet, since becoming a monster and living alone, my mind had begun to think differently than it had in the past.

"I'm a music major."

"Really?" I'd never done anything artistic in my life, and I'd always thought music a field more for women. There was nothing feminine about Mark though.

"Yeah, a lot of people look shocked when I tell them that." Mark raised a brow.

"Well, I mean, after you told me how you're planning on hunting down a monster I just figured—"

"Um, you're looking at a guy who grew up on hunting." Mark

chuckled, but it wasn't a happy sound — more bitter. "So what are *you* majoring in?"

"I'm going to be a history professor." It was out before I thought about it. I'd been so used to telling everyone with pride what I was going to do in life. "But I'm taking a semester off."

"Why?"

"Why what?" I blinked.

"Why are you taking a semester off?"

"Oh, well, I-I was tired from high school. Really worn down and…." There had to be a better excuse than that if he was going to believe me. "And I also needed time to recover from….from posttraumatic stress disorder." Good save, Jeanine, I thought. Pat yourself on the back.

"Oh." Mark looked to the fireplace. "I know how that is. I'm sorry."

My eyes glued themselves on him. He'd had posttraumatic stress disorder? I guess my assumption that weird-looking people were full of mysteries was true, and now I wished he'd explain. "How long ago?"

"A couple of years ago," Mark said, so low that I could barely hear. "What happened to you?"

"I'd rather not talk about it." Since Mark hadn't told me his probably true story of the experience, I wasn't going to tell him my nonexistent situation.

Abruptly, Mark leaned forward and fixed his gaze on me again. Without warning, my heartbeat began thumping against my rib cage. There was just something about those eyes. "Wait, so you're suffering from posttraumatic stress disorder, and you've decided to come out to Hayward to live by yourself? Am I getting this right?" His dark brows arched inward with confusion and narrowed his beautiful eyes.

He made a pretty good point. "My parents didn't want me around," I said, because I knew he sort of knew this fact already. "They couldn't live with my problem, so they sent me here."

"That's horrible."

I wanted to hug him. Finally, someone recognized how terrible my parents were treating me! "Yeah, I know."

"When will you be going back?" Mark leaned back again in his recliner. "To tell you the truth, I thought you'd already be gone."

"Well, it looks like I'm going to be staying here awhile. Especially because my parents don't want me back anytime soon." I sighed and already felt my stomach begin twisting.

"Miss your friends, huh?"

"Yes," I said, surprised that it was true. "My friend, Diana, she was a model, and we used to talk about everything. Guys, clothes, future plans—" My voice stopped, and I suddenly felt like crying. I swallowed hard and turned my face to look out the window so Mark couldn't see my eyes glass over. If I started crying, I didn't have to worry; for some reason, water my own body made didn't trigger a change.

"I'm sorry," Mark said, his voice holding sincerity I didn't think capable from a guy.

"I'd better get going now," I said, rising from the couch.

"Okay." Mark stood from the recliner as well.

"Thanks for chatting with me," I said, and gave one more glance into those eyes.

"It's not a problem. Actually, thanks for visiting. My parents left, so I've been sort of alone, too."

This made me halt in his doorway. "Your parents left? So soon after she died?"

"Well, they're in a lot of pain because of it, and I sort of convinced them to go back to Florida. It'll keep their minds busy and not thinking about Jessie." Mark's voice almost seemed to crack when saying his sister's name, and that broke my heart.

"Are you sure you're going to be okay?" I asked, wishing I could put my hand on his shoulder.

"I'll be fine." Mark smiled vaguely. "I just want to figure out what happened to her. That's why I'm staying. I'm sort of self-employed, so it doesn't matter where I am."

"Don't you have a girlfriend or something in New York?" I found myself asking this question more because I was curious if he was single.

Mark shook his head. "Haven't met 'the one' yet."

"Oh." My heart did a little flutter, and I wanted to slap myself. What the hell was wrong with me? I bit my lip.

"But I miss my friends." Mark opened the door for me. "Have a good weekend!"

"Yeah, thanks." I began out the door but jumped when his hand touched my shoulder.

"Hey, I was wondering, do you want to go to this party on Saturday?" Mark smiled slightly.

Wow, was he asking me on a date? "When is it?"

"Around seven. I'll pick you up."

"Okay." My voice had risen in pitch. What was I thinking? Had I just accepted?

"Cool. I'll see you then." Mark smiled.

"Yeah." I stepped from his doorway and walked to my truck, or stumbled as it were. I must be going crazy. I'd promised myself that I wouldn't get into any new friendships. But talking with Mark had almost made me forget what happened when water touched me. Water....no! Anyway, Mark wanted to kill me. But for some reason, that only made hanging out with him all the more appealing, in a perverse sort of way. Images of Greg involuntarily floated into my mind. Especially the face he'd given me when he'd seen me turn into a monster.

11

I sat alone at my dinner table eating a fancy meal of macaroni and cheese. The sound of frogs croaking by the lake serenaded me from outside. I'd be going to a party with Mark in two days! For a fleeting moment, I thought of calling Diana. But, oh wait, Diana thought I'd killed myself. I didn't have any phone service anyway. The ambience in my cabin was unbearable that night. There was no one to talk to in the darkest hours of the night, and I wanted to spill my guts to someone, cry on a shoulder, and tell them about how frustrating it was to live for nothing, to *be* nothing! But I comforted myself that now I had a small purpose. Saturday night I had something people expected of me.

After finishing the mac and cheese, I placed my dishes in the sink. I washed them after putting on elbow-length gloves. I couldn't have my kitchen looking dirty, just in case Mark wanted to see inside the place on Saturday. There was an excitement creeping into me. My family, who didn't want me, didn't have to know about what I did anymore. They had even faked my suicide, so they didn't have to bother with me ever again. I didn't even care if they visited. Okay, sometimes I wished I could see Corrine. She'd seemed sad when I left. Did she still think of me? It was silly of me to miss a kid whom I'd often thought of as immature and annoying, but when it came down to it, she was the only member of my family that I missed, besides Grandpa of course. But he didn't live with us, and for some reason, I suspected that I'd see more of him than anyone else in my family. I tucked myself into bed but didn't fall asleep for another hour. My mind kept returning to Mark's unique face and the way he'd seemed interested in what I had to say, which seemed an alien notion to guys like Greg.

*

Ten times. That's how many times I'd looked in the mirror to check my hair and makeup. I'd used dark brown eyeliner and mascara. I was wearing the blue dress I'd worn after my green one had ripped at the party. One disadvantage to not having my Mom around was that I didn't have someone to check with who could say I looked beautiful. Tying my long hair back in a ponytail, I let a few wisps hang loose to frame my face. In the mirror, I pictured my monster-self staring back and jumped away, my heartbeat racing. "Just stay away from water," I told myself aloud, as I'd gotten into the habit of doing, so I could hear a human voice in the silence of my cabin.

A knock on the door sounded, and I hurried to it after smoothing my dress once more. Feeling a rush of anticipation, I opened the door.

Mark stood in the doorway, dressed pretty casual, wearing jeans, which hung loosely on his slender frame, and a T-shirt. "Hey," Mark said.

I wished for a compliment but didn't get one. "Hey," I answered back, giving him a little smile. "Am I dressed up too much?"

"No." Mark laughed and put a hand to the back of his neck. "Actually....yes."

"Oh, no." Feeling my face heating up, I placed my hands on my cheeks. "What sort of party is it?" I asked.

"Well, it's just a bonfire."

"A bonfire?" I repeated.

"Yeah, and there's going to be a movie afterward. Some of my friends invited me." Mark's grin was lopsided. "I'm sorry; I should have specified."

My dismay was showing on my face. "It's okay," I said.

"Maybe if you want to change," Mark said, shrugging, "you

can do that quickly."

I nodded and walked into the cabin. Motioning toward the couch in my living room, I said, "You can sit here if you want." It was a good thing I'd made sure the place was spotless.

"Thanks." Mark sat down, and I hurried into my room.

Switching into a more casual jeans and blouse, I hurried back to Mark.

"Perfect," Mark said, smiling at me.

"Good," I said, raising my chin a little.

There was silence for a minute, and then Mark clapped his hands together. "Well, let's go."

"Okay," I said, getting an impulse to giggle.

Mark's car was no longer the rental. It was a truck, but much newer than mine, with very comfortable leather seats.

"How's it been?" Mark asked.

"Fine," I answered. This was general conversation, the kind that one makes when they feel obligated to talk to one another. It bothered me. "Thanks for inviting me."

"No problem."

Another silence followed.

"So you have friends around here?" I asked.

"I did grow up here." Mark's gaze stayed on the road at all times, and I worried that he might be bored with me. I found my hands were again twisting strands of my hair, ruining the hard work I'd done earlier.

"So, what happens at a bonfire?"

"Well, there's a bonfire." Mark's laugh after saying that made me jolt. "And then we're going to watch a movie. Nothing complicated. I don't know what kind of parties you attended in New York, but here in Hayward we don't have any special names for things."

Realizing that he was picking on my upbringing, I stuck out my bottom lip. "In my defense, we don't call bonfires and movie nights 'going to a party'."

"What did you think we would be doing? Heading to a club?"

"No. Do they even have any of those here?"

"Ha!" Mark said laughing. "Stuck up city girl, huh?"

I giggled. "Yep, and proud of it."

"Well, that's just great." Mark gave a dramatic roll of his eyes. "How come I always get stuck with people like you?"

"You're the one who invited me," I said, sticking out my tongue. "Anyway, I think that you secretly like it."

The truck turned down a gravel road. "This is called a *driveway* in Hayward, Jean." Mark drew out each syllable as if I were a little kid.

It made me giggle again. I couldn't remember when I'd last laughed like this. "Are you serious?" I asked, widening my eyes and blinking. Mark chuckled, a deep, throaty sound. I also liked that he called me "Jean".

"Here we are." Mark parked the car, its wheels crackling against the gravel.

A small house that looked like a traditional log cabin sat atop a steep hill in front of us. Mark offered his hand to me to help me up the hill. His grip was strong and warm and his fingers long. He'd said he was a music major. Maybe he was a piano player.

"How many people are going to be there?" I asked.

"Oh, about six or seven. I don't know for sure," Mark answered. With his free hand, he flicked his hair back. I wondered if there was a girl at this bonfire that he was interested in; I hoped that wasn't the case. Once over the hill, a dancing fire and a circle of chairs around it came into view.

"Hey!" Mark called out, waving his free hand.

Some of the people sitting around the fire stood. One of them, a short guy with dirty blond hair hanging over his shoulders and a goatee, spoke. "Mark! It's been a while."

Mark let go of my hand, much to my dismay, and embraced a couple of the people in the group. One of them was a girl.

"Who is this?" The girl asked, giving Mark a smile and then looking toward me.

Before Mark could say my name or introduce me, I spoke up. "I'm Jeanine Stafford."

The short guy with the long hair was the first to extend his hand. "Luke Perry."

Another young man rose to shake my hand. He'd grown a beard to hide acne. I could make out a few red dots on his jaw in the flickering light of the fire. "Jordan Miller."

Mark had been right about the number of people; it was a small group. The girl was the next one to greet me. "I'm Hayley Adams." Her dark hair was cut short in a pixie cut, but it suited her oval face.

"Nice to meet you all," I said. A quiet guy and girl didn't greet me personally. They nodded at me with a small wave. They looked like a brother and sister pair, both with white-blond features.

Mark sat in one of the chairs between Hayley and Luke. There was another empty chair between Luke and the blond girl, so I sat down there. It was nice to be nowhere near a lake. This cabin was situated in the middle of the woods.

"How's it been going?" Jordan asked Mark. Jordan lifted a

beer bottle to his lips and took a swig. He opened a cooler next to him and lifted another bottle out. "Want one?"

Mark shook his head and raised his hands. "No thanks. It's been going fine. I have a picture that I think all of you should see."

Oh god, he wasn't going to bring out that picture he'd taken of me, was he?

Mark brought his iPhone into view, and I began to panic.

"Nice gadget, dude," Luke said. "What is it?"

"It's an iPhone, Luke," Hayley said, rolling her eyes.

"I took this picture by the lake." Mark held up my picture for all to see; I could feel my face flushing.

"What the heck is it?" Jordan stood and squinted his eyes at the screen.

"Wow, that's the worst phony monster I've ever seen." Luke chuckled.

Hayley didn't say anything; she just stared at it.

The blond girl spoke up, though. "Where was this?"

"It's real, man, so real. Its tail moved like a whip," Mark said to Luke, and then he turned to the blond girl. "It was just off my dock, Meg." So the blond girl's name was Meg, and Mark knew her.

Luke shook his head, crossed his arms. "Mark, you're too old to be pulling pranks like that."

"Yeah." Jordan slouched back into his chair as well.

Luke leaned over toward me. "Jeanine, right?"

"Yep." My hands kept fidgeting.

"Where are you from, and how did you end up going out with a freak like Mark?"

"I'm not going out with him," I said, shrugging.

"Then you're single?" Luke grinned. I didn't like him; he reminded me of Greg.

"I'm not looking for anyone," I said, crossing my legs.

"Oh." Luke stopped smiling at me and gazed back into the bonfire.

I caught onto the conversation again that Luke had distracted me from.

"This monster in the picture you've got here, Mark, isn't real," Jordan said articulately. Did I see a stretch of concern wringing on Jordan's brow?

"Why not?" Mark's face was serious. "Why can't there be a monster in Teal Lake?"

"'Cause they don't exist, and even if they did, how would it get into Teal Lake?" Hayley spoke up now.

"Teal Lake is connected to a river, and that river is connected to another. I mean, for all we know this creature could've come from anywhere." Mark shrugged. "But I don't need you guys to believe me; I'm going to prove you *all* wrong when I kill it."

"Why are you going to kill it?" Meg asked. Her brother still remained mute; his eyes didn't travel to the other members of the group. They seemed blank or far away, as if he were in a different place, a place that troubled him.

"Because I think it's what killed Jessie," Mark said, his eyes unblinking.

Everyone around the bonfire grew silent. Hayley rubbed her eyes, and I wondered if she was wiping a tear away. Luke continued to stare into the fire, and Jordan shifted in his chair. Hayley stood and put a hand on Mark's shoulder. "Mark, maybe you need to see a doctor or something."

"Why?" Mark frowned, and his brows arched inward and downward.

"You need to understand that Jessie was not murdered or killed by a monster," Jordan put in slowly.

Mark's face went blank. "You don't understand."

"Of course we don't, but I was best friends with her, Mark," Hayley said, her light eyes flashing with the fire. "So don't tell me that I'm not mourning her and frustrated either!"

"Are we going to watch a movie soon?" I asked, because I was getting uncomfortable now.

All eyes turned to me, even the silent blond kid's.

"What?" Mark asked.

"When are we going to watch the movie? And what are we watching?" I noticed Mark's faint smile, as if he knew I was trying to steer the topic off his sister.

"I don't know, but I want to watch a thriller," Jordan said. Then he gave Luke a look. "It's your house though, Luke."

Luke shrugged. "Yeah, we can put in a movie."

"Better not watch a monster flick," Hayley said rolling her eyes. "Mark might become even more convinced that there are monsters all over the world."

"Just because you've never heard or seen something doesn't mean it can't happen or that it's not there." Had I just said that? What was wrong with me? Dump some water on me now.

Mark's eyes connected with mine, and the corners of his mouth twitched. He didn't say anything, but I could tell he was giving me a silent thank-you.

Hayley snickered, not put down or convinced of what I'd just said. "Where are you from, Jeanine?"

"New York."

"What are you doing in Hayward?" Hayley narrowed her eyes at me.

"I'm taking a break from school," I said. Hayley annoyed me, and her smug expressions made me want to say, Don't make a monster pissed off with you.

"From what?" Jordan asked, returning to the conversation.

"Guys, come on. Stop asking her all these questions, and let's just watch a movie." Mark stood from his seat.

They agreed with him, and we began up the hill to Luke's cabin.

12

Luke's family's cabin was a little bigger than mine. There was a large high-definition television in the living room. Mark sat on a couch and motioned for me to sit beside him. I hoped Mark wouldn't notice my shaking hands as I sat next to him.

"So, are we gonna watch a thriller?" Jordan asked, chuckling a little. He'd brought the cooler inside with him, and Luke took a bottle from it.

Hayley kept glaring at me, making me shift in my seat and my hands shake even more. "Yeah," Hayley said, still keeping her eyes on me. "Let's watch something that'll make us scream."

Mark leaned over near my ear, making my spine prickle. It was weird that I felt so nervous around him. When Greg had done stuff like that, I'd been brave and defiant. "Are you okay?" Mark asked.

"Of course I'm okay," I said, rolling my eyes.

"Thanks for covering for me earlier." Mark straightened up in his seat, a genuine smile on his face.

"No problem; thanks for doing the same for me," I said, returning his smile and continuing to feel attracted to him, especially when he looked at me like that. His expression held a growing fondness, and I'd never had anyone look at me like that, nor looked at anyone in this way. I wanted to cry.

"What's wrong?" Mark's brow knit.

My emotions gave me away in the blink of an eye. "Sorry," I said, putting a hand on my cheek and looking away from Mark.

"This will be good," Luke said, as he turned on the movie. I'd missed hearing which movie they'd picked, but I didn't care.

*

"Did you enjoy it?" Mark asked later. We had been driving along in silence for the past five minutes. My eyelids felt as if they were made of iron.

"Hmm?" I asked. I'd heard him, but my mind wasn't processing information at this point. My body burned with achy tiredness.

"Did you enjoy the movie?" Mark chuckled this time.

I tried to remember all that had happened. It had been a werewolf flick, and I'd hated it. "I don't feel like they got enough emotional depth into what it's like to be a monster," I answered him drowsily.

"Why do you say that?"

The sound of rain beginning to patter against the car woke up everything inside me. "It's raining," I said, clutching my seatbelt in my hand.

"Yeah," Mark said. He hadn't caught the tension in my voice, which happened to be a good thing for me. "Anyway, why didn't you think it had enough emotional depth?"

I tried to bring myself into our conversation again. "He wasn't horrified enough."

"Why do you say that?"

"Well, he let being a monster not freak him out." I shrugged.

"How would you handle the situation?" Mark asked, raising his brows in challenge, and grinning.

Was I really being asked that? I laughed at myself, but decided against answering the question. "He could also not look at the full moon. It's not that hard; just lock yourself up."

"Don't have much sympathy for him then, huh?" Mark turned the car off the gravel road onto a curving paved road. There were ten short minutes until we'd arrive at my destination. I hoped it'd stop raining. Talk about déjà vu.

"No," I said. "I don't have any sympathy for some guy who isn't horrified by the fact that he's a monster." For some odd reason, my adrenaline began pumping. The rain continued in its tantalizing rhythm against the windshield. "The idea that forever your life will be changed, taken from the human race, and there is no going back…." My voice trailed off. "It is extremely horrifying."

Mark chuckled. "You make it sound as if *you're* a werewolf."

"Not quite," I said dryly.

"Did you have a fun time?" Mark asked, keeping his gaze on the road.

"Yes," I answered. "Thanks for taking me. So, Hayley mentioned that you go to church?" I normally wouldn't have brought the subject up, but I wanted to hold a conversation that would keep my mind away from the rain outside.

"Yeah," Mark answered. "What are your beliefs on that?"

"I'm…." I had no idea what I believed in that sense. There had to be something going on besides the natural world. I was convinced of that now especially. "I believe that things happen around us that we can't explain," I began, "but I've never made a clear conclusion to what it is, or if there is a Greater Being out there." I laughed. "Hayley seemed pretty annoyed that you go to church."

"Yeah, she's never seen the point."

"Did Jessie go?"

"Yes. She loved God a lot."

"She loved God? What is your god, Mark?"

"What is yours?"

"Water," I said, before thinking it through.

"Water?" Mark gave me a confused look. "Why?"

"I love being in it. You didn't tell me what your god is yet," I said. Water had become my god while out here. It was the thing that I feared, wanted, and loved all at the same time.

"I'm a Christian," said Mark.

Trying to force back a laugh, I said, "Good for you."

Mark chuckled. "But I didn't believe."

"What?" Now he'd caught my interest.

"It's sort of a long story."

"Long story?" I cast a quick glance at the rain. "I've got time."

"Well, my parents raised us to believe in God, but I hadn't accepted it until only a few years ago. God really changed my life."

"Why did you accept it?"

"Remember how I told you that I had suffered from posttraumatic stress disorder in the past?"

"Yeah."

"Something happened to me that really woke me up a couple of years ago," Mark said.

We were almost to my cabin. Again, I'd have to wait for the rain to die down before leaving. Maybe he'd talk long enough to keep me with him. "What happened to you?"

"It doesn't matter." Mark's voice trailed for a moment before he cleared his throat. "But it brought me to the realization that I needed to do something. Life is short, and I have no control of what happens."

"No control," I repeated. His words caused me to think. You

have no control over what happens. I'd thought I'd be going to school by the time autumn came along, but I'd been very wrong. In the past I had counted on predictability in life. Now that I thought about it, I didn't remember a time when I hadn't known what the next day would bring, except now.

"It looks like we're here." Mark pulled up by my cabin. "Do you need an umbrella? I can walk you to your door."

I folded my hands in my lap and took a quick glance out the window at the rain. "No," I said. My voice came out as a gasp, and I hoped Mark didn't noticed.

He rubbed a hand against the back of his neck. "Okay. Well, thanks for coming. Hey, you want to come to church with me tomorrow morning?"

"Sure," I mumbled, not really thinking about his question, just about the droplets on the glass of the windows. There was a silence, and then I realized that Mark was waiting for me to get out of the car. "Thanks for the fun time," I said mechanically, resting my hand on the door.

"Don't mention it." Mark watched me as if he knew what would happen when I opened the door.

I remained in my seat and tried the door, letting it open a crack.

"Are you afraid of something?" Mark asked, furrowing his brows and leaning toward me.

"The monster," I whispered, the hair on my neck prickling at the word.

"What? Oh…." Mark's eyes softened. "I'm sorry; I shouldn't keep bringing it up. I'm sure you'll be safe once you get inside. The offer still stands to walk you to the door."

The monster was waiting to take me when I stepped out this door. I couldn't allow that to happen in front of Mark. "Listen, Mark,

I need your help."

"What do you need my help with?"

"Can you close your eyes while I walk to the cabin? Can you…." I had to think fast. I knew that he'd mentioned going to church, and I'd always seen people closing their eyes when they prayed. An idea struck me. "Can you pray for me?"

"Um….okay," Mark raised his brows as if surprised. "Sure."

"Close your eyes. Please, pray that the monster doesn't get me." He did as I'd said as if by magic.

I made a dash from the car and toward the cabin. The first splashes hit my skin, beginning to change me. Opening the cabin door, I rushed inside. My tail was just lengthening itself out when I shut the door, and it barely missed being slammed. I curled it back and breathed a sigh of relief. It had been too dark and rainy for Mark to see anything when I'd run. Anyway, I'd set up the fact that I was scared, so it wouldn't surprise him that I'd rushed into the cabin. He would come inside if he'd seen anything, so when I heard his car start I knew everything was fine. I stood straight in my monster form, trying to walk upright, using my tail for balance. It'd been something I'd been practicing. I might as well take a shower, since I was due for one, and I didn't want to go through two transformations in one night.

*

A loud knocking sound made my heart pound when I woke. "What?" I said aloud, blinking my eyes, then rubbing the sleep out of them. I stood on the creaky floorboards of my bedroom. Waking up in the cabin had begun to feel normal. The knocking continued. I hurried out into the main room and peeked through the window next to the door to see who was waking me up so early on a Sunday. Mark was waiting at the door dressed in khakis and a button-down.

What was he doing here? I opened the door. "Hey," I said, brushing away the hair that hung over one of my eyes.

"Are you ready for church?" A smile crept onto his face, and it irked me. He thought this was funny?

"I'm sorry, I forgot," I mumbled, turning back into the cabin.

"Are you just going to go to church only wearing a T-shirt?" Mark asked, raising a brow, his grin growing by the minute. "I mean, we have all kinds of people there, but I'm pretty sure that this is pushing the limit."

I grabbed hold of the bottom of the oversized T-shirt and yanked it down. "Sorry, I'll be right back," I said sheepishly, blood pumping in my face. As I began searching for clothes, I came to the realization that I hadn't been wearing a bra, either. Mark had been right yesterday. You never know what tomorrow will bring or be able to control it. Pulling on some pants and then putting on a bra and shirt, I hurried back into the living room where Mark stood. This was the second time he'd had to wait for me to get dressed. It was becoming a rather rude bad habit.

"Have you eaten anything?" Mark asked, amusement in his strange eyes.

"No," I said.

"The service starts in fifteen minutes." Mark glanced at his watch. "We can be a little late."

"It won't take me long," I assured him, hurrying into the kitchen.

Mark laughed. "You know, Jean, it was boring in Wisconsin before you showed up."

13

They sang songs at Mark's church that were okay and of course the church songs were about Jesus. A man stood for about half an hour talking about forgiveness of sins. Thinking back, I couldn't recall any sins that I'd committed. I'd never killed anyone or stolen anything, and heck, I hadn't even gotten laid. It looked like my track to heaven was pretty sure. The church itself had a pretty amazing appearance. It was a big log building with beautiful glass windows and a cross in the archway of the entrance.

I'd sat with Mark during the service. A man I recognized, the one who'd given me the truck, approached once we'd been dismissed.

"Mark Calvin, I see that you and Jeanine Stafford are getting along fine."

Mark smiled at the chubby man that I couldn't remember the name of. He'd cleaned up since the last time I'd seen him; probably because he was at church, and they'd have thrown him out. "Yeah, I decided to take her to church with me, Tom."

Oh yeah, his name was Tom.

"How's the truck working for ya?" Tom asked, his gaze shifting to me. His bushy brows nearly touched in the middle.

"I haven't had any problems," I said with a shrug.

"Good, good." Tom waved. "Well, I'll see ya'll later then."

As I watched Tom lumber away, I noticed other familiar faces. Meg, her brother, and Luke were among the rest of the congregation.

"Mark, why doesn't that kid ever talk?" I asked, pointing to the brother of Meg.

"Oh, Charlie?"

"Oh, so that's his name."

"Don't know why he never talks," said Mark. "Charlie used to be quite the chatterbox."

"What?" The hair on the back of my neck prickled, and I couldn't place why. Something about that kid just freaked me out.

"Who knows?" Mark shrugged. "Hey, I'm going to talk to Luke for a minute."

"Okay," I said, sitting down again in one of the rows. Being talkative had never been a forte of mine, and since living in the cabin and becoming a monster, people made me feel even more uncomfortable.

"You're Jeanine, right?" a tenor voice said from behind me.

I turned to face whoever it was. It was Meg's brother, the one whom Mark had said was called Charlie. "Yes, and you're Charlie?"

The kid nodded and crossed his arms. "Are you living in the Stafford cabin?"

"Yes." I blinked. "I am a Stafford."

Charlie kept fidgeting as if he were nervous. "Do you know Frederick Stafford?"

"He's my grandpa," I said, smiling. "Do you know him?"

"I used to clean the cabin for him when he was away, so I guess I know him." Charlie didn't give me eye contact.

"Oh," I said. "Then I guess you live nearby?"

"No, I live on the other side of Teal," Charlie said. "Hey, um….I…." He seemed as if he were about to tell me something, but instead he said, "I have to go. It was nice meeting you, Jeanine."

"Yeah." My gaze followed him as he hurried off. There was something wrong with that kid.

"Jean!" Mark called. He stood next to Luke. Luke had his hair tied back in a ponytail for the service. "Over here!"

I rose from my seat and approached them, still feeling dazed over encountering Charlie. "What is it?" I asked.

"We were wondering if you want to go to coffee," Luke said.

"Coffee?"

"Yeah. We only have one place in Hayward, but it makes the best coffee," Luke announced proudly. I longed to tell him that I'd been to a Starbucks, thank you very much.

I shrugged. "Okay, sounds great."

"Hayley, Meg, Charlie, and Jordan are going to meet us there," Mark explained.

So they weren't just a bunch of friend-of friends. Mark had come back into their clique when he'd returned from New York, and for some reason he was including me. I had grown comfortable with talking to Mark, more comfortable than I'd ever been with any guy. It made me wonder if this friendliness he showed me would last.

Following him and Luke outside, I grew uneasy and realized Charlie was watching me. It bothered me that I'd have to see him at the coffee shop. Why were they friends with him, anyway? I got into Mark's car and sat next to him.

"Did you enjoy the service?" Mark asked, giving me a quick, encouraging smile.

"Um….sort of." I shifted in my seat and folded my hands in my lap.

"What's going on?" Mark asked. "Do you *want* to go to

coffee?"

"Oh, yes, of course," I assured him.

"Then what's wrong?"

"It's Charlie."

"Charlie?" Mark furrowed his brow as he continued to look at the road. "What did he do?"

"He came up to talk to me, but it was really weird." I took a deep breath. "He acted like he was speaking to a ghost when talking to me, all nervous and stuff."

"That is weird," Mark muttered. "Don't worry about it. I think something is wrong with him, like he's partially not all there upstairs, if you know what I mean."

"But he still hangs out with you guys."

"He used to be fine. Something happened to him, and he won't say what. The guy has got a problem." Mark shrugged. "I've tried talking to him. He used to be one of my closest friends."

"Do you think he saw your sister get killed or something involved with that?" The words were out before I could stop them.

"What?" Mark glanced at me for a moment, taking his gaze away from the road. His interesting face contorted in bewilderment, and his jaw dropped a little. Maybe he hadn't expected me to bring up his sister like that. "No, he got messed up before Jessie was murdered. While I was in New York, we used to e-mail and call each other, but then he stopped one day. It was like two months before Jessie died when that happened." Mark sounded a little pissed about this.

"How long did you live in New York, Mark?"

"I lived there about six months."

"You told me on the plane that you went to New York to run

away. What were you running from?" I felt I'd known him long enough now to ask this but braced myself for an angry reaction.

"Oh, just stuff," Mark said, brushing the question off. "I don't know why I even told you that." He chuckled.

You're not fooling anyone, I thought. There is a big reason that you're not telling me. But I'm going to figure it out. It's my mission.

"I'm going out on the lake tomorrow," Mark announced, changing the subject.

"Oh?"

"I know you're sick of me, but would you like to come with?"

"I'm not sick of you." I laughed with him. "I'd love to come with—" Crap! I'd forgotten about the curse.

"Great! Just come down by my dock tomorrow in the morning sometime." Mark's grin reminded me a little bit of how Greg had been so pleased when he'd thought he'd won me over. This brought to me the fact that I really didn't know Mark that well yet. All of this nice-guy stuff could be an act to get me to sleep with him. We were in downtown Hayward now, if it could even be called "downtown," and Mark parked next to the coffee shop. It certainly didn't look like a Starbucks. Upon walking in, the first thing which caught my attention was a heavyset Native American guy sitting at a table playing a guitar-like instrument with a hat resting on the table for tips. The smell of coffee beans and chocolate greeted me warmly. Luke, Jordan, and Hayley stood waiting for us in line.

"Wow," I found myself saying, as I took in the rustic originality of the coffee shop. "This looks good."

"Knew you'd like it," Mark said, and waved to the group. "Hey, guys, look who decided to join us again: the city girl."

Beginning to wonder if that was the only title Mark was going to give me, I followed him toward the group.

Hayley smiled at me. "Nice to see you again, Jeanine."

I disliked her, and now her fake way of greeting me caused the feeling to grow. "Where are Meg and Charlie?"

"I'm sure they'll be here soon." Jordan shrugged, and when I looked toward him I realized his eyes were focused on my chest. How nice.

Luke, whom I had put off the other night, still didn't grace me with a smile or eye contact.

Hayley linked her thin arm with mine and took me to a table. "The guys know what kind of stuff is best. In the meantime, let's get to know each other."

"Okay," I said, drawing out the word and wishing I could pull myself away from her and stay with my new best friend, Mark.

"So tell me, how old are you?"

"I'm eighteen," I said.

"Me, too! I'm in my last year of high school. What are you doing with school? I know you're taking a year off," Hayley continued, talking a mile per minute. "But what are you studying?"

"I'm a history major."

"Well, that's cool. Do you have a boyfriend in New York?"

"No." Biting my lip, I looked down.

"Do you like Mark?"

Whoa! Where had that come from? I didn't know her, and she was asking very personal questions. "Um, excuse me?" I couldn't help the shock in my statement or voice or my face as I brought my gaze back to her.

"Well, a lot of girls end up liking Mark until they figure out who he really is and why he *really* left here," Hayley said smugly, crossing her arms and nodding toward him as he stood in line.

"Who is he?" Someone was going to give me an answer.

"He's almost as much of a mess as Charlie. They were best friends once, but then he — well, Mark, left."

"What do you mean?" I looked in his direction. His tall figure slouching slightly, his dark hair waving across his forehead, his ghostly blue eyes, and his strong jaw gave him a bad-boy aura. This guy went to church and seemed to have higher moral standards than your average Joe. But Hayley was right in the fact that he wasn't a whole person, and that didn't surprise me; he'd just lost his sister.

"Did he tell you about Jessie and Jordan?" Hayley touched my arm.

"What about Jessie and Jordan?" Someone needed to write me a guide that could explain to me the complexities and workings of this little group's drama. Granted, Diana and I had encountered drama over the years with our friends, but none of it had ended in a death or someone moving a thousand miles away.

Hayley's voice went to a whisper. "Jordan and Jessie were dating, and Mark had some sort of problem with it."

"He had a problem with his sister? He said that he was close to her." My mind needed time to suck in and process all this new information.

"He may say that now because she's dead." Hayley shrugged. "But I guess they were close at one point." She paused and her expression grew pained. "Jessie loved Jordan."

"Why doesn't Jordan seem that upset then? Did he love her?"

"Jordan broke up with her a week before she died."

"That is so strange," I murmured. "Why? Did he give a reason?" Out of the corner of my eye, I noticed Meg and Charlie entering the coffee shop.

"Jessie called me up the night it happened; the breakup, not her death."

"Was there anything strange that you noticed about her around the time of her death?"

Hayley narrowed her eyes at me. "What are you, the investigator?"

"Sorry, I was just wondering. You seem to be one of the last people she spoke to while still alive." I began fidgeting. Hayley made me uneasy.

"We're going water tubing, Jeanine. You wanna come?" Jordan asked, breaking into the conversation. He sat himself down next to me without an invite.

Mark handed me a cup. He'd ordered me a frozen coffee with a spoon. Without thinking, I brought the moisture to my lips. Upon feeling the liquid touch the tenderness of the skin on my lips, I jolted. The water part of the beverage began taking effect. My mouth needed to be dried *now*. Without a choice, and no napkins in sight, I used my shirt to wipe the liquid away. When I raised my head up, all eyes were on me. Instinctively, my hand touched my cheek to make sure it was smooth and scales had not appeared on its surface. The softness of it brought me relief.

"You need a napkin?" Mark asked, amusement in his voice.

"Yeah, um....I'd like a straw," I said.

"Are you sure? It's sort of like ice cream." Mark chuckled.

"I'm sure." My teeth clenched.

"All right, no problem," Mark said, raising his hands and heading back to the counter.

"Anyway," Jordan began, "did you want to go tubing, Jeanine?"

"No," I said, doing a very good job of acting, if I do say so myself. "Sorry, I can't swim."

"You'll have a lifejacket on," Jordan said winking. "You won't sink."

"I don't like water sports. It sounds sort of scary."

"Are you thinking that there is a monster in the lake? Is that why you're scared?" Hayley giggled. Mark had just returned, and this remark was more toward him than me. What was with her constant digs at him?

"No, I don't believe there is a monster," I said laughing. "That would be silly."

Mark shot me a glance, and I remembered what I had done the other night. His expression was one of being betrayed, and I felt my heart fall into my feet. "Here's your straw," Mark mumbled, placing the straw in the cup. Then he set a napkin in front of me. Icy blue eyes stared into my soul while he sat back in his chair.

"Jeanine doesn't want to go water tubing," Jordan announced to Mark.

Mark narrowed the daggers he called eyes at me. "Why?"

"Can't swim, and I don't like being in the water."

14

Mark's brows furrowed, but he didn't say anything. Hayley began glaring at me, and I couldn't place a reason. I wished they'd just talk like a normal group instead of obsessing over whether I was involved in the conversation or their ventures. Charlie and Meg arrived with their drinks at our table. Charlie glanced at me before sitting down. His eyes were blue in color, but there was nothing incredibly striking about him: His blond hair lay handsomely, but his boyish body and plain features didn't make him distinct. He'd worked for my grandpa, though, and he probably knew my cabin better than me. Sometime I'd have to invite him and Meg over just to learn more.

"You want to go water tubing, Meg?" Luke asked. Meg was a little blonde, cute but not beautiful.

"Sure. Charlie, do you want to come with?" Meg turned to Charlie.

Charlie shook his head. "No, you can go without me."

"Why don't you want to go, Charlie?" Mark surprised me by asking.

"Got plans for the afternoon already," Charlie whispered. For a moment his eyes met with Mark's, and then his gaze shifted to me. Creepy. I noticed his sister take note of this and how she folded her arms across her small chest before narrowing her eyes at him.

I stood from my seat. "Well, thanks for inviting me to coffee, but I think I need to get home."

Mark stood as well, his face stony. "Come on, Jean. I'll take you."

*

"You are such a liar," Mark said, parking the car next to my cabin and shaking his head. We'd ridden in silence almost the whole way back to the cabin, and it worried me but had not prepared me for that accusatory statement.

"What?" I could feel myself growing warm.

"You told my friends that you didn't like water, and then you also said that you didn't believe there was a monster. Am I just someone you're using to get yourself around and know people?" Mark's eyes were killing me now.

"No," I said, feeling tears begin to well up involuntarily. Why was I crying for someone I'd just met? In my past life I hadn't cried for anyone.

"Then why are you lying to me or them?"

Now I just wanted to scream. "I was lying to them, not you," I said, wishing I felt more offended and less guilty toward him.

"Why are you lying to them, then?" Mark's intimidating stare remained on me.

Wiggling in my seat, I brushed back my hair. "I don't want to go water tubing, and I don't want them knowing that I believe in a monster," I said, opening the door of his car. "I'll see you tomorrow, I guess."

"Wait a sec." Mark opened his car door and hurried after me as I walked toward my cabin. He grasped my upper left arm, sending a shock through me. "Did Hayley tell you something about me?"

"What?" I whirled around to face him, glaring up at his threatening eyes. For some reason, I was out of breath.

"Did she tell you about Jordan and Jessie?"

"Yes, but how did you know?"

"She would tell you that." Mark let go of me and rolled his eyes.

"You left for New York just 'cause your sister went out with some guy? I should say *you* were lying to *me*. You said you were close to her!"

"I was. At the time I was confused," Mark said. He ran a hand through his hair and turned his back to me. Now *he* was out of breath. "I feel like it's my fault she died."

"What?" My brow knit. "Why?"

"I didn't come! I didn't rescue her!" Mark exclaimed. His teeth sounded as if they were clenched, and he continued raking his hands through his black locks. Taking a deep breath, he calmed and shook his head, and his shoulders slumped.

"Here, let me explain." He faced me again, dug in his pocket, and brought out his iPhone. "I want you to hear this."

"What is it?" I leaned forward to look at the phone.

"It's a message Jessie left me. I refused to pick up the phone," Mark said, his voice cracking. He pressed a button on the phone, and the sound of a girl's voice came through. It sounded frightened and small.

"Mark, can you please pick up? It's Jessie....I-I know we haven't talked in a while....but please, just listen to me. There's something strange that's been going on....um....you were right about everything. Something or someone comes by the cabin every night. I think whatever it is wants to hurt me. I don't want to bother Mom and Dad, and I just thought that maybe if you'd come home for a little bit...." Her voice sounded distressed at the end, and she'd started crying. "Please, call me back. Please! I'm sorry about everything....um....I love you."

We both stood next to my cabin quietly after the call. My skin had begun prickling into goose bumps while listening to the message, and I found myself shaking. "Something or someone?"

"Yeah." I noticed that Mark's voice sounded muffled like he was trying to keep himself from bursting into tears.

"Did you ever call her back?"

"Yes, but she never picked up. I got this call the night of her death." Mark placed the phone back in his pocket. His eyes had glazed over.

"It killed her that night? You mean it'd been haunting her for a while? Whatever it was, had she talked about it before?"

"She'd asked me to come back before, but I hadn't. This was the last message she left me. She'd left ones earlier as well. I'm such an idiot!" Mark's face became strained and suffused with red. "You want to know the truth about her and Jordan?"

I nodded, not able to speak. I still wondered what he had meant by not being able to rescue her.

"I told her Jordan would let her down, that he was no good. I told her that he only wanted to get at her because she was innocent and untouched." Mark shook his head and leaned on his car. "She wouldn't listen. She thought she loved him and told me that he loved her. We argued for days about it, but Jessie was so stubborn. Hayley and I were going out at the time, and one day....one day...." Mark stopped talking for a moment. "Never mind. Why am I telling you all of this? You probably agree with Hayley. I was being a jerk."

"But Jessie didn't know Jordan like I did. He was the first guy who had ever asked her out. She didn't deserve someone like him." The first tears sprung from Mark's eyes. "I told her there was a great guy out there who would sweep her off her feet someday. She was so special, Jean. She didn't deserve what happened to her. She didn't deserve to die." Mark slouched back, his body shook, and I realized he was trying to hold back a sob.

I stepped forward and put my arms around him. "I'm so sorry, Mark. I'm so sorry," I murmured. "You couldn't know." Before I could stop myself, I kissed his cheek. The stubble just enough that its touch differed against the smoothness of my lips. Hitting me like a bullet was the realization that my desire to be with Mark was more than of just being friends.

Mark gently took himself out of my embrace. "I'll see you tomorrow, Jean," he said, his tone deeper than I'd ever heard.

My mind beat into me as I parted ways with him and heard the rev of his car's engine. If there was a God out there, I wanted to scream at Him. Why had He made me so attracted to this guy and without warning? And why did He allow me to make stupid mistakes like kissing a guy I barely knew, who had given me no indication of desiring me back? For all I knew, Mark could still have feelings for Hayley; they'd been going out, after all.

*

The sound of someone tapping on my door awoke me from a fitful nap, making my heart pound. I remembered Jessie's message. *Someone comes by the cabin every night....I think whatever it is wants to hurt me.* "Snap out of it," I told myself. "Worrying about that sort of thing will kill you and make your life unlivable."

Tap. Tap.

The knocking increased my adrenaline, and I forced myself toward the door. Much to my dismay, Charlie's figure stood on the porch.

I opened the door. "Hey."

"Can I come in?" Charlie smiled.

Like hell you can come in, I thought. Not with a murderer out there somewhere! I have no idea who you are. "Um, no," I said instead.

"I'm sorry. I should explain myself. I know your grandpa pretty well." Charlie kept shifting on his feet.

"Oh?" I leaned against the door, holding it half open. "And...?"

"I know why you're here." Charlie's eyes met mine. They were lit with a frightening inner fire.

"And why is that?" I folded my arms now. If he was going to say I had posttraumatic stress disorder or some other aliment, I'd laugh. That wasn't dirt he could use on me.

"You're a monster."

"I know I—" All words left when what he'd said settled in. I blinked. "What did you say?"

"You're a monster." Charlie chuckled and smugly walked further toward my cabin as if he owned the place. "Your Grandpa told me."

"Get away from my cabin," I breathed. "You are demented."

"Jeanine, you're a monster, and your parents banished you. That's why you're all the way out here." Charlie took a step toward me, invading my personal space. "Tell me that isn't true."

"That is a bunch of bull," I said with determination. "Now get away from me. You've watched too many movies."

"I just want to become friends. I'm the only one who knows your secret. I won't tell anyone. I swear."

Grandpa had told him that I was a monster? But why? I've always trusted Grandpa's judgment; maybe it would be good to have someone who knew. "I still don't understand what you're talking about. I don't have a secret."

"Jeanine." Charlie took my hand in his. "You can trust me, okay?"

"No." I yanked my hand from his.

"You're not like the other people here, and it's refreshing. I also have a special favor to ask of you." Charlie smiled. "And pardon me for being so bold as to say this, but you are the hottest girl in the Northwoods."

"Um....thanks, but no thanks. I'm totally not attracted to you," I said, wrinkling my nose.

"You like Mark then?"

"No," I snapped. "And for the last time, I'm going to ask you to leave!" I turned and slammed the door in his face. Upon locking it, I breathed a sigh of relief and slumped back onto the couch I'd been napping on. I was more popular up here as a monster in northern Wisconsin than I'd ever been in New York.

*

After eating a meager meal because I hadn't felt like cooking, I headed to bed. The darkness of the cabin that night shadowed over me. I kept hearing Jessie's message playing again and again, whispering in my mind. Every little noise outside put my senses on alert. I wrapped my covers around myself and shuddered when an owl began hooting outside my window.

I think it wants to hurt me.

Closing my eyes, I began humming a tune. There was no one to protect me during the night. Shivering in my bed, I realized how Jessie must have felt, knowing that something was out there stalking her, waiting in the shadows to pounce. It sent me wishing that Grandpa would come and visit again soon.

15

The memory of Charlie's brief visit and thoughts of a murderer disturbed my sleep. I rolled over for the fiftieth time under my covers and wondered why Grandpa had told him. There was a bright side to all this craziness, though: It hadn't given me time to think about how alone I was. Lacking cell phone service frustrated me because I couldn't gain quick access to Grandpa to ask him if what Charlie had said was true.

"Tomorrow I'll go into town and call him," I said aloud, comforting myself in the dark. "I'll ask him again about the murderer too."

*

Birds singing, the sound of water lapping, and rain hitting against my windows awoke me. Something was different about today. The wind had caused the water on the lake to become louder than usual. Maybe Mark and I wouldn't go out on the boat today! This prospect lightened my heart as I rose from bed and stumbled into the kitchen area of my cabin to make breakfast. Still rubbing sleep from my eyes, I felt a drop of water hit my arm, bringing every part of my being awake with pain. Where had the water come from? Another drip fell on my head. There was a leak in my cabin's roof. How wonderful.

Flinging my now-ruined nightgown aside, I pushed a chair under where the leak was and climbed on top of it. A small crack through the wooden boards of the ceiling was the culprit. Gum would seal this up until I could find someone to repair it. Another drop hit me in the face as I glared at the offensive area. Hissing for no reason at it and pinning my ears back, I hopped off the chair and grabbed my purse from the living room's end table to dig for a stick of gum to chew.

Smash!

Rolling my eyes, I turned to see what my tail had knocked over. My lizard-like features were not made to live indoors. The lamp, my source of light in the living room, had fallen and shattered. Growling under my breath, I bent to examine where the glass had scattered. Climbing on top of my recliner, so as not to step on glass, I made a leap back into the kitchen and stuck the gum in my mouth to chew. Another drop of water spilled on my forehead, and I realized that there was more than one leak in this old cabin. What a great way to begin the day, I thought.

*

Knocking on my door made me sit up on the couch with wide eyes. What time was it? Had I fallen asleep? Ugh, why was I naked? Then another thought hit me. Oh crap — Mark!

The rain had stopped and the wind had died down. Taking the quilt off the couch, I wrapped it around myself and hurried to my room.

Knock! Knock!

Mark would leave if he thought I wasn't home, and I couldn't let him down. Rushing myself into shorts and a T-shirt, I opened the door to see him turning his back from the door and heading back to his car. "Wait!" I called.

Mark turned around. "Hey." His hands were in his pockets. "What's going on?"

"Nothing," I said. "Come in." I motioned for him to follow me, glancing at the sky to see if it looked like rain would fall soon.

"Okay," Mark said, trudging through the mud toward my door. He didn't seem to be in the best mood, maybe even a little shy toward me. I didn't blame him after our discussion yesterday.

"Please, wipe your feet," I said.

Mark gave me a wry smile and did as I'd told him. He lifted

his gaze toward me. "Why didn't you answer the door right away? I was afraid something had happened to you."

"What?" His concern made me wonder and again feel that flutter I'd felt the other day. "Oh...."

"You made me worried, Jean." Mark rubbed his temple with one hand and sat down on my couch.

"I'm so sorry; you wouldn't believe the morning I've had," I started to explain. "First, there was this leak in my roof and—" I stopped. I'd been about to talk about my curse. It hurt that one of the most defining things about me I couldn't explain to my best friend in this place.

"What happened to your lamp?" Mark pointed at the remains of my late lamp.

My cheeks flushed. "It broke."

"I can see that," Mark said. The corners of his mouth twitched. "What happened?"

Oh, my tail knocked it over, I thought. A statement like that would be a shock to him. He'd think I was talking about a birth defect. "Like I said, it's been a pretty crazy morning." I laughed, more because of my thoughts than the statement.

Mark chuckled. "Okay, I believe you. But please don't scare me like that again."

"Aw, you're worried about me," I said, using a baby-talk voice.

Rolling his eyes, Mark shook his head. "Jean, you're so weird sometimes."

"Thanks, you've told me that before," I said grinning.

"You want to go hunt down that monster or not?" Mark said, rising from my couch.

"I want to eat breakfast and change into something a little more appropriate for monster hunting." I giggled.

"How 'bout I make both of us breakfast, and you go get ready." Mark walked into my kitchen.

"Okay," I said, giving him a smile. "Thanks."

"No problem," Mark said. "You're worth it."

His statement nearly knocked me over. Was I really worth it? If only you knew, Mark. I'm a monster.

*

Turns out Mark's family owned a pontoon boat. As we walked down to the docks, I was relieved that my waterproof boots went up to my knees because of how muddy the rain had made the ground. Mark took my hand as we got on the dock, and I glanced at him to see why.

"I'm going to help you onto the boat; it can be a little rocky," he explained. He must have noticed the curiosity in my expression. "I don't want you falling in."

"No, that wouldn't be cool." I laughed.

"You're shaking?" Mark gave me a lopsided smile and raised his thick brows. "Don't be afraid." He squeezed my hand. "Have you ever been on a boat?"

"No," I said. It was true. Crap. Why did my emotions have to give themselves away? It was a constant flaw of mine.

"Here." Mark pulled the pontoon closer in, and I hopped on.

The water sloshed against the boat, calling my name. This had been an awful decision on my part.

"Are you going to be all right?"

"Yes. I'll be fine," I said, but found that my hand was gripping his so tightly that I could feel both of our pulses. Stop me from giving in; hold me tighter, I thought toward him as I stood on the boat's rocking surface. His hand on the small of my back sent prickles of life into my body, almost making me forget about the calling water supporting our vessel.

"Are you sure you're going to be fine?"

"I'm fine! Now please stop asking!" I snapped without meaning to.

His warm hand stopped touching me, much to my dismay, and I felt guilty for bringing my frustration out on him when it was my fault. The pontoon boat was like a room. Shaped in a rectangle, it had a sitting area with a table on one side, and the technical and steering whatnots on the other side.

"Do you think we'll see the monster?" I asked, trying to get his mind to focus on his own recent obsession.

Mark brought out his cell phone and held out my picture once more to me. "It's going to be hard to see in the water, but if we can lure it up to the boat we can maybe shoot it."

"Shoot it?" I felt the blood drain from my face. Note to self: Don't go near Mark when a monster unless you want your brains blown out.

"Yeah, it brutally killed my sister, and it's not going to get away with that." Mark frowned.

"Wait, when did the police find her and where?"

"On the dock; parts of her were scattered everywhere. They said that she was killed within the first five minutes of being attacked. It took out her throat." Mark shuddered, and I felt a chill run down my spine. What a horrible way to die.

"That's so...." I shivered.

Mark started the motor of the boat. "Enough talking, let's get out there and see if we can find any evidence."

"It's such a large lake, Mark. How will we find such a small creature?"

"It's not that small. And who knows? It must live near here since I found it sleeping on my shore." Mark shrugged. "We've got to start somewhere."

Try next door. "You're right."

I relaxed in the sitting area while Mark sat behind the wheel. Water churned underneath the boat as it propelled itself across the surface, continually bringing my mind toward how it would feel to have the water brush against me like that, with my aquatic form sleekly moving through the light waves. The wind from the speed of our boat brushed my face, the moist fragrance of it tempting me. "Tell me something, Mark. Why are you so nice to me?"

The boat began slowing down. "What do you mean?"

"I've never had anyone be so nice to me." I laughed. "You gave me a ride to my cabin, you took me to that bonfire, you took me to your church, out to coffee, and now we're on a boat together."

"Maybe it's because I instantly liked you." Mark grinned.

"Why did you *instantly* like me?" After saying this, I was caught by surprise at how flirty that had sounded. I'd even leaned forward.

"Because you're different and weird." Mark winked at me, then turned his attention to something among the technical junk in front of the steering wheel.

"What are you looking at?" I asked, afraid that if I stood and walked over toward him I'd want to jump overboard.

"I'm checking to see if we have anything swimming underneath us."

"Oh." I'd been unaware that such instruments existed that allowed you see beneath a boat. "Does it tell how big the creatures swimming under the boat are?"

"Not mine. It's not that advanced," Mark answered.

For some reason, I took a moment to study Mark once again. His hair blew in the wind, his brow furrowed, studying the monitor, and his blue eyes that didn't match the rest of him continued to stare at the device.

"Do you want to know something?" I asked out of impulse.

Those blue eyes looked up at me. "What?"

"You're a handsome guy." After saying this, I realized that it sounded awkward.

Mark blinked. "Really?" He rolled his eyes. "What do you want, Jean?"

"No, Mark, I'm not saying that to flatter you. It's true." I bit my lip.

"Do you want to know something?" Mark stood from his post and let the boat float.

"Yes?"

"You're a beautiful woman." Mark walked up toward where I sat and sat down next to me, closer than he'd ever been. Those words sent thrills of joy into me, and I was frustrated with that. I'd known him for three weeks, and here I was wondering if he would kiss me.

"Thank you," I said. I felt like crying and laughing at the same time but held myself from doing either.

"Hayley and I were going out," Mark announced.

The good feeling vanished. "You told me that. Why did you break up?"

"She broke it off with me over the whole Jordan and Jessie thing. I know this is going to sound harsh, but I was relieved. I would have broken it off around the same time."

"How long had you been going out?"

"About a month or so. I also realized something about her that made it so that she could never be an option in my future. The fact that she didn't share my beliefs about God and stuff became a constant source of mockery for her."

My heart fell down to my shoes. I wasn't a believer. Well, I might believe that there was a supernatural power, but I wasn't sure what that was, or who that was. Mark knew that. So why was he even flirting with me? Keeping my eyes down so as not to show my disappointment, I asked, "Why did you start going out with her then?"

Mark shook his head and shrugged. "I was sort of stupid, I guess. I just don't want—" A splash in the lake made both of us jump, for different reasons. The noise created a longing inside of me. Mark rose from his close proximity to me and squinted into the sunlight from where the splash had come from. "Whatever that was, it was huge!" he exclaimed, hurrying toward the wheel again. "Let's follow it."

Hands wringing, I stood from my seat. I stepped toward the edge of the boat and stared mesmerized at the water. Mark started the engine of the boat again.

"Jean, what are you doing?" Mark asked.

"Water," I breathed.

"Jean?"

His voice seemed far away — miles away. The water on the other hand shouted and screamed for me. I dove into the lake, the water swirling around me as I sunk to the bottom. Pain cut into me, and I let out a roar. But it was over fast, and I darted under the water. My sanity returned at that moment. Mark was still above, he was hunting me, and it had just looked like I'd drowned myself, for I wouldn't be rising to the surface anywhere near here. The sound of a splash above caught my attention.

16

Mark had come in after me, probably to rescue me. He was diving deeper, coming closer, and grasping at the water. "Jean!" he shouted, his voice bubbling out. He swam upward, for breath most likely. There was a thud that my acute ears picked up. His body abruptly stopped moving.

Fear caught within me, sending adrenaline up my veins. I swam like a torpedo toward him. His body floated lifelessly when I reached him. Wrapping my arms around him, I swam for the surface and broke through within seconds. I hoped he was still alive and hadn't breathed in a lot of lake water. With no expression on his face and his eyes closed, he looked frighteningly dead.

"No," I said, patting his face with a clawed hand.

His heart beating against my body indicated, much to my relief, that he was only unconscious. I noticed a ladder up into the pontoon boat from the water. I hauled him onto the deck of the boat, using my tail as a fifth limb, and laid him gently on the floor. My scales, now out of the water, burned in the warm summer air. "Mark," I whispered. "Mark, please be okay." He'd left his phone on the carpeted floor of the boat. I used my tail's length to reach it while I sat watching Mark. I dialed 9-1-1 but naturally there was no service. "Perfect," I muttered. Isn't that just how my life went? I ran a hand through Mark's hair, and it came back with blood sticking to my fingers. His head was bleeding! "Oh no! No!" I gasped. "This is all my fault."

I stood and scanned the boat, looking for something I could wrap his head with. Finding a towel, I used my claws to rip a perfect strip and wound it around his head. Minutes continued to pass, and still he remained unmoving.

"Mark, come back to me, please. I don't know how to get this boat back to shore," I told his unconscious face. My body was drying fast, and the scales continued to burn in the direct sunlight. Mark began stirring, giving me the urge to leap for joy. He needed medical attention, and if he could just get us back to shore we could call an ambulance for him.

"Jean," Mark murmured.

"I'm here," I told him, taking his hands in my clawed fingers. I tried not to grip him too tightly so as not to hurt him, even though I wanted to hold him close to me. "I'm so sorry." The claws on my fingers reduced and sucked themselves back, and the scales began fading and shifting back to smooth skin.

Mark's eyes opened halfway. "Jean. You're okay. Why did you fall overboard? What happened?" He smiled with a dazed expression on his face.

"Shh…." I said, placing a now-human hand on the side of his face. "You hit your head."

"I must have really hit my head hard," Mark murmured and chuckled, his voice groggy and eyes closing, "'cause you're really, *really* naked."

"What?" My hands released his face, and I crawled back. I grabbed hold of the reduced towel and wrapped it around myself. "You need a doctor," I ordered. "I don't know how to get this boat back to shore."

Mark moaned. "Oh, my head. What happened to my head?"

"Mark, I just told you that you hit your head." I sighed.

"What did I hit my head on?" Mark scrunched his eyes and then opened them. His hand reached for where it hurt. "What the—" He must have felt the towel wrap.

"I bandaged your head. It was bleeding."

Mark groaned. "No wonder my head hurts."

"I need your help getting this boat to shore so we can get you a doctor," I repeated.

"Okay." Mark lifted his head shakily and brought himself up to a sitting position.

"Don't move!" I ordered and rushed toward him, putting a hand on his chest to stop him. Although I hadn't been trying to feel how firm the muscles under his shirt felt, I couldn't help but be pleasantly surprised.

"You're only wearing a towel," Mark said, his eyes wide.

"Stay still! I'll drive the boat back. Tell me how to get us to shore."

"Why are you only wearing a towel?"

"Yes, I'm only wearing a towel, Mark. Thank you for letting me know that." I rolled my eyes. "Now tell me how to get us back to shore."

Mark laid his head back down on the floor of the boat and closed his eyes again. "Okay, sit behind the steering wheel. I'll tell you what to do."

*

I hopped from his boat and took his iPhone with me. "Stay there," I ordered, still wrapped in the towel. "I'm going to get some help."

"Go to the north side of our house; you'll get cell phone service there for whatever reason," Mark called after me. "At least, I've always been able to get one or two bars."

I hurried over to the designated spot. Much to my delight, I found that Mark was correct about the cell phone service. After dialing 9-1-1 and explaining the situation, I hurried back to the boat that I'd docked by myself. "Mark, they're coming! The ambulance is on its way!" I exclaimed.

Mark had remained where I'd left him. "Good," he said.

I sat down next to him. "I'm sorry."

"Sorry for what? You fell in." Mark smiled at me and took my hand. "Thanks for rescuing me."

"Yeah, but if I hadn't fallen in, you wouldn't have jumped in after me to rescue me. You wouldn't have hit your head, and we would never have been in this fix." I realized my words were coming too fast to understand.

"Jean....uh....what happened to your clothes?"

"My clothes?" Think fast. "They ripped when I fell." Fail.

"Ripped?"

Sirens sounded in the distance. They'd be here soon, and Mark would be okay. "Yeah. I'm going home now because I really don't want to meet the paramedics while wearing a towel." I had to ignore the water under the boat beckoning me. It hadn't taken long for it to call me once again. "Don't move; I told them you were on the pontoon boat."

"Oh, all right." Mark closed his eyes. "My back and limbs are working perfectly fine, though."

"All the same, stay where you are. You really scared me, and I don't want you getting hurt even more."

He gave me a silly grin. "Jeanine."

I laughed when he said my full name. It sounded funny. "Take care of yourself, Mark."

*

It was a miracle. I kept replaying the scenario in my mind, and that was the only conclusion I could make. He'd not seen me as a monster! Maybe Mark's God was looking out for me after all. Driving into town to call Grandpa, I wondered if I should tell him about Mark and me. When I'd mentioned Mark to him earlier, Grandpa had seemed bothered and cold to the idea that I wanted to be friends with him. I pulled my car over at the coffee shop since I'd been there already, and the coffee that I'd had yesterday had been more than just good. While going through my list of contacts, I came upon Diana's name, and then I came upon my old home's number. Pressing the call button, I closed my eyes, listening to the phone ringing.

"Hello?" Corrine's voice asked.

For some reason words didn't come.

"Hello?" her voice asked again.

"Corrine," I said.

"Who is this?"

I'd only been gone for three weeks! How could she not recognize my voice? "Corrine, it's Jeanine."

There was silence on the other end of the phone. "Jeanine who?"

"Your sister." My eyes felt like tearing up. "Your older sister. The one who left on vacation."

"You can't be Jeanine; she's dead." Corrine sounded angry and frustrated. I could picture her round little fists balled up and her brows wrinkling her smooth skin.

"They told you I was dead?" My breath caught in my throat. Why had they told my little sister I was dead? What sort of sick parents were they? "I'm not dead, Corrine. Mom and Dad pretended that I was dead. Like a joke."

"It's not a funny one."

I couldn't believe I was having this conversation with Corrine. "I'll even visit you guys. I'll come home for Christmas."

"Christmas is a long way off," Corrine said.

"Yeah, but I'll be there. I promise you that. Can I talk to Mommy or Daddy now?"

"Daddy isn't home, but Mommy is."

"Good; go get her," I said.

"Okay. Bye, Jeanine. I miss you. I wish you wouldn't have pretended to die. They all cried."

Those words hit like a sledgehammer. They'd cried for me at my funeral? People had been sad that I was gone? I'd never felt that those people even cared. "Well, I'm alive, honey, so you don't have to cry anymore. Goodbye, Corrine." Why was my throat tightening? I waited a few seconds before I heard Mom take the phone from her.

"Jeanine, why are you calling us?" Mom's voice was high pitched and angry.

"Um....I don't know." Then I added with emphasis, "Oh, yeah, I miss my family!"

"You weren't supposed to call us." Mom's voice held no sympathy. "We'll visit you when we want to talk."

Even though I'd already known they didn't care, this hurt more than I'd expected. "What if *I* want to talk?" Sucker that I am, I still had to ask that question. Silence on the other end confirmed that Mom didn't know what to say without sounding heartless. "Never mind," I said. "Take care." Then I hung up on her.

A second later, my phone buzzed, showing my old home number. I ignored it and ordered the coffee.

"It's hard, isn't it?"

I turned to see Charlie standing next to me.

"Why do you keep bothering me?" I asked, crossing my arms over my chest.

"Can't help it." Charlie shrugged. "You fascinate me, Jeanine Stafford."

Rolling my eyes, I was relieved to hear that my coffee was ready. Much to my chagrin, Charlie followed me to my table. "Can I help you?" I asked.

"Yes, you can go to dinner with me."

"I was just going to call my grandpa."

"Really? Give Fred my best."

"Fred?"

"That's what he told me to call him. He was like a grandpa to me." Charlie's face was so smug that I wished I could punch it.

"That's great," I mumbled. I'd never heard of anyone calling Grandpa Frederick "Fred", except for Tom. Maybe everyone around here knew him by that name.

"So tell me, what is it like to be hunted by Mark Calvin?"

"What do you mean?"

"Romantically and physically hunted." Charlie shook his head slowly, the grin still stuck on his face.

"I have no idea what you mean."

"It's sort of funny, isn't it? He's hunting you as a monster and also trying to get you to sleep with him." Charlie laughed. "I don't think I've ever heard of a more ironic situation."

"If you're trying to be my friend, you're doing a lousy job of it," I muttered, sucking on the straw I'd put in the coffee.

"Why do you always drink out of a straw, Jeanine?" asked Charlie.

I thought fast. "Because that's what I prefer. This way it doesn't burn my mouth. If I took a big gulp of hot coffee, I could burn my tongue."

"I see." Charlie gave me the look that parents give you when they're questioning your honesty. I got the sense that Charlie didn't quite believe me. "Really, I just want your help."

"What?"

"I'm blackmailing you." Charlie got up from his seat next to me and winked.

"I thought you said you were friends with my grandpa." Wow, this kid really was disgusting. "Why are you blackmailing me, then?"

"There are things you have no clue about, aren't there?" Charlie leaned toward me. "I can tell everyone, including Mark, that you're the monster he thinks killed his sister."

"You're scum," I said narrowing my eyes. "Mark said you used to be his friend."

"I'm glad that's over. Didn't ever want to have fun anymore since....well...." His voice trailed off, and I wondered what he'd been about to say.

Maybe Charlie knew what had happened to Mark and had given him the posttraumatic stress disorder.

I got up from the chair. "If you'll excuse me, I'm going to call my grandpa."

"You'd better meet me tonight, or I'm going to...." He held up his cell phone and tapped it.

"You can't force me to do anything."

"Yeah, well, I'll call up your precious Mark first." Charlie turned from me and walked out the door. Taking a moment to think, I decided it best to figure out where he wanted this little meeting.

"Where do you want to meet?" I panted.

"Ah, there's the spirit. My boat will come to your dock around 10:00 p.m. We can talk and get to know each other a little better."

"So you want me for sex?" I decided to be blunt. If that were the case, my life was going to become quite degrading. In some ways, I'd rather have him expose me as a monster.

"Actually, I was going to have you help me with my history homework. But now that you mention it…." Charlie shook his head, chuckled, and put a hand to his forehead.

"What?" I felt dumbfounded.

"Yeah, that's what you specialize in, right?"

"Yes…." I said slowly.

"Do you specialize in sex, too?" Charlie winked, but upon seeing my look of horror, he threw up his hands. "Jeanine, what sort of scum do you think I am? But who knows; you might become quite a sweet blackmailing deal." He waved and got into his truck.

Breathing a sigh of relief, I leaned against my own truck. So he hadn't wanted to use me in the way I'd expected. How nice of him. What a decent guy. Turning my attention to what I'd originally intended by coming here, I dialed Grandpa's number.

"Hello?" Grandpa answered the phone.

"Grandpa, hey!" I said, smiling at the sound of his voice.

"Jeanine!" Grandpa laughed. "I'm so glad to hear from you. How is the cabin working out? Are you feeling any better?"

"I'm actually doing—" Thinking the question through for a moment, I realized that I was once again enjoying life, even though I hated to admit it. "Good."

"Really?" Grandpa sounded surprised. "Seclusion feels good sometimes, doesn't it?"

"I haven't been that secluded," I protested, giggling. "I have

Mark."

"Mark?"

"Yeah, the guy I mentioned before. We're actually becoming quite good friends. He's introduced me to this group of people around my age." I paused, thinking, and then added, "There's this kid, Charlie, who claims to know you quite well."

"Oh, yes, Charlie." Grandpa seemed happy suddenly. "He's a good kid."

"He's blackmailing me," I said.

"What?"

"He's making me do his history homework for him, and I don't know what other things he'll want me to do in the future. He even suggested sexual favors." I realized this was a lie, but he had implied it, and that frightened me.

"No, you can't be right. Charlie and I are good friends. I even told him about your situation because I knew he'd understand. I thought you needed a friend who knew." Grandpa's voice was filled with shock.

"Yeah, I know. That's what he's blackmailing me with. He came to our cabin the other night and tried to talk, but I wouldn't let him. I'm still afraid there is a murderer on the loose. Charlie met me today in the coffee shop."

There was silence on the other end of the phone. Finally, Grandpa spoke: "Don't worry, Jeanine. Everything is going to be all right."

"Thanks, I've heard that before." I sighed and glanced up at the sky, hoping I'd make it back to my cabin before dark — before I felt vulnerable again. I hated being alone and feeling unprotected in a place where I was reminded constantly that a murder had occurred. "Are you going to visit soon?"

"I might do that for you," Grandpa said cheerily.

"Good," I said. "When?"

"How about in two weeks? Does that sound like a good time?"

"It sounds great. Thanks, Grandpa."

"Don't mention it."

"I talked to my parents," I said.

"Oh?"

"They're busy, I guess," I mumbled.

"Jean, I wish I could make them see that you're really the same girl they know." Grandpa's voice held compassion. I needed that. It felt good to have someone helping me through all this, someone who knew and understood what I was going through.

"I'd better go now." My mind had remained on Mark the entire time.

"No problem," Grandpa said. "Love you."

"I love you, too. Goodbye, and see you soon."

"Yep," Grandpa answered cheerily. "'Bye."

I ended the call and started my car. Time to make sure Mark was fine before the suspense of worrying about him killed me. My face reddened when I thought of what had happened on the boat. It all seemed so surreal to me still. The phone beeped again, and I glanced at it to see who was calling me. Mom. Still? Did she feel guilty now? For some reason, the thought of that made me feel better.

17

"Hello?" I said into the phone. After letting it ring a few times, I'd finally decided to answer it. Mom could be persistent.

"Jeanine, I'm sorry about what happened," Mom said, her voice apologetic.

I waited for what sort of excuse she'd come up with.

"And I wanted to tell you why we faked your suicide."

"That would be nice to know," I said.

"Rumors started spreading that you'd left because you were pregnant, and then your grandpa told us that—"

"Wait, Grandpa?"

"Yes, Grandpa told us that would be the best solution."

"Are you serious?" This was a shocker. I'd thought Grandpa viewed my situation in a more positive light than that. At least he had the decency to not make me feel like a hopeless case or a freak — of which I was both.

"Yeah, didn't he tell you?"

"No. But no one tells me anything anymore, Mom."

"Oh, honey, I'm sorry. It's just too strange to be real. Sometimes I don't think it's happened." Mom's voice was filled with emotion, but it seemed faked. I wished she'd stop pretending.

"Believe me, it's a reality."

"Is it true that y-you don't remember what h-happens when *it* happens?"

"What are you talking about? Who told you that, Mom?" Taken a little bit by surprise at her question, I tried to think of a time when I'd said that. I'd never had that problem, so I decided not to worry.

"Never mind, dear. I won't bother you anymore about this; you're under enough stress as it is. I hope that you're—" She paused. "—having a good time in Wisconsin."

"Um, yeah. I love it here. There's a murderer on the loose, and this guy is blackmailing me, but I'm good otherwise."

"What do you mean there's a murderer on the loose?" Did I hear a hint of concern in her voice?

"This girl got murdered next door. Dismembered, throat torn out....it was pretty gruesome," I said, feeling a shiver run through me. How could I talk about Mark's sister like she was just another nameless girl? Her voice on his answering machine ran through my head. It still haunted me. "Her name was Jessie," I added.

"Does Grandpa know about this?" Mom's voice had risen in pitch, and I was sure she was worried about me now. Even though I was a monster, she really didn't want me to die. Knowing this made me miss her. Why did she have to care?

"He does, but he said the authorities thought it was a bear." I nodded, trying to assure myself that it was a bear. "And he's right; they did say it was a bear. I've gotten to know the brother of the girl who died."

"I hope you're not letting anyone else know about your problem," Mom said.

Your problem. Sometimes I had to remind myself that I'd done this to myself. I really had no one to blame for the thing that held me back from everything. If I'd been pregnant, I could've blamed it on the guy. If I'd been sick, I could've blamed it on the disease. If I'd been defective, I could've blamed it on my parents or an unknown cause. But *I* had brought this curse on myself. I had washed myself in that basin, bled myself…. "I'm not," I said.

"That's good." Mom's worry had disappeared as quickly as it had come. "I have to go. The Harrison's are having a party tonight. We're all going."

"Okay," I said. "Will you do me a favor?"

There was silence on the other end of the line for a moment. "And what is that?"

"Could you give Corrine a hug for me and tell her that I miss her?"

Another pause, then, "Yes, I'll do that."

"Thanks. Bye, Mom." I hung up the phone, and fortunately I'd arrived at the hospital to distract my guilty and spinning thoughts. Upon arriving at the desk, a lady who wore scrubs and horn-rimmed glasses glanced up at me.

"Is a Mark Calvin still here?" I asked.

"Let me check." She pointed her long nose down at her computer. "He just left, dear."

"Left? Is he all right?"

The lady chuckled. "We wouldn't have let him leave if he wasn't."

"Oh, good." I sighed. "Thanks."

"Have a great day, hon."

"You too." I turned and walked out the door and back to my truck. It seemed like a load had been taken from my mind, but then I remembered Charlie and how he'd be waiting for me that night.

*

I thought about dropping in on Mark but decided against it.

The doctor said he'd be fine after all. Pulling up to my usual parking spot, I exited the car and started for my cabin. After fumbling in my pockets for the keys, opening the door, and stepping inside my home, I realized how normal this life of solitude felt to me now. The weird events going on around here felt normal. Heck, being a monster had even become normal, and I hated that. Was it only just a month ago that I'd been a normal girl finishing her final year of high school? Now I felt years older than that girl I'd known. Collapsing on my couch, I glanced at the clock above the fireplace. Less than four hours until Charlie would arrive for his cheating session.

An image of Mark's drenched, unconscious form entered my mind involuntarily; how his dark, damp hair had clung to his forehead, droplets dripping down his face; how his soaked shirt had stuck against his skin and the lean muscle underneath. A flutter inside made me want to slap myself. He'd never know what I was, and he'd never want to be with me anyway because we didn't have enough in common in ways that mattered. Like being human.

Thunk!

Something had banged against my window. I rose to my feet. What had that been? *Something comes by the cabin every night.* Why was I living alone? Didn't Grandpa and my parents think this dangerous?

Thunk! Thunk!

Whatever it was, it stood on my porch. A snuffling noise outside my window reached my ears, then a low growl. Something *was* out there, and it wanted in. Closing my eyes for a moment, I tried to think of what I would and could do if something got into the cabin. How could I fight off whatever it was?

An idea stuck me. Running to the sink I turned on the water and dunked my head under the faucet before I could even feel the water's pull. Water trickled down my face, changing my appearance and my body, but most importantly, it caused my fingers to lengthen into claws and my teeth to become pointed. I crouched on all fours for a moment; I could hear whatever it was creeping around the cabin. Its footsteps were soft, but I wasn't fooled; whatever this thing was, it was big. A snarl rose in my throat without warning — my monster body reacting to an intruder, more primitive than my human mind willing it to remain silent.

Scrape! Sniff, sniff. Thunk!

Whatever it was, it was near the front door now. Hitting me with horror was the realization that I hadn't locked my front door upon coming home. Hurrying toward the door, I could almost feel the presence of the intruder outside as it searched for a way in. My clawed hands slid across the metal of the knob, making it difficult for me to turn the lock shut.

Snuff. Growl. Thunk! Thunk!

It had reached the door, and now it was banging against it! Somehow I managed to get the lock to click in place at that moment. The sound of the knob turning hit my sensitive ears. This definitely was not a bear or cougar. Pinning my ears back, I backed away from the door, ready to spring into action if for some reason this thing succeeded in getting in. The burning in my skin indicated to me that I needed to douse myself in water if I wished to remain a monster. Quick as a wall lizard, I darted to the sink once more and wet my hair and hands. Returning to my post at the door, I listened for sounds of the intruder trying another way in. There was silence, but I knew it was still there. This creature didn't strike me as stupid.

In my mind, I could play out Jessie's situation, picturing her terror at being helpless and stuck, like a mouse in a trap with a cat prowling outside. New fear enveloped me. Should I talk to Mark about this? *If* I lived, I'd have to.

It began snuffling again, and then came a gurgling noise. Finally, I heard it back away from the door and halt.

SCREE-EECH!

An unearthly, ear-shattering sound I'd never heard before turned my insides cold. "God, protect me," I found myself saying. There was no one else to ask for help from. The monster part of me took over and hissed, then let out a high-pitched scream-like screech back.

SCREE-EECH!

One more threatening noise, then it was crawling or slithering away. My breath remained frozen in my lungs until I could no longer sense its presence. Rising to stand on two feet, I noticed that only the many stars above in the pitch-black night shone as the source of light out here in northern Wisconsin.

Glancing at the clock, I realized that this whole process had lasted for over an hour. Charlie would have to be disappointed tonight. I wasn't leaving this cabin, and I wasn't going to allow myself to look like a little defenseless girl during the night. Walking carefully toward my bedroom and making sure my tail didn't knock anything over this time, I entered my bathroom, turned on the shower, and sat next to the drain. The water fell over me, and I closed my eyes, trying to block out the constant ringing of that blood-curdling screech.

*

Thump! Thump!

The shower still ran against my scaly skin, but it had turned icy. Shivering, I reached for the spigot and turned it off. Had I imagined that noise? Was my mind playing tricks on me now?

Thump! Thump!

No, my mind hadn't played a trick. Wearily, I traveled from my bathroom to the main room once again. This noise wasn't from my previous aggressive visitor. It was a human, and I knew right away it had to be Charlie. Longing to scream at him that he shouldn't be outside my cabin, I ran to the door. "Who's there?" I still asked.

"Who do you think, Jeanine?"

Yep. It was Charlie.

After opening the door for him, I realized that I was still a monster.

"What the heck?" Charlie's shocked face turned to a smile and he laughed. "Ah, I see, you don't feel like hiding yourself from me anymore? What happened to change your mind?"

"Charlie, you have to listen to me. It isn't safe to come to my cabin at night," I said, ignoring his mocking attitude.

"What do you mean?" Charlie asked, stepping inside without an invite. I rushed to lock the door behind him.

"There's something out there."

Charlie chuckled. "I doubt there is anything out there freakier-looking than you."

The dig hit me hard. I glared at him, my concern for him dissipating. I growled, "You want to know something, Charlie?"

"Yeah?" Charlie raised a brow in challenge.

"It's people like you who make people like me want to be with people like Mark. There is no pity inside you, no concern." The words were out before I could stop them.

"Do you think your precious Mark would look at you any differently? You look like a monster, Jeanine, but that's not a bad thing. I was just stating a fact. By the way, you've got some nice tits for a monster."

"What?" Mortification drained the blood in my face.

"You may look like a monster, but that's a very human-shaped body of yours. Mmm." Charlie smiled and pursed his lips a little.

"Shut up, pervert," I said, wrinkling my nose in disgust and turning toward my room to dry off and get some clothing on. "Sit on the couch and wait for me. I'll be right back."

"Okay, no problem. I wonder what that skin would look like

without scales," Charlie said.

"Yeah," I mumbled. "Don't get your hopes up."

Charlie laughed. "I won't. I'm just here to get help with history homework. I have to take summer classes 'cause I'm behind."

"How unfortunate for you," I said under my breath, slamming my bedroom door shut. At least there was more than one person here now. It almost was comforting, even if that other person was someone as demented as Charlie.

18

"Seriously, you don't know the last ship's name?" I rolled my eyes. "We just went over them!" Apparently, Charlie had an upcoming test on the discovery of the Americas. Truth be told, he sucked at history.

Charlie shrugged. "Sorry, we're going to have to go over them again."

"Okay." I took a deep breath and then closed the book.

"What are you doing?"

"I'm going to write flash cards for you," I stated and extended a hand toward him. "Hand me some paper."

Mumbling something under his breath, Charlie obeyed.

"So, let's write them all down," I began. "The Niña, the Pinta, and the Santa María are the names of Christopher Columbus's ships."

"Oh, the Santa María," Charlie stated slowly.

"Yup. Which was the biggest of them?"

"The Pinta?"

Laughing, I shook my head. "The Santa María, weirdo." Upon seeing his disappointed face, I decided to explain my method of remembering. "Just think of it like this: Niña means 'little girl' in Spanish, and Pinta....well, I don't know what that means, but let's just say it's a pin, and those are pretty small. But the Santa María is named after a saint, so she must be the grandest of them all."

There was silence. "Jeanine, you're pretty good at tutoring," Charlie finally said.

Shocked by his compliment, I tried not to think of him in a positive light. "Yep."

"I think I'll take off now. Thanks for your help. I should ace this test."

"I hope so," I said dryly. "I was blackmailed into doing it so...."

"You know what? I'm sorry, Jeanine. You're really a decent girl." Charlie stood and put out his hand. "I'm sorry for hating on you."

"Why do you hate me?"

"'Cause I hate your grandpa."

"What? But I thought—"

"He's had me clean this shack for him with hardly any pay for a long time," Charlie interrupted. "I sort of lied to you about him being like a grandpa to me; he told me about you, but that's because I've earned his trust through sucking up. He's really strange." Charlie inhaled a deep breath, and worry lines formed on his brow. "You won't tell him I said that, right?"

I blinked but shook my head. "I guess not. I'm sorry he used you. He's really a great guy if you get to know him a little better."

Charlie's face grew like stone, and he nodded. "Yeah, he is," he mumbled and turned around. "I do mean this when I say it to you: thanks."

"Okay." Not able to let go of my resentment toward him, I waved. "See you later, maybe at one of those bonfires."

Charlie waved back and left me alone in this cabin to think about the creature that was still out there stalking me. I began to worry for Charlie but then closed my eyes and locked the door after him. Forget about that; I needed sleep more than anything.

*

Sleep hadn't been easy. I figured I'd drifted off around two. Trying to stay my wandering mind from thinking about the intruder outside my cabin last night, I began making breakfast. I still had it in my mind to go to Mark's house and ask him if he could perhaps come over and make me feel safer, at least before Grandpa came. Then a thought struck me that hadn't occurred before: What if he'd had the same experience last night? After all, our cabins weren't too far from each other. My heartbeat thumped in my chest as I quickly began dressing, completely dismissing the idea of breakfast.

*

Upon my first knock on his door, I held my breath. Answer, Mark, please answer. My breath let out when I heard footsteps approaching.

"Jean!" Mark had a bandage around his head, but he looked fine besides. "What are you doing here?"

"I wanted to make sure you were all right," I said, my heart settling its beating.

"Why?" Mark's brows knit with concern. "What happened last night, Jean?"

Surprised that he could tell that much from looking at my face, I bit my lip. "I think whatever killed Jessie was at my cabin last night."

Mark's already pale face grew white. "Are you sure?"

"Yes. It crawled around my cabin, sniffing, scratching, banging, and trying to find a way in."

"It has to be that monster. What else would do something like that?" Mark shook his head. "I'm so sorry, Jean, but the best thing for you would be to go home."

My heart sank down to my shoes. The thought of leaving northern Wisconsin killed me. Not only because I technically couldn't, but also I realized I didn't want to, even if it meant I'd die if I stayed. There wasn't anything left for me in the world if I left northern Wisconsin. Here I was a somebody: a friend. No one except Charlie knew my secret. But in New York, I'd be a freak, one of those people who lurked in the shadows away from everyone else. My parents didn't want me living at home, and I didn't want to live with them now that I knew what it was like to be independent and no longer wrapped in their lies about how they "loved" me and wanted the "best" for me.

"I can't," I said aloud.

Mark blinked. "Um, yes, you can."

"You don't understand," I said, finding myself growing angry. Why had I even bothered telling him? "They don't want me to come back, and I don't want to go back!"

Mark's face softened. "Listen, you've got to tell the police about this, at least." He placed his hands on my shoulders.

Shrugging him off, I shook my head. Deep down I knew that the less I exposed myself to other people, the less chance there was that my monster self would be revealed. "Mark, I just don't want to be alone over there."

"That is completely inappropriate, Jean, and you know that," Mark said. His seriousness killed me.

Yes, I knew that; but still, it was life or death, and I didn't want to be alone. "I need someone to protect me, just until my grandpa comes up again. He'll be here in a couple of weeks, anyway, and then maybe I can change my situation a little bit. Get better security."

"Not only would it look bad to everyone around us, but it would be difficult for me to maintain....um...."

Maintain what? I wrinkled my nose. "I just need someone to

protect me. I....I don't want to end up like Jessie. Whatever that was that came to my cabin, it wasn't in a friendly mood." Very much aware that my eyes held convincing fear, I felt a little bad that I was nearly pleading for this. "Besides, you're the only person I trust around here; I know that you'd protect me if anything happened."

Mark grew silent, closing his mouth and staring at me blankly. "Okay," he finally said. "You're right."

"Thank you so much! And I promise I'll be on my best behavior," I assured him, giving him a smile that nearly hurt my mouth.

"We don't have to tell anyone about this, either. No one will have to know." Mark shrugged, and I wondered if he was thinking of his ex, Hayley.

Nodding, I already felt my fears dying down and relief settling in. "You won't even know I'm there. I'll give you a lot of privacy."

"Somehow, I don't believe that." Mark chuckled. "If you want, you can even stay here instead. It's a lot bigger than your place. There's more than one bedroom." His good humor was returning.

This hadn't occurred to me. "That sounds like a good plan."

"I'll even go with you to get your stuff, okay? You can sleep in Jessie's room." Mark walked with me to his front door but paused before turning the knob. "First, can you tell me *exactly* what happened?"

Taking a deep breath, I thought about what I should and shouldn't say about what had happened. One thing was for certain: I wasn't the only strange creature out here. "The creature crept up to my cabin last night. It tried to find a way in, but I locked the door. After a while, it gave this ear-shattering screech and crawled away." I shuddered upon remembering my brief but terrifying encounter.

"It came up to your house and you heard it? Did you check for footprints this morning? The ground has been sort of soggy."

"You're right!" I exclaimed, quite curious if the odd creature had left any signs of its existence. Mark was so much smarter than me.

"Come on," Mark said, opening the door.

We walked to the cabin. The distant sound of thunder reached my ears, but I didn't flinch. Water's intoxicating presence around me persisted, but I found that if I kept my mind off it, the temptation held less power. Even though I'd told Mark there was no chance we'd sleep together, he'd become a temptation in and of himself. I thought of telling him the entire truth: I knew there was another monster out there besides me that wasn't so friendly. If there were tracks, I'd have to tell him; right there, let the rain soak me, or maybe—

"If we find tracks, I want to get the police out here," Mark announced, studying the ground by my cabin. "Who was here last night?" Mark asked, pointing at one of Charlie's footprints.

"Charlie," I said under my breath.

Mark raised a brow. "Okay…."

"And, Mark, if you're thinking what I think you're thinking—"

"Hey, I didn't say anything." Mark raised his hands in a defensive gesture.

"Yeah, sure, but it was in your eyes and in your tone of voice." Placing my hands on my hips, I took a step closer to Mark. "Charlie and I were not doing anything….ungodly, if that's what you're thinking."

"Sheesh, Jeanine, you're making me out to be—"

"Judgmental?"

"Yes, and I wasn't thinking that. I'm just a little jealous that he's hanging out with you." Mark laughed, and then grew serious again, narrowing his eyes. "I do not see any animal or monster tracks around here, though — wait!" He pointed at a clear print in the mud next to my bedroom window. It looked like a human footprint, except the toes were long and webbed. Claw marks were in front of each toe. The familiar appearance of it sent shivers up my spine, although it must've been about three times bigger than my feet when they were clawed.

"Let's call the police."

Fear hit me. What if the police figured out too much about me, or what if water somehow—thunder echoed again. It was closer than before. "Let's get my stuff and go inside," I said.

"Okay," Mark said. "But don't you want to catch this creature?"

"It's going to rain any second, Mark, and that track will be gone," I stated.

"You're right!" Mark exclaimed. "Wait right here. Do you have a box in your house?"

"No," I said.

"We need to find a way to cover this print before the rain comes. It's my only evidence that a creature killed Jessie."

I was beginning to get agitated over Mark's new obsession but held it in. After all, his sister had just died three weeks ago. "Come on, Mark, we need to get inside." A flash of lightning in the distance made me jump, and my nostrils picked up the scent of incoming rain. "Please." I realized my voice sounded whiny, but couldn't help the fact that if I stayed outside a minute longer, my secret would be blown with Mark. "Come on."

He glanced up at me with hurting eyes. One thing I noticed about his face was guilt written all over it.

"Mark, I'm sorry," I said. "But I don't want to be caught out in this storm; it's going to be bad."

"I know," Mark said, sighing. "Let's get inside." He cast a longing look at the footprint then opened my door for me.

"Thanks," I mumbled.

"You can pack up."

"My grandpa is coming in a week," I explained, "so I can move back then."

"Sounds good," Mark said. He was silent after this for a moment, and we stood in the living room of my cabin awkwardly.

"Mark, have you met my grandpa ever?" I asked, trying to escape his quietness.

"Actually, I've never met him. I saw him a couple of times before I moved. Actually, he was spending a lot of time at the cabin before I left—" Mark halted what he was going to say next, and I wondered why.

"Hey, what were you going to say?" I asked.

"Nothing...."

"You were going to say something, Mark." I laughed.

"Jean, your grandpa was sort of creepy."

"Why do you say that?" What was with people's differing views of my grandpa?

"He would sit outside the cabin watching the water in a weird, hypnotic way, and then one day, he disappeared for like a week with his car still sitting in the driveway." Mark didn't give me eye contact while saying this, probably because he didn't want me to look into his eyes with hurt over him not liking my closest family member.

"Grandpa was the person who really cared about me once I was cursed," I said, before I realized that I'd used the word "cursed".

19

"Huh?" Mark's blue eyes flashed at me; his dark brows nearly met in the middle in a quirky, amused expression. "Cursed?"

"I mean, this problem I have." I laughed, trying to put off the word. "You know how it is....it feels like a curse."

"What exactly happened to you?" Mark narrowed his eyes and sat on my couch. The rain began pouring on the roof of my cabin and he winced. I realized he probably was picturing the evidence of the footprint washing away.

Think, Jeanine, what could have happened to you? I asked myself, turning my gaze down. I noticed the scar on my hand from the cut I'd made when I'd cursed myself. "This is sort of embarrassing, but I used to cut myself." Inspiration had struck!

"Really?"

I lifted my hand and wrist for him to observe. "See, this is where I would cut."

"That's horrible," Mark said, and I hoped he wouldn't be too judgmental over this.

"Yeah, I know. I didn't like my life very much, but I didn't want to kill myself. I just liked punishing myself." This statement was quite true, and it hurt.

"So once you did something—" Mark began.

"Yeah, and that made me even worse. My parents were horrified and disgusted, so they decided it'd be best for me to get some rest and come up here."

"Have you cut yourself since that time?" he asked.

"Nope," I answered. I could tell him a truth. "I came too close. It sort of scared the self-loathing out of me."

"Why did you hate yourself? Does it have something to do with your ex-boyfriend?"

Never had he brought up that I had a boyfriend besides earlier on in our relationship, but he gave me a very nice explanation without me having to think it through. "Yes," I said slowly. "I realized I was going out with a jerk, so I felt angry with myself. It sort of got me to the point where I cut myself."

"If it's not too personal of a question, how long did you guys go out?"

"Um....I don't know if you'd call it going out, even," I said, then bit my lip. I was sick of lying to him. Why did I have to lie to him, anyway? "Mark—" A clash of thunder shook my cabin and the rain grew harder.

Drip.

The sound of a leak in my roof, allowing water to get through, took all my attention away, and I couldn't remember at the moment what we'd been talking about. This caused the hair on my arms to prick. My attraction to water grew stronger every time I noticed it. "Mark....Mark...." I began saying, closing my eyes.

"Jean, what's wrong with you?" Mark stood and rushed to my side, concern in his voice.

"Mark, please, talk to me. I'm—I wish I wasn't such a freak," I blurted.

Mark put his arm around me.

Drip. Drip.

My eyes shot open and watched the water splotch onto the floor in a little puddle.

Drip. Drip. "Come over here, Jeanine. Touch us, Jeanine."

"What is wrong with you?" Mark asked again, bringing me closer and shaking me. "Please, you're kind of scaring me."

His words snapped me back to reality. "I have a leak in my roof."

"Is that what this is all about?" I noted the worry lines on his face. "I'll patch it up while you pack. We kind of got distracted from our original mission." He laughed.

"Okay," I said, walking to my room. I covered my ears with my hands until I could close the door.

*

It'd been two weeks of Mark and me living in the same house. At times, I felt like I'd go mad with the tension that was building up inside me at how hard it was to keep a secret from someone who had become your best friend. Mark had shown me his music, which also happened to be his career. I learned that he played the guitar and had a decent singing voice. He wrote songs and was paid by famous composers to provide them with lyrics. I shared with him most of my story about Greg and growing up in New York, even about being a débutante. Somehow he'd never learned the truth about me being a monster, even though I was constantly feeling distracted by water. He still liked to tease me about drinking from straws all the time. He called me a freak. Better than being called a monster, though.

Today, however, I stood in Jessie's room alone. Mark had told me, before leaving, he was going out grocery shopping and wouldn't be back till later tonight. Jessie's room was on the top floor, large, painted a bright pink, and had photos of her and her friends doing crazy things taped all over the walls. There was a queen-size bed, a desk, and dressers, along with a mirror. One thing I had noticed about Jessie through staying in her room was that she had her brother's blue eyes, but her hair was a light brown. She had long lashes, a medium-sized nose – similar to but less manly than Mark's — and freckles.

I studied the picture of Mark and her standing by the lake the longest because Mark's appearance seemed almost unrecognizable. His haunting eyes held laughter and light inside of them. The smile on his lips seemed so genuine. It hit me that Mark really was still mourning. He may not be expressive or talkative about his hurt, but he was mourning her. These thoughts brought me pain, so I focused again on the photos.

Jessie could be characterized as a light that shone in every picture, and I could barely stand the realization that the same person, who seemed so full of life and merriment, was also the source of the scared, small voice on Mark's answering machine.

In the photo next to the one of Mark and her, I finally saw what appeared to be the entire Calvin family. Sometimes I wondered if I'd ever get to meet his parents. The picture was blurred a little, but I could make out the figures. Mark had an arm around Jessie in the picture. His mother was a short, skinny woman with dark hair much like Mark's, and his father was tall and broad-shouldered, but still Mark stood taller than him in the picture.

Since Mark was gone, and I was bored, I guiltily turned to Jessie's desk. A pencil lay half-used on its surface along with the book *Pride and Prejudice*. To me, it seemed as if the room had been left untouched by Mark and her parents, giving it a sacred aura. A sketchpad lay under the book.

Glancing about, even though I knew no one was there, I picked up the sketchpad and opened it to see what she'd been drawing. The first one I flipped to was of an American Robin, the next a Blue Jay, then a wolverine. I had to admit, the girl had talent, because the drawings were so lifelike. A drawing of Jordan appeared next. Her ability to draw people was not as perfected as her talent for wildlife, but it was still pretty well proportioned. The next drawing disturbed me, for it was of a wolf killing a deer. Its teeth were sunk into the animal's neck. Sort of morbid for this girl, but I wondered if she'd drawn it during her and Jordan's break-up. Flipping the page so as to escape from that sketch, I found that the next one disturbed me even more, for at first glance it looked like my type of monster! This monster, however, appeared masculine. The muscles were ripped, and it didn't have a curvaceous body like mine. Its hair hung over its forehead, cut short, and its tail was shorter than mine. Eyes, serpentine like mine as a monster, stared back from the sketch.

Cryptic writing on the bottom of the sketch stated, "No one will believe me."

Had Mark seen this sketch? If he had, maybe that was why he was so convinced that there was a monster lurking. I turned the page of her sketchpad and found yet another drawing of the same creature. Another note at the bottom said, "Mark, if you ever read this, it means I am dead. Please, get as far away from the cabin as possible. Don't stay. I'm pretty sure it is going to come for me tonight. It knows I saw it, and now it wants me. I tried calling you, but you didn't pick up, and I want you to know that YOU WERE RIGHT. Love you and miss you. Don't feel guilty, because I know it's my fault. You've always been the best big brother a girl could have. Your loving and sorry sister, Jessica Calvin."

Horror shuddered through me as I read the note over again. Mark needed to see this, and if he had already seen it, I had no idea why he hadn't hightailed out of here. Another hope began playing in my mind. If he did see this drawing, I could show him that my monster appearance was very different than this monster's.

I'd confront him at dinner. In the meantime, I didn't feel safe being alone anymore, because now I knew for a fact that whatever had visited me the two weeks ago had murdered Jessie.

*

"The gang has invited us to the annual summer dance," Mark announced, breaking the quiet of our supper. The sun had set by the time he'd arrived back, and Mark had prepared some chicken soup for us. "Would you like to come? It's on Saturday."

"Sure," I said, putting a chunk of chicken in my mouth and chewing, careful that the broth didn't touch my skin.

"Did I do something, Jean?" Mark asked.

"I'm fine," I said. "It's just that I have something to show you."

He set down his fork. "What is it?"

I got up from the table and walked up the stairs.

"Where are you going?" Mark called after me in a bewildered voice.

"Upstairs. I'll be right back," I answered, and hurried my steps until I reached Jessie's room. Upon opening the door, I felt a draft and heard a clattering noise along with a low growl.

I did what any red-blooded woman would: I screamed my lungs out.

SCREECH!

It was a familiar noise. I backed away and continued to scream, turning on the lights. The last thing I saw was a scaly, alligator-like tail disappearing out the broken window.

Thumping footsteps coming up the stairs assured me that Mark was coming to my rescue. "Jean!" he shouted, appearing in the doorway. "Are you all right?"

"It was in this room!" I screamed, my heart pounding. I wrapped myself around Mark and began sobbing from the adrenaline.

"What was in this room?" Mark knew already, but I knew he needed to ask.

My hands shook as I released Mark's shirt and looked again to the window where the intruder had disappeared. Shattered glass glistened on the floor from the light in the hallway. The entire window was obliterated and claw marks appeared in the wooden frame. *Now* I wanted to go back home to New York, where creatures like that were found and taken captive or killed. My pathetic little life seemed so much better than I used to view it. I wasn't ready to die. But then I remembered, Oh yeah, Jeanine, you're a creature like that. "Th-that creature that J-J-Jessie drew in her b-book," I stuttered.

"She drew the monster we've been hunting in her book?" Mark's face grew confused. "What book?"

"Her sketchbook. It should be under *Pride and Prejudice*. She had all sorts of pictures and a note for you in there, even. Here, let me show you." I grasped his hand in my own and, finding new strength, stumbled toward the desk. There lay *Pride and Prejudice*, but the sketchbook had vanished.

20

"She wrote me a note?" Mark followed me up to the desk and stood looking over it.

"Haven't you come in here since her death?" I asked, still feeling the pulse throbbing in my hands.

"Yes, but only briefly. Jean, I didn't want to touch any of her things; they seemed so sacred. Why were you digging through them?" Mark's brow furrowed.

"I wanted to figure out more about her, I guess....and you were gone." I felt heat rush to my face; I had disrupted a dead girl's room, but still, it made me realize even more that Mark's assumption that a monster had killed his sister rang true. "There was a drawing of a creature, much like the one in your picture that you took," I said slowly. Tell him your secret now, I thought; you have nothing to lose. But what if, when I revealed the monster to him, he thought I had made up "another monster" to divert suspicion from myself? Also, I now didn't have that drawing of Jessie's to back me up. "It took the drawing," I said, clenching my teeth; rage was replacing my fear. "Mark, we're going to find that thing and kill it."

"We already have come to that conclusion," Mark said, putting an arm around me. It was a protective gesture, but to me it felt so much more than that. "I'm going to call the police," he said, letting go of me, much to my chagrin. "It broke a window, so if it wants to get in again, it will. Maybe the police will be able to track it."

It broke a window. If it wants to get in, it will. What had been with me the other night then at my cabin? Why had the creature not gotten to me if it could break windows so easily? I wished Grandpa would hurry up and get his butt over here. Come to think of it, he should be here now. He'd said two weeks last time I'd talked to him, and it had been two weeks.

"Jean, let's get back downstairs and call the police. I'll lock the door here so we can hear if it tries to get in through there."

"Maybe we should go into town," I suggested. Was there an escape from that creature here, and why was it stalking us but not wishing to kill me....yet?

Mark brought out his iPhone and began dialing. He locked the door of Jessie's room before heading down the stairs, and he motioned for me to follow him.

I did as indicated, glad to be away from that room and its haunting memory of sweet Jessica Calvin and an image of the beast that had killed her. Where would we go now? Was it safe to stay in this house anymore? Why was the creature back if it hadn't shown its face earlier? These questions rang in my mind when Mark returned from his talk with the police.

"They're coming out here; you have to tell them everything, okay?" Mark said. He walked to the sink and turned on the faucet, reminding me against my will of how delicious water sounded. I could forget everything if I just doused myself in it. Without thinking, I slapped myself across the face.

"Jean, you're kind of freaking me out when you do stuff like that," Mark said, taking a step closer. "Like what happened in the cabin when we were getting your clothes....and why did you just slap yourself?"

"It's from my disorder," I mumbled in a cover.

Mark crossed his arms and narrowed his eyes. "Jean, I need an answer: Do you know more about this than you're letting on?"

"What?"

"I'm bringing you to stay at the hotel tonight; you'll be safer there." Mark turned from me and placed his glass under the current; the glass filled, bubbling with the air that caught under its flow until it reached the rim. Turning off the faucet, Mark took a gulp. I watched as his Adam's apple bulged while swallowing and how the muscles in his neck flexed. Again, I could picture his wet shirt sticking to his chest, and for a moment I wondered what he'd look like shirtless. But my conscience rebuked me. Relationships that deep would be dangerous; plus, once he knew my condition there would be no way he'd want a relationship like that with me.

I scrunched my eyes shut for a moment, then composed myself and nodded my approval to his idea. "I don't want to go outside yet, though."

"We'll wait for the police to arrive. How does that sound?" Mark stated more than asked.

"Okay." Walking into his living room, I plunked myself down on the couch.

"I don't understand why you sort of searched my sister's room," Mark said, and I realized that his tone was annoyed. Why hadn't I read that before? Gone was his usual flirtatious mood around me. That hurt most.

"I wanted to know more about her because, after talking to you, I felt like I knew her somehow." Pressing my fingers to the back of my neck, I felt guilty now. He had a point about my snooping, and my explanation didn't seem to suffice.

"It's all right....but it's just that I hadn't looked through her stuff....yet," Mark admitted, staring at the floor.

"She told you that she didn't feel like it was your fault," I said. "She said—" I tried to remember the exact words so as not to dishonor her, "—you were always the best big brother a girl could have."

Mark chuckled, his eyes far away. "She had a good heart."

"She certainly did," I said, smiling at him. "It made me wish I had a big brother like you."

"What day of the week is it?" Mark asked aburptly.

"Um, I don't know. Why do you ask?"

"It's Tuesday, I think," Mark said, settling into a chair.

It was then that I realized I didn't keep track of time anymore. To me, it felt as if I'd been in northern Wisconsin forever. More had happened in my short time here than in my eighteen years in New York. "Is it really?" I asked, half dazed.

"Yeah."

"How long will it take the police to arrive?"

"I don't know."

"Did Jessie call the police the night of her death?"

I'd caught his full attention once again. "No, why?"

"She wrote in her journal that no one would believe her that there was a monster."

"I know you want to play detective now, Jeanine, but we can't. All I know is that there is a monster out there that murdered my sister and recently broke one of my windows." Again, he pulled out that image of me from his cell phone. "It's like when you see it with your own eyes, you just know that it's what killed her, you know?"

At this point I wanted to shake Mark and say, "That was me," but there really was a cold-blooded killer out there that looked like me. Exactly like me. Maybe some other poor soul had gotten caught up in the sect my ancestors followed. Grandpa had said that those people had moved to America to escape persecution. Someone else was out there, cursed like me, cursed to be something dreadful. They were now taking advantage of the very thing that damned them. Come to think of it, that really was understandable and twisted at the same time. I could see how someone would want revenge on the human race if they themselves had been cut off from it. Their normal life had ended, and they wanted to thrive on that abnormal. The sound of cars arriving alerted us to the fact that the police were here.

"I'll take you to the hotel after this," Mark said, standing from the couch and walking to the door.

I followed him, feeling my stomach turn. He couldn't be upset with me; I didn't want him to be. "I'm sorry for snooping around," I said, touching his shoulder once we stopped at his front door.

"It's okay. I would have done the same thing, Jean." Mark gave me a vague smile. "I don't know why I hadn't searched her room if I was so convinced."

"The monster must have known I'd seen the sketchbook picture. It must have been…." Nausea set in. "It must have been watching me."

"You're right!" Mark's blue eyes flashed with fire. "It's stalking you now, I just know it!"

"Maybe it has a thing for women." I shrugged. This assumption sent a chill through my spine.

"That's why you're staying in a hotel tonight. You're too close to the lake here at the cabins." Mark sighed. "I'm not sending you to a hotel because I'm mad at you. I'm sending you because I want to protect you. I like you, Jean."

"I like you, too" I answered him under my breath, knowing he wouldn't hear.

Mark swung open his door. With a slam of their car doors, the policemen began walking up the path to the cabin. They seemed bored.

"What seems to be the problem, Mark?" the tall, handsome officer asked. He appeared the exact opposite of his partner, a short and squat man with adult acne.

"I've had a break-in," Mark explained, motioning for them to come inside. "Let me show you."

"You mentioned there was an eyewitness to this break-in?" the short officer asked.

"Yes," I said, and Mark allowed me to step forward. "Something strange broke in; it wasn't—wasn't human." Noticing how Mark shot me a look, I continued when an idea struck me. "I have to go now. I'll see you later, Mark."

The tall policeman chuckled. "Wait, miss, could you explain this nonhuman for us?"

"Could you hand me your notepad? I'll draw it for you," I offered, stretching a hand toward the short officer who held the pad in hand.

"Um, sure," the short man answered, giving it to me hesitantly.

It'd been awhile since I'd taken any art classes, but I began describing myself, in a manner of speaking. The drawing wasn't too good once I finished it, but hey, I wasn't an artist. I put notes on parts of the drawing: scales, pointy teeth, tail much like a lizard's, claws growing from its hands, webbed hands and feet. "Its scales are brown- and greenish-colored," I commented after handing the pad back to the short officer.

"Well....well...." Those were the only words that came from his mouth. He looked to Mark. "Is she serious?"

"Yes," Mark answered. "I have a picture. I think it's what killed my sister."

The tall officer immediately put a hand to the back of his neck, and his expression grew pained. "Now, son, we know how much you beat yourself up about this, but we've told you before and we'll tell you again, that entire lake was searched after your accident."

His accident? My curiosity sparked into flame. The lake had been searched after his accident? The accident that had left him with posttraumatic stress? Casting my gaze on his perfect face, I waited for him to say something in response, maybe explain this further, but he didn't; instead, his face grew determined and his blue eyes cold.

"I have a picture of it on my phone. You have to see it," Mark said, digging in his pockets for the slim iPhone, then bringing forth again my monster face for the world to see.

"Kid, you're pulling pranks!"

"Officer O'Brien, does this look fake to you?" Mark shoved the picture into his face.

"It's amazing what you can do with Photoshop these days." The tall officer shrugged.

"Come inside, at least." Mark stepped inside his cabin, they followed, and I decided now was the time to put my plan into action. If they just saw a monster, maybe it'd be enough to convince them. They didn't have to catch it; I wouldn't let them, anyway.

"I'm going to check myself into the hotel," I said, starting toward my cabin. "If you need any backup support, just call me."

"But I don't know your number," Mark admitted.

"Oh." I chuckled. "Here, hand me your phone. I'll leave it on the table after I add the number."

"Okay," Mark said, continuing with the officers up the stairs. I heard them fumbling around up there but knew I only had a small space of time to accomplish my scheme. Adding my number into Mark's phone, I ran out the door and toward the lake. The sun was beginning to set, but the light was just strong enough for them to see. Glancing up at Jessie's bedroom window, I shuddered remembering the other monster could be lurking anywhere. Lapping waves on the shore of the lake called my name.

Yes, come to us!

My mind became lost in them, and I made a dash for their soothing embrace. Enveloping me on all sides, the water burned the scales onto my body. Strange, but this time the pain was quite minimal — in fact, it barely existed.

"Ah." I sighed with contentment. Now, to get the officers' attention once they came from the cabin, then dive under the water and not return, but give them something to think about. That aught to let them know Mark wasn't a crazy person.

The sound of the door creaking open as Mark allowed them back outside caught in my sensitive ears; I listened for what they were saying.

"Someone is pranking you, Mark," Officer O'Brien told Mark, his long-legged stride headed straight for the car.

Opening my mouth, I emitted a loud shriek. "EREEK!"

Officer O'Brien, his short partner, and Mark froze in place.

"EREEK!" I called again.

"Hey, what are you trying to pull, Mark?" the short guy growled.

I rose from the water and slapped my tail against its surface. Their attention turned toward me; I could hear their hearts pumping and smell the sweat forming on Officer O'Brien's brow, even though the distance between us was expansive. "Oh my—"

"—Sweet Mother of Mercy," the short officer finished for Officer O'Brien. "What the hell is that?"

"SCREECH!" — my final note to the situation, before someone pulled out a gun. I dove beneath the surface of the lake, unable to hear what went on above, only sure that they wouldn't be thinking Mark so crazy anymore. Smiling to myself, I enjoyed some water play, doing somersaults, closing my nostrils so that I could be completely free in the murky depths of this lake. My body sensed movement beside it and, without thinking, I caught a fish in my claws, stabbing it through with their sharp points and killing it. I feasted on its flesh under the water. The taste didn't bother me; in fact, it tasted good, and I couldn't think about what I'd just done. After swallowing the fish, I realized with a thrill of fright that I'd just eaten bones. The bones would puncture my stomach walls and cause me to bleed internally. Why was I taking all of that so lightly? I couldn't think clearly; my mind felt fogged over. Something large appeared in my vision, startling me. Its freakish gaze met mine with similar eyes to my own. The eyes almost glowed in the darkened water, but it darted away, slipping into the murk, its crocodile-like tail trailing last behind. For a moment, I willed myself to take pursuit, but another fish swam past. I caught it in my claws and feasted. Why couldn't I think clearly anymore? My mind faded into an instinctual abyss. Grasping at strings to return, I finally allowed myself to succumb to its freedom of no worries, no regrets, and no real thoughts.

21

Bright sunlight warmed my face and blinded my eyes as they blinked away sleep. Where was I? Why was I always waking up with a hazed mind and memory? Come to think of it, that happened a lot. Shifting my body, I felt mud underneath me, squishing and sucking at the spaces of air the movement created. As I rose, I tried to concentrate on what I'd done. I had allowed the authorities in this state to actually see me! What had I been thinking at the time? The answer: I didn't want them thinking Mark insane anymore. The guy had a tough enough life without people thinking him out of his head.

I stretched from head to tail, trying to wake myself up some more and maintain my bearings. The ever-present question on my mind was, Where on earth was I? My stomach felt full. Had I eaten more than one fish? Rubbing my temples, I tried to remember what I'd done after the officers and Mark had seen me. I'd seen Jessie's killer again — or had I imagined him? Shaking my head, I realized I needed to figure out where I was before someone else found me. I had to stop contemplating the alarming fact that I didn't always remember what I'd done as a monster. Out of the water I could think, but in the water things became surreal, as if I, Jean, did not exist any longer. Jean....I'd begun to think of myself with that name. Jeanine Stafford was dead.

"Hey, Fred!"

I almost jumped out of my skin. Whoever it was, they were directing their voice toward me. Flopping off the shore and into the water, I glanced up to see Tom by a nearby dock in a pontoon boat. "You see anything down there worth catching, bud?"

I dove under into the depths of the lake. While down there, I heard the motor of Tom's pontoon boat starting up. Where was I? And why had he just called me Fred? Fred....

If Tom knew something, maybe I could get him to talk. Resurfacing and trying to relocate his pontoon boat, I watched it move away from the dock. Get ready there, slob; I'm coming to get you. Maybe he'd mistaken me for a swimmer. There had to be another explanation, unless he called the monster of this lake Fred, which didn't go with Teal at all. I mean, the Loch Ness monster they called Nessie, and the Chesapeake Bay monster was called Chessie. Why not call me Tealie or something like that? I almost laughed at how silly these thoughts were but restrained myself. I surfaced next to Tom's boat and grasped hold of its side. A red flag went up in my brain about this.

What are you doing? my mind asked. Are you trying to let every soul on Teal Lake know a monster does exist?

Here I was about to talk to this guy who could have just mistaken me for a swimmer. The boat began speeding up, and I knew the time was now if I wanted to get some answers from Tom. Inhaling deeply, I thought of what I should do once visible to him. Speak to him? Demand an explanation for why he'd called me Fred? On all fours, I leaped onto the deck of the boat.

Tom's back was to me. He stood at the wheel, but he froze when he heard the splatters of water dripping from me. "Fred?" He sighed as if relieved. "Buddy, you gotta stop doin' that. Scared the livin' daylights outa me." Tom's head turned just in time to see me lunge on him.

Pinning him to the floor of the pontoon boat, I growled in his ear. "Who is Fred?"

"I beg your pardon. I don't know you, do I?" Tom's voice sounded shocked, and his face contorted with fear.

Guilt for my rude way of asking him flooded in, and I hopped off of him. "I'm sorry, but I need an answer!" My voice continued to hiss, but I'd toned down the anger in it as much as my lizard-like body would allow. "Who is Fred?"

"Fred?"

"Whom were you talking to? You were talking to me, but you must have mistaken me for someone else."

"Yes, I did think you were somebody else. I'm sorry. I'm sorry!" Tom covered his head with his greasy hands. "I'm sorry!"

"Shut up!" I snapped. What had come over me? I was *acting* like a monster! Trying to tone my temper down another notch, I asked, "Who is the 'someone else'? Who did you think you were talking to?"

"Fred," Tom answered. He was trembling, and although I'd always thought him quite round and large, he looked very small and shriveled to me at that moment. It was as if I could overpower him if I wanted to, and that knowledge surged in my veins and the tips of my claws.

"What's wrong with me?" I asked aloud.

Tom's eyes grew huge. "Listen….Fred, Frederick Stafford. He's a friend of mine and used to fish with me a lot. He sure knows how to fish."

"That doesn't make sense! Why did you call me Fred?"

"He looks like you a little bit….sometimes. I mean, you are obviously a female, but he looks like you," Tom blubbered, his fat face squished into chins; I could smell the sweat beading on his brow.

Snorting with disgust, I let that information sink into my thick, scaly head. "Frederick Stafford looks like me?" My skin began prickling dry, and I realized that if I wanted to keep my identity a secret, I'd better dive back down into Teal. "Are you sure you're not lying?"

"I'm p-p-positive," Tom choked. It was then that I realized I'd gripped his neck in one clawed hand. Letting go with shame, I backed away from him.

"I'm sorry, and thank you," I said, flopping over the boat's side and allowing the water to swallow me. As I drifted to the bottom, my mind became lost. My own grandpa was also a monster, according to Tom. But he couldn't be Jessie's killer; there had to be another creature out there.

Get real, Jean, my brain complained. How many monsters do you think there are in this lake? Your grandpa killed Jessie.

*

It was nightfall when I reached the shore near my cabin. No longer did I fear to live alone there. My mind hardly processed as I fell onto my bed and closed my eyes. Grandpa, my idol growing up, had killed an innocent person, and who knows what else he'd done. A chill of regret, betrayal, and hopelessness struck me. If he was cursed like me, then everything about that room could be a lie. What if he'd planned it out all along? I could envision again the moment I'd told him about the room. I'd seen his eyes light up. Maybe he'd hoped that he would no longer be the only freak living among humans. But it didn't add up. Why didn't he seem addicted to water like me? All my muscles ached, and it wasn't long before my consciousness drifted away into nightmare-filled sleep.

*

I had it in my mind to visit Tom, tell him an update on the truck, thank him again, and maybe get a few more answers to how he knew that Grandpa was a monster. The sun shone into my cabin's windows today, filling me with relief. At least I wouldn't have to worry about rain. A knock on my door made me jump. Who could be at my cabin so early in the morning besides Mark? But I hadn't invited Mark over. Rising from my seat at the kitchen table and my breakfast, I walked to the door and peeked through my curtains. I could feel blood rushing in my ears, and my hands went cold: Grandpa stood at the door. Questions rose in my mind. Should I answer the door? Should I accuse him now? Should I remain silent about the entire thing and first figure out if he *was* the killer? After all, it was one dirty backwoodsman's testimony. The guy could be crazy for all I knew. "Breathe....just breathe," I told myself.

"Come on, Jean, open the door. I've got a treat for you!" Grandpa's voice rang muffled but cheery behind the door, but to me it sounded phony.

Gathering courage, I turned the knob of the door, not sure whether I was doing the right thing or not. "Hey," I said, afraid that it sounded faked.

"How's my favorite granddaughter?" Grandpa asked, smiling from ear to ear.

"Good, I guess," I mumbled.

"Good?" Grandpa chuckled and stepped in.

"Has it really been two weeks since our last phone call?" I asked.

"Nope, you called on Monday, and it's Friday now."

It took a moment for that to sink in fully. Then everything froze, and my heart raced harder. "It's Friday?" I asked him.

Grandpa raised his brows. "Yes, Jeanine, it's Friday."

"I must be losing my mind," I said, forgetting for a moment that the man before me was a killer. "I thought it was Thursday!"

Grandpa's expression grew curious. "Why?"

"Well, I was at Mark's on Tuesday and then—" It was Friday, and I'd missed a complete day in my muddled monster form. Why didn't I remember two days passing? Fear gripped my stomach, making it turn.

"Are you all right, honey? You're as pale as a ghost." Grandpa touched my arm and led me to the couch, concern written all over his face.

"Why are you here early?" I asked. My poor thoughts were so jumbled about that my head hurt as well as my stomach and racing heart.

"I was in the neighborhood. Now, you need to tell me why you thought it was Thursday," Grandpa said, rubbing my back.

I pulled away from him and stood. "I was swimming and lost track of time."

Grandpa nodded gravely. "That doesn't surprise me. The more you become this creature, the more you'll begin to give in to its desires and instincts."

Shuddering at his words, I tried not to think that the reason he knew this was because he'd been through the same experience. "Will it get any easier?" I asked, but wished I hadn't.

"I don't know. That will depend on you; you can control this thing, Jean. I know you can. Now, you said you were at Mark's. You're not sleeping with that boy are you?"

"No." I rolled my eyes.

"Just wondered if you still were trying to find true love," Grandpa murmured.

"True love?" Oh yeah, true love supposedly broke the curse. I'd given up long ago, though, during the whole Greg episode.

"So, tell me this business about Charlie," Grandpa said, his bushy brows arched inward.

I narrowed my eyes at him. "It's nothing. It's completely over now." Shrugging, I decided to brush off the subject. I couldn't trust him anymore.

"What did he make you do?"

"What do you mean?"

"You said he was blackmailing you."

"Oh yeah, um….he wanted me to tutor him on history for an evening," I said. Why had I never noticed the darkness in Grandpa's gaze? He was like a snake hunting its prey; one couldn't know when it'd strike.

"Is there something wrong, Jean?" Grandpa smiled at me in his usual way, but I couldn't breathe. I kept picturing his teeth sharpening to points and the rounded pupils in his eyes narrowing to slits.

"Nothing," I answered quickly, turning my gaze from him in case I threw up.

"Jeanine, there is something I have to tell you."

These words brought my face back to his. Maybe he'd come clean, feel sorry about what had happened, and explain that he hadn't meant to kill Jessie. Maybe he *hadn't* meant to. After all, I hadn't even noticed that I'd been gone two days when I was a monster. Perhaps I needed sympathy instead of anger toward him. "What do you have to tell me?" I asked, returning his smile.

"Your parents told me that you called."

Dismay filled me, but I nodded.

"Corrine was greatly disturbed. She thought you were dead."

"But why did Mom and Dad tell my own little sister that I'd died?"

"They told her so that she wouldn't tell anyone else that they'd faked the suicide." Grandpa shrugged. "It doesn't make sense exactly, but it's understandable."

"Understandable?" I'd made up my mind to charade that I didn't know anything about his curse; instead, I'd pretend as if I were still angry with my parents and obsessed with my situation of being a monster.

"Jeanine, as much as it shames me to say this since your father is my son, I don't think they want you to come back." Grandpa's eyes held sadness and sympathy in them, but it didn't look real to me anymore. "It's a good thing I'm around to look out for you."

"Yeah," I said, taking his hand in my own, glancing at his wrist and hand to see if there was a tell-tale scar anywhere; not any that I could see, but still, that wasn't the only place blood came from, and maybe his cut hadn't left a scar. A memory flooded me. I wanted to research, and now that he was here, I might as well take advantage of that. "Hey, will I ever get some Internet around here? You said you'd get it to me earlier when I first came."

A perturbed look spread across Grandpa's face, but he nodded. "Oh, yes, I'd forgotten. I'll call the internet service providers up today."

"Thanks." I let go of his hand and rose to look out the window. Fear didn't grip me anymore. Grandpa wasn't going to hurt me.

22

"Has anything else been going on around here that I should know about?" Grandpa inquired. I assumed fishing for information.

"Nope," I said.

He narrowed his eyes. "Are you sure?"

I sensed that he was trying to get me to mention that I'd heard the monster by my cabin or in Mark's house, but I decided to pretend that it wasn't important anymore. I smiled, hoping that it looked sincere. "Yep."

I detected suspicion in his features for not owning up that I'd heard the monster. "That's good. So, everything is going well now?"

"Of course." Now please, go away! I willed.

There was a silence, which was odd for us. We'd always had something to talk about in the past. "Do you want me to stay a couple of days?"

Think fast. "Are you doing anything else in the area?"

"I decided to pay Tom a visit. He and I have always been good friends, and there's a musky tournament going on that he wanted me to be a part of."

Not sure how to answer that, I just said, "Oh."

"Jean, I'll see to it that you get a wireless connection out here. If there is no need for me to stay, then I guess I can leave again."

Despite my newfound disgust with him, I almost wished I could ask him more about being a monster. I wanted to ask what being a monster could do to you over a long period of time but restrained myself. If I were to become a crazed killer like him, though, I would end my life now while I still held on to sanity. "You don't have to leave yet; why don't you stay for supper?" It would make me look suspicious if I out-of-the-blue started disliking him.

"That sounds good." Grandpa got up from his seat and grinned. "In fact, let's go out for dinner."

"I know of a really great coffee shop, too," I said, realizing that I was becoming addicted to that place.

"So the truck is still holding out for you?" Grandpa asked, as we walked to his car.

"Yeah, it's been nice to have a way to get around."

"You know, I'm proud of you, Jean. You seem a lot more in-control of everything." Grandpa opened my door for me. "It's almost like you're a new person."

"I went to church for the first time, too. Maybe that's why." I chuckled and Grandpa shot me a look.

"You did? How was it?" He seemed grouchy with me now.

"It was fine," I mumbled. Grandpa's reaction to the idea of going to church was interesting — very interesting. "Tom was there," I added.

"Good ol' Tom. Poor sinner; if he's going to heaven, then I'll be damned," Grandpa snorted.

I almost wanted to point out to Grandpa that his word choice wasn't well put in that statement. Still, it was odd to hear him swear. I'd always thought him sophisticated. Maybe here in Hayward he didn't feel he needed to put on a pretense.

"Grandpa, I've wanted to ask you about something for a while," I blurted, feeling my cheeks redden.

Grandpa had gotten in his car beside me and turned the key in the ignition. "What is it?"

"Why do you know so much about the curse?" I shrugged. "It's like you almost know how I feel."

"My dad told me stories of that room, remember?"

"And?"

"And…?"

We both looked at each other, and there was silence between us.

Grandpa turned his head back to the road. "I've studied our family history quite extensively."

"Extensively," I repeated.

"Jean, maybe I should come clean on something here," Grandpa began, and my heart lifted a little. I was sure he'd fess up now. "I'm very familiar with the cult our ancestors followed."

"Huh?" My gaze snapped back to him. He hadn't confessed! But the fact that he was familiar with the cult our ancestors had followed was an interesting detail I hadn't known. "What do you mean, 'familiar'?"

"I guess you can say I sort of follow its rules." Grandpa shrugged. "You can learn more about it, too, if you'd like. It might even help with your curse."

"How so?"

"They're the people who made up the curse. They did know a thing or two about how it worked." Grandpa chuckled as if this were funny. How could he laugh about my serious situation unless he knew a way out of it through the rules of the cult? Maybe there *was* a way!

"Do you know anything about my particular curse?" I asked, hope beginning to sprout. "Is there something that….can break it?"

Grandpa scratched his head and adjusted his spectacles. A

nervous gesture. Hmm. "If you were to pledge your soul to—"

Wait a second, Grandpa, I thought. I am not about to give my soul to something that has cursed me. "Pledge my what?"

"Your soul." Grandpa grinned. "I know it sounds weird, but look at what that curse did to you. It changed your physical appearance. There is so much power in this sect's rules. All you have to do is…."

A chill prickled through me. There was no way I'd ever do something like that. It felt so wrong and evil, I could've thrown up. In the past, I hadn't thought much about any religion or sect, but now I could almost see the demons, which dwelled in the words Grandpa spoke. I didn't listen to the rest of what Grandpa said about what I had to do. Instead, I stared out the window thinking about Mark. Through all of Grandpa's talk, I realized there was no doubt in my mind that Grandpa, whether or not he was a monster, had lied to me for too many years.

"….You then need to promise that if you do not obey that rule, you will remain cursed in that monstrous form the rest of your life…."

Little tidbits I caught made my mind burn and my stomach turn over. Shut up, Grandpa! I don't want to hear about this, I thought toward him; but he continued, describing what I needed to do to rid myself of the curse through the cult. He'd finished talking. Clearing my throat, I said, "I'd rather find true love."

"What?" Grandpa appeared annoyed that I'd allowed him to go through what I needed to do, only for me to go back to the alternative.

"True love. Like you said when you translated those walls."

"Oh, yes, I remember," Grandpa laughed. He turned into the parking lot of a restaurant. "Good luck with that." Sarcasm dripped from his tongue while saying those words.

"I don't want to be a part of something that cursed me in the first place. That would be like giving up," I stated, getting out of the car and slamming the door behind me. The raising hair on the back of my neck was subsiding after an assault that I could only describe as spiritual.

Grandpa followed me into the restaurant. "It wouldn't be like giving up, Jean; you don't understand. It's like coming to a compromise."

"I'll find true love or stay like this the rest of my life, Grandpa. I've made my decision."

"Jean, you're a different girl." Grandpa half smiled. "I don't know whether I know you anymore."

"I don't think I know *you* anymore," I said with a bitter laugh.

We sat down at a table and there was silence between us once more. The waitress brought out glasses of water for us, and I watched to see if Grandpa felt attracted to the liquid as much as me. It looked to me as if he didn't give it a second glance, which made me wonder more about him.

"Are you—" I began, but halted myself from asking the question that continued to haunt my mind.

"Yes?"

"Never mind." Maybe I'm being a horrible granddaughter for suspecting the worst of someone who loves me more than anyone else in this world.

The waitress had put straws in our glasses, so the water wouldn't touch either of us. There went my plan to see if Grandpa turned into a monster when he drank from his glass. He sucked on the straw, gazing at me while drinking the tempting liquid, a smile plastered on his face. "Aren't you sick of it?" Grandpa asked after setting down the glass.

"Sick of what?"

"Uncontrollably becoming a monster? Feeling obsessed by

water every second of the day?" He shook his head.

I shifted my gaze down to my own glass of water.

"It's dangerous, isn't it? You could spill on yourself right now and frighten everyone in this restaurant." Grandpa spread his hands.

"Grandpa, not so loud," I ordered, pleading him with my gaze to at least show a little compassion.

"I just told you a way you could control it all, and yet you refuse my advice."

So that's what this was about. He was angry with me for not giving my soul to the cult. He should be proud of me; I'm not that easily…. Then it struck me like the plague. How could I have not read this from his earlier speech in the car? Grandpa had sold his soul! That's why he didn't feel tempted by water. His words floated back up in my mind. *I follow its rules.* Without thinking, my hand touched the cool sides of my water glass. I wanted to be anywhere but here.

"Jean, did you hear me? You're being stupid. I found out a way for you to be rid of the curse." Grandpa's voice was down to a growl, and his eyes flashed at me.

"You've heard my answer, Grandpa," I said, still under the spell of the water in my glass. I was aware of its swirling when Grandpa rocked the table as he slammed his fists against it.

"Is this a bad time?" The waitress's voice interrupted us.

"Of course not," I said, smiling at her, grateful that she'd rescued me, in a way of speaking. My hand released the glass.

Grandpa's face twisted in frustration, but they softened a bit because of the waitress, making me feel more comfortable. It felt so foreign to see him cross. "I'll have a bacon burger with fries," Grandpa announced.

"And you?" The waitress looked to me.

"The same," I said, handing her my menu. "Please, don't add onions though."

"Okay," The waitress said, taking our menus from us.

Out of the corner of my eye, I noticed Hayley and Jordan enter the restaurant together. How strange.

"Jeanine, I don't know what to say if you don't take my advice," Grandpa said, shaking his head. "Is this about you going to church? Did they tell you our ancestors' cult was demonic or something? Did they tell you you'd be damned to hell if you followed it?"

A shudder went through me again. "Demonic" was a word used in horror stories. My life had felt like a horror story recently. "Actually, I think I figured that out without going to church, thank you very much," I said.

Grandpa gripped me by the shoulder, sending adrenaline running up my spine. He looked as if he were about to eat me. "Jeanine, you're so naïve! Just you wait, and you'll be *begging* to hear how you can rid yourself of the curse. It'll get worse. After this lunch, I'm going to go back to New York. But I shall return in a few months. If you want my advice again, I'll give it to you then."

"Why are you upset with me?" I asked. "I'm strong; you even said that yourself back in the cabin when I was crying my eyes out about being alone."

Grandpa did not say anything. Instead, I could see him studying my face, as if he were looking into my soul. He opened his mouth. "I shall return in a month."

As we got in the car, my phone rang. It was an unknown number to me, but I knew it had to be Mark. Grandpa glanced over. "Aren't you going to answer your phone?"

I gave him a look. Was it dangerous to let Grandpa know I was still communicating with Mark? "No, I don't know the caller. If they're worth my while, they'll leave a message."

"Oh," Grandpa said. The snake returned its focus to the road.

The rest of our ride to the cabin was silent. "Don't forget the Internet," I told him right before he left.

"Of course," Grandpa assured with a half-smile. "I love you, Jean; remember that."

23

After Grandpa's surprise visit, I was left in a type of shock. My grandpa had sold his soul to the sect that had cursed him in the first place! In a month he'd return, but what could and what would I do about that? With too much information to process, my head felt like it would explode. Should I tell Mark that I knew who had killed Jessie? Or did I really know? Between Charlie, Tom, Mark, and Jessie's journal, I knew. In my heart, I was sure, and that chilled my blood.

I lay on the couch in my cabin and pondered all the decisions I had before me. How had I gotten myself into such a tangled mess? It caged me in on all sides. If I told Mark about Grandpa, I also would have to tell him about me. I couldn't talk to Grandpa anymore about anything or ask him about anything because he was on the wrong side of the playing field. Charlie still confused me as to whose side he was on, and Tom knew about Grandpa as a monster, for some unknown reason. The most irking realization on my mind was that I was positive, as a monster, that I was losing my mind. Plus, my attraction to water was becoming worse; the smell of water alone was becoming enough to make me dive in.

"Don't think about that," I told myself as my heart began pounding for the lake's waves outside my cabin. "Oh Lord, what should I do?" I asked the air, but in reality, I guess I was hoping God would give me an answer; send a hand to write on the wall or whatever He did to make His will known. My phone beeped, making me jump.

"You have two new messages," my phone announced.

Well, maybe a hand hadn't been sent down, but those words were clear. I put the phone on speaker and listened.

"Hey, Jean, it's Mark. There's something I'd like to talk with you about. I don't know where exactly you're staying, but there's an annual church dance that we can talk at tomorrow. Remember?" There was a pause, and I could picture him searching for words to say. He was one of those awkward answering machine people of which I was too; it made me smile. "I'm sorry I acted so weird the other day. I am sort of looking forward to seeing you. It starts at five, by the way, and you can—" A dry chuckle sounded. "—be as fancy as your city-girl heart desires. Okay, um, 'bye." *Click.*

How nice. He "sort of" was looking forward to seeing me. Why couldn't I stop grinning? Gosh. I needed help when it came to Mark. So the dance was at the church and it was tomorrow — I'd forgotten. Although I couldn't blame myself; I'd missed a complete day of my life, lost in the mindless snacking of fish and swimming in the depths of the lake, unaware of the present complications in my life. The next message was from my grandpa, much to my surprise, and I held it to my ear.

"Look in the stove," Grandpa's voice said without emotion. *Click.*

Huh? Okay, Grandpa, I thought, walking toward the stove in my kitchen and opening the stove door. A journal greeted me — Jessie's journal. Why had Grandpa told me this unless he wanted me to know that he was also cursed? Now I could tell Mark and—but no, no, no! What could I do? Walk up to Mark and say, Hey, my grandpa is the monster? There was a concept that everyone else around here except me held: People don't transform into monsters. Also, it came to me that I was accusing my grandpa of murdering someone. What sort of demented and cruel granddaughter was I? But the answer came as quickly as I'd asked it: One with a demented and cruel grandpa who'd be back in a month. That meant I had a short amount of time to make my decision. Why was Grandpa allowing me to know he was a monster? Why did he *want* me to know?

"Give the diary to Mark," my conscience seemed to say. "He deserves to see this."

My relationship with him was just beginning, and if I told him

I was a monster now, it would end. He wouldn't be able to look at me without thinking that my grandpa had been what had murdered Jessie. Then there was the factor that if Mark knew about my curse, he would only see the monster lying under my skin, waiting for water to wash away the human appearance and reveal itself. A flash of Greg's face when he'd come back to the house appeared in my mind. Charlie knew, and for some reason it hadn't disgusted him, but he'd mocked me for it. What would Mark say if— The faucet dripped and interrupted my thoughts. I placed my cell phone on the coffee table, and without thinking, I walked toward the sink. I wanted water again, and my monster wanted to be let out of its cage.

*

The creature of me knew that something was wrong. I surfaced and heard the noise of a boat approaching me. The waves from the motor splashed against my chest, and I curled my tail and hissed in anger at its oncoming assault. I ducked under the water and swam about ten feet under, watching all the while above. The sound of something loud and booming going off above the water reached my sensitive ears, and I winced. My heartbeat rushed, and a roar of rage sounded in my ears. I wanted to kill the noise. Propelling myself upward as fast as my strong limbs would allow, I broke the surface in a splash and hopped onto the boat. A young man with dark hair stood on the deck, shirtless, with a long device in his clawless hands. Something strange I noticed about his bare chest was a red scar that ran in three marks swiping across his left pectoral muscle and angled down his well-muscled side. His blue eyes met mine with fearlessness, like a monster lay inside him as well. For a moment, I felt afraid of him.

"I knew you'd come back one day for me," he growled. His body was in a threatening position. "Let's see how thick that skin of yours is."

Bringing the long device up, he pointed it at me. Sensing there was something dangerous about it, I ducked low and darted around him. I stood behind him, breathing into his ear. His scent caught in my nostrils, and I recognized it; it relaxed everything inside me and lit an attraction toward him. My tail wrapped around his right leg, and I continued to inhale him. I licked his ear. A low growl sounded in my throat, and my lips touched his in a long and delicious kiss. I released him and gazed into his face.

The young man had frozen, as if not sure what to do. "What the—" he began, as if unable to say anything else. "You can't be the—" None of his sentences finished.

I placed a hand on his neck and felt his pulse rushing underneath the skin. It pumped rhythmically, enticingly, and….Mark. This man was Mark! What in the world was I doing? My tail released him, and my body shook in shock. What the hell was wrong with me? What sort of siren was I? "I'm sorry," I blurted, feeling tears reach my eyes. "I'm so sorry. I'm not what you are after." After saying this, I dove under the water and made back for my dock. His boat did not pursue me, and I could feel my blood growing hot. How had I gotten all the way out here? And what had I been doing on Mark's boat? What had I just done? What day was it? How long had I been a monster? This habit of getting wet and forgetting my actions was becoming an incredible bother.

After I found my dock and scrambled out of the water toward my cabin, I began sobbing. By the time I reached the back door, I was bawling. Such a crybaby I could be, I scolded myself. It wasn't like Mark knew who I was in that form. The door was locked. Where had I put the keys? The keys — they must've been in the remains of my clothing that I'd ripped! I'd have to go shopping again once I was.... What was I thinking? Here I was, the clock ticking before I was naked outside, not looking for the key or the remains of my clothes.

"Looking for these?" Charlie's smug voice asked. He held up my keys, a smile on his face. "How've you been, Jeanine? I heard you almost ended up staying at Mark's for the night."

"Charlie!" I growled. "Give them to me!"

"Don't raise that spine of yours at me!" Charlie snapped. He tossed the keys toward me. "Here, I don't want to stop you from getting inside. What were you doing out there?"

"What are *you* doing here?" I screeched as I caught the keys in one of my hands and put them in the lock.

"Let me come inside with you, and I shall explain myself." Charlie swaggered toward the door.

"Please, do," I muttered as I pushed the door open and clambered inside, my body still dripping wet.

"I actually like you, Jeanine, and I wanted to ask you to the dance," Charlie began his story. "When I knocked on your door, I noticed you were gone, so I walked around the back, found telltale ripped clothing on the dock, and I knew where you were. Your keys — which almost fell into the lake, by the way — I saved."

"How gentlemanlike of you," I said dryly. "Why are you asking me to the dance?"

"Well, the guys are supposed to ask the girl they are interested in and—"

"You're interested in me?" Arching my brows inward, I focused on keeping my human mind alive by talking with him. I wrapped a blanket around myself and found myself unable to stop the smile that spread across my lips.

Charlie's eyes met mine. "Yeah."

"Charlie....I-I've already been asked."

"By Mark?"

"Yes."

Charlie turned away from me and crossed his arms. "He's not going to ever be anyone that will stick with you, not if he knew what you really were."

What you really were.... That wasn't what I really was; that was a curse, not me. "Maybe I should give him a chance before I make a judgment like that."

"He was the first guy you met here, am I right?"

"Well—"

"What if I had been on that plane with you and taken you home. What then?"

"Charlie, you're a different person than Mark," I stated, shaking my head.

"I'm not so different. Sure, I don't believe in any of his mumbo jumbo about God, but I—"

"You may not believe that, but I think I'm beginning to," I said, surprising myself even for admitting that. But it was true. I'd become very much open to the possibility that God did have a hand in things; in fact, ever since my chat with Grandpa and sensing the demons in the cult he followed, I could feel the difference on which side of the playing field I wished to be part of.

"What do you mean?" Charlie's eyes grew wide and confused, as if he thought me insane.

"Look at me. Now tell me that's a natural thing!"

"I don't see what you're getting at." Charlie shrugged.

"You're blind, then," I said, facing myself toward my bedroom door. But I turned my neck and looked Charlie in the eyes again. "There are things going on in this world that we can't explain, but the devil still fools us into thinking we can." I pointed to my face. "This. This can't be explained, and yet you still think that talk of God or the supernatural is mumbo jumbo. Realize this, Charlie: I was once like that, but then *this* happened to me. I know better now. Please, don't fall victim to the same trap I did."

"Jeanine, what did you do? How did you make yourself like this, because I want it." Were his eyes clouding up?

This statement caused pain inside me for him. "You don't know what you're saying."

"I do, though." Hurt filled his voice and facial features. "I want to be extraordinary like you, like….like Fred."

"You know about Grandpa?" I bit my lip.

"Yes, I've known about him for a while." Charlie shrugged. "Ever since Mark's accident, I've known."

"His accident?" My human appearance sucked the monster away at that moment.

"That is incredible." Charlie's eyes lit with an inner fire. "You're so beautiful, Jeanine." The words were said sincerely, and something inside me fluttered a little, even if the compliment came from Charlie. I wanted to slap myself for being so vain.

"Please, tell me about Mark's accident; what happened? He hasn't talked about it."

"Then maybe he doesn't want you to know," Charlie said. "I may not be his friend anymore, but I'm not a squealer."

"Was it that bad?" An image in my mind appeared of Mark's bare chest, and the angry red scars which were etched into his otherwise perfect skin made its way into my mind. How did I know this? I'd been on his boat, and he'd almost shot me, and then I'd— Shaking my head to get rid of the shame and image of what I'd done while still in monster form, I forced myself out of my thoughts.

"If he wants to tell you about it, I'll let him." Charlie sighed. "Well, I guess you don't want to come with me, then?"

"Wait, you're not going to blackmail me into doing this?"

He shook his head.

"Thank you for asking, but I'm already going with Mark." I took his hand and squeezed it.

"I guess there might be hope for me, the less handsome and charming one," Charlie mumbled. He walked to the door.

"What are you talking about?"

"Mark always got all the girls' attention. It's part of the reason why I just couldn't hang out with him anymore. I want to be like you, Jeanine. I don't care if you call it a curse. To me it looks more like a blessing." Charlie stalked out of my cabin, his shoulders slumped.

"If only you knew that I'm losing my mind," I whispered softly after him. A rush of wind hit my face as he closed the door, and I closed my eyes. Mark and I needed to talk.

24

Staring into my closet, I came to the conclusion that I needed to do something about this constant clothes-ripping problem. Now I had one pair of jeans, two T-shirts, one pair of shorts, two dresses, one bra, and two panties left in my meager wardrobe. Sure, that sounded like it could suffice for a desperate person, but when one has grown up to be a débutante, that amount of clothing is pathetic and depressing. I placed my dress, the blue one I'd changed into the night of my first transformation, on. Styling my hair to perfection, I stared into the mirror at myself. My physical appearance since living in New York hadn't changed much. Perhaps it had grown wilder. Having taken a very short, very cautious shower, so I wouldn't lose my mind while a monster, I felt clean enough to go with Mark to the church dance.

As I hopped in my truck, I thought about what I could say to Mark. First, I'd have to hear what Mark had to say and figure out if he thought the female monster he'd seen in his boat had killed Jessie. I remembered telling him that I wasn't what he was looking for. Would he believe me? I'd taken Jessie's journal with me. But how could I explain to Mark that I'd found it?

*

My eyes scanned the crowded bunch of people in the gym of the church. Where was Mark? Was he even coming? Sometimes I wondered why I was so attached to him. Like Charlie had said, what if he hadn't been the first guy I'd met? My attraction to him I realized was perhaps slightly perverted because I felt a thrill of danger whenever around him. Maybe I just liked getting myself into dangerous and/or deadly situations. That had to be it. I couldn't be falling in love with a guy so soon after meeting him.

"I'm so glad you made it." Mark's voice behind me caused my

spirits to lift.

I turned to face him. "What do you think?" I asked, holding up the skirt to give him a curtsy.

"You look great," Mark said, smiling. "You know, I've sort of missed you."

"Yeah, just like you 'sort of' were looking forward to seeing me."

"Okay, I have missed you." Mark chuckled. "Sheesh, Jean."

"That's better," I flirted back. "So, what did you want to talk about?"

"Let's go somewhere a little more private first," Mark said, taking my hand in his. I thought of what Charlie had said about Mark always getting the girls' attention. That bothered me for just a moment. I didn't want to be another one of those silly girls whose attention was so easily won. I spotted Charlie staring at us shamelessly just before Mark and I walked outside the building and into the nighttime summer air.

"So, you've got me alone…." I said.

"Something happened yesterday," Mark explained. "And then once you left, you know, when the police came, the monster showed up! The police saw it, too."

"Are you serious?" I tried to do my best at feigning shock.

"Yeah, it was weird, like on cue, you know?" Mark gave me direct eye contact. "Jean, where are you staying?"

"I'm staying in my cabin," I said.

"What!"

"I've decided I'm not going to let it frighten me away."

"Then at least let me stay with you," Mark said. "I can't bear the thought of that monster coming in at night to get you."

"Huh?"

"I want to protect you." He seemed a little embarrassed to say this, and I wondered why.

"Aw! You like me don't you?" I said, regretting it immediately because of how childish it sounded.

"As a matter of fact...." Mark poked me in the ribs. "Now shut up. I've got another story I need to share with you before I explain anything else."

"And what is that?" I asked seriously.

"I think there are two of whatever that creature is living in Teal Lake, like a male and female pair. Maybe even more of them exist." Mark shuddered. "But the female one jumped aboard my boat and acted really, really friendly. It was odd."

My cheeks began to redden, and I was glad we were outside in the dark so Mark wouldn't see.

"Anyway, the creatures, they can speak English."

I opened my mouth.

Mark stopped me from saying anything. "I know! I know! I'll bet someone has already told you that I'm crazy."

"Of course not! Besides, with the monster picture you took, I doubt anyone would think that. Anyway, you've forgotten that *I've* seen it myself."

"Well, there is my accident to consider. It caused quite a stir," Mark mumbled.

"Tell me about it then," I pleaded.

"I'd rather not," Mark answered, rubbing a hand across his chest for no reason, and then I thought about his scars and knew why.

"It's okay. I won't talk about it to anyone. Anyway, before I let some crazy guy live in my house, I'd really like to know why he's thought crazy." I laughed a little, hoping humor would open Mark up a little bit more.

"This monster that I saw today wasn't the one that attacked me on my kayak."

"A monster attacked you on your kayak?"

"Yeah. I think I accidently hit it while it was swimming, and it got pissed with me." Mark shook his head. "I got out alive, but when I went to the authorities and my parents and even Jessie, they all thought that I'd hit my head or something or gone insane. I know I told you that I left for New York because of Jordan and Jessie's relationship. Well, that is true, but it's also because….because Jessie did think I was crazy. She treated me so differently. Everyone did." Mark went quiet, and my heart went out to him. I laid a hand on the back of his neck and, without thinking, stood on tiptoe and kissed him on the mouth. My head began whirling, and then it pounded when Mark surprised me by kissing back. His warm lips against mine threw all of my senses to the wind. Our perfect kiss ended, much to my dismay.

"Jean," Mark said, his voice hoarse and eyes wide.

"Yeah?" I was out of breath. A strong sense of wonder filled me.

"You're my best friend." Mark touched my face, running a hand along my cheek.

Best friend? Maybe the man really was crazy! Come on, Mark, we just kissed; doesn't that mean more than a friendship to you? It seriously wouldn't work with me if he wanted to be friends with benefits. "We're only friends?" I asked aloud and nearly put a hand over my mouth for it.

Mark grinned sheepishly. "I meant to say, I've never had the girl I liked also be my best friend." He put a hand under my chin and lifted my face to his again for a kiss. It was short but sweet, and Mark looked toward the church. "You care to dance with me, Miss Stafford?"

"Miss Stafford?" I asked, trying not to laugh; heat still pulsed through my entire being. "Now that I'm your girlfriend, you address me by my last name?"

Mark shrugged, chuckling. "You're right; that was lame. I was pretending to act like those guys in your high-society circles."

I rolled my eyes and took his hand in my own. "Please, don't. They don't act any more civilized than you, or Jordan, for that matter." It was at that moment that I remembered Jordan and Hayley walking into the restaurant that Grandpa and I had gone to. "Do Hayley and Jordan have a thing for each other?"

A bewildered look crossed Mark's face. "Not that I've known of. Why do you ask?"

"I saw them eating together at that restaurant in town. I was there with my grandpa."

"Huh." Mark shrugged. "Maybe they were just hanging out."

"You're right. I guess they are friends." I decided to dismiss it from my mind. Mark didn't seem bothered by it, so it wasn't going to bother me. "Let's dance, Mr. Calvin," I said dryly, making Mark roll his eyes; but he slipped his arm around me, sending thrills of electricity through me. Mark was so different from any guy who'd touched me in the past. Our friendship before our relationship had to be to blame, I concluded, as he swung me about the dance floor. He danced in a way that made me wonder at the fluidity of it. He'd probably be great in bed, I found myself musing, what with his dancing and the way he kissed.

After our first dance had ended, I noticed Luke with Meg on his arm approaching. "Hey, Mark. I see that you and our city girl are now a thing."

"What makes you say that?" Mark grinned and put an arm around my waist. I loved how his large hand slid against my slim waist as if it could wrap itself around me.

"I saw you and her lip-locking." Luke elbowed him.

"Luke." Mark lowered his voice to a warning tone.

"It's okay, man! I'd have done the same thing with someone like her." He looked to me and winked. "Congratulations to you both."

Mark rolled his eyes but continued to hold me close to him. "So what really brings you over here, Luke? You're not just here to hit on my girlfriend, are you?"

A flutter of delight went through me when I heard him call me, for the first time, his girlfriend; it made me feel silly.

"We're having a party at my house next Tuesday, and I wondered if you wanted to come with Jeanine."

"Okay." Mark looked to me, an amused look on his face. "Do you want to go?"

"Yeah, sure," I said, trying to be casual but inside still rejoicing over Mark's and my romance. A loud crash sounded along with the sound of water splashing everywhere, and the happy feeling inside me vanished. Water.... But how had it found me here? I almost felt as if it waited for the opportune moment to sneak up on me. Dripping sounded, and laughter rang from pretty much everyone in the room. Their laughter mocked me; it was as if they knew that the liquid tempted me so. The source of water was from a cooler that had fallen against the smooth floor. Ice cubes spread out in all directions, sliding about everywhere, just like I would do with my own slippery, serpentine body if I touched it.

"I wonder who knocked it over." Mark laughed along with everyone else. My eyes darted everywhere, trying to avoid the water, but I couldn't help it, and almost magnetically I was drawn to the shimmer cast on the puddles from the lights. Charlie stood next to the fallen cooler, a smile on his face. He was looking at me. I should have known. Blood burned in my face as I controlled the urge to go up and lay in the shallow puddles. Already, churchwomen were bustling about with towels, paper towels, and other means of soaking up the remaining liquid. The music stopped, and Charlie began walking away from the mess. He tossed his blond hair back with a type of pride. I touched Mark's arm. "Excuse me a moment."

"Sure," Mark said. He was preoccupied with watching the people who were trying to clean up the mess.

Slipping out of the gym and through the door Charlie had walked through, I found myself in a small lounge room. Charlie stood, arms folded, in the center.

"What is wrong with you?" I asked.

"You and Mark are now together officially." Charlie narrowed his eyes.

"Yes, but that doesn't give you a reason to act like a little kid."

"Jeanine, Mark is all wrong for you. Have you forgotten? He doesn't know that you're, as you call it, cursed." He shook his head. "I don't care."

"Seriously, I'm not attracted to you that way, Charlie."

"But I'm attracted to you! Every time I see you, I can't help but feel drawn to you." He sighed. "You're what I want."

"You don't even really know me," I said, throwing up my hands. Why was this kid so persistent?

"And you think Mark does?"

I couldn't answer him.

25

"Look, I don't know if we're supposed to be together, but I at least want a chance," Charlie said.

"Why is this happening to me? Why do I have people like you and Greg hitting on me and growing attached after such short periods of time? Maybe Mark is similar to you guys in the way that he's attracted to me, but he's gone about it in the right way: by actually becoming my friend," I said. "You started out by blackmailing me. Then you told me you hated my grandpa...." My voice trailed off. I'd forgotten to give Jessie's journal to Mark!

"Don't you hate him too now?" Charlie interrupted my thoughts and met my gaze. He must have noticed the troubled look that I knew had appeared on my face. "What's wrong?"

"Nothing," I said, finding myself gripping folds of fabric from my dress. "I think I am starting to pity Grandpa," I whispered in answer to his first question.

His eyes widened. "Why? Your grandpa is a *real* monster."

"Because he can't help it. Because I'm becoming one, too," I said, but the stupidity of such a statement struck me. This wasn't information I should give out, especially since Charlie had no idea that I didn't have control over myself as a monster.

"What do you mean?" Charlie's voice had dropped to a whisper like mine.

"Never mind," I said, shaking my head and laughing. "Forget I said anything. I don't pretend to like my grandpa now. He's a monster."

"Jean?" The sound of Mark's voice behind us made me jump.

Charlie grinned vaguely. "Hey, bro, how's it going?"

"Hey, Charlie," Mark said, giving Charlie an odd look. His gaze shifted to me.

"Mark, I know who spilled the water," I said, smiling at him; but I realized that my smile was faked, which caused me to feel shame. I really did want to be transparent with Mark.

Charlie knew I was faking the smile. I could tell by the way he stared at me minutes after without saying anything.

"Man, you sure made a mess." As Mark approached me, he chuckled to lighten the mood. "They got it all cleaned up now, though."

"Oh, good!" I said, feeling my stomach turn inside-out as I thought of the journal sitting in my truck once again. Did I have the courage to give it to him now that he had declared his interest in me and said that I was his best friend? I couldn't bring myself to imagine what sort of reaction I would get if I let him know the complete truth. My grandpa....my own grandpa, a flesh and blood relative, had killed Mark's beloved sister. Tears involuntarily began welling up in my eyes. It annoyed me that I cried so easily.

"Jean, are you okay?" Mark asked, putting an arm around me.

"Yes," I said, sniffing and rubbing my eyes. "This room is very dusty." Really lame explanation for that, Jeanine, I thought.

"Okay, well let's get you out of here," Mark said.

"Yeah, don't step in any puddles," Charlie said, bursting into laughter before walking out. He brushed by Mark.

"What's his problem?" Mark asked, looking to me.

"He likes me, I think," I admitted, gaining control over myself.

"I didn't even know he knew you that well." Mark's blue eyes grew dark. "Is there something going on that I don't know with him?"

"I don't like him, if that's what you're asking."

"No, I didn't mean that. I meant, like, is he treating you badly without my knowledge of it?"

Mark walked toward the exit of the lounge, and I followed behind, feeling as if my defenses were weakened. Any amount of water left on that floor could be enough to put me over the edge. It frightened me so much that I couldn't concentrate on Mark's question. "No," I answered, but I had to think it over again. "Well, actually, he did blackmail me about my grandpa for a while."

"Why?" Mark asked.

"He's cheated during some of the fishing tournaments." Another lame explanation, but it would have to do. I hated myself now for lying to Mark, but telling him about the journal would probably end our relationship. Plus, if I remembered correctly, he'd seen me as the female monster, and I'd acted in a way uncharacteristic to myself that I couldn't explain without telling Mark I was crazy. After these thoughts jumbled through, I realized with dread that the hole I'd dug to hide myself in was only getting deeper.

"Weird. I didn't know your grandpa fished." Mark shrugged. "All those years of living next door to him, and I never saw him on a boat."

"He always went with Tom," I said.

"Come on, let's dance some more," Mark said, smiling. He took my hand in his again and rubbed it with his thumb.

We danced two more dances, but the entire time I could not enjoy being with him. A picture of that journal remained in my mind. I knew it was sitting in the passenger seat of my truck. I knew that if Mark saw what I was keeping from him, he wouldn't be holding me so close against him.

*

"I'll meet you at your house; you don't even have to get out of your truck until I make it there," Mark said in an assuring voice. "I've got my gun in the back of my trunk." His eyes held such concern when saying that. "Did you have fun at the dance?"

"Yes," I answered. "It was wonderful."

"I'll see you back at your cabin," said Mark, as he walked away toward his truck. It was on the other side of the church's parking lot, and I stared at his back as he walked toward it.

"I'll be waiting for you!" I yelled after him.

I'd never felt this loved before. Maybe Mark did love me. Maybe, just maybe, the curse would break because of—but that couldn't be true. Mark might be fond of me, but he couldn't *love* me. He didn't really know me. He didn't know what water did to my physical appearance. Charlie's words about that very subject kept ringing in my mind, haunting me as I drove my truck home. The curse kept reminding me that it existed everywhere I went. I now knew Grandpa had sent me here to live on a lake because he wanted me to give in to the curse, just as he'd done, so he wouldn't be the only one trapped in the cult he'd sold his soul to. One thing he hadn't figured on was my surprising strong will. I wasn't weak like him. I would never sell my soul to some devil's spawn to get rid of this curse, even if I lost my mind from the curse. I glanced at the passenger's seat and took note of the journal. It lay there, with Jessie's drawing and my lies wrapped inside.

"You're an idiot," I told myself, as I parked near my cabin. "Do you think you'll never tell Mark about this?" With determination, I grasped the journal in my hands and opened the door.

I don't *have* to tell him that I'm a monster, I thought. I don't even have to mention that I know Grandpa is the one behind Jessie's murder.

My thoughts were leading me into denial. Who was I kidding, though? Mark would want to know how I'd gotten the journal back, and it could even put more suspicion on me and—oh, bother! My life was so screwed up I could scream. The sound of Mark's vehicle approaching made the decision for me. The journal lay in my hands, and I gripped it with one hand and swallowed.

Mark walked from his car to me. "You ready to go in?"

I nodded. In the dark, I knew he couldn't see the book in my hands. My phone beeped at that moment. Mark's face turned downward at my glowing phone.

"Did you get a text?" he asked.

"No, I don't have a texting plan. I think I missed a call, though," I said. Taking my cell phone out of my purse with my free hand, I checked who the caller was. Grandpa had tried to call me while I'd been dancing. I hadn't heard the phone over the blasting music. He'd left a message. "Let's go inside so I can take care of this," I said.

We walked in together, and Mark turned the lights on before I could run to my room to stash the journal.

"I'm going to go put this—" I began but realized I couldn't keep it from him without my conscience nagging me, so I handed Mark the book. "I found Jessie's journal."

Mark's eyes narrowed as he stared at it; then his eyes went to me. "Where did you find it?"

Ignoring his question I opened it for him. "Look, is this the thing that attacked you on your kayak?" I asked.

"Jean," Mark said, almost in a whisper, which caused me to meet his gaze once again. "Where did you find this?"

"Mark, to be honest with you, I found it in my oven." Sheepishly I looked away, knowing that I had just blown most of my cover by telling the truth right away.

"Your oven?" Mark ran a hand through his hair and turned from me, walking further into the cabin. "What is going on?"

"I don't know," I said, taking a breath.

"What do you mean by saying that you don't know?"

"Mark, I—"

"Jean, please, I like you a lot. In fact, like I said before, you really are my best friend…." His voice trailed off and he looked at me, blinking his haunted eyes; I could read the confusion in the muscles of his face. "But I feel like you're not being honest with me."

I couldn't say anything, but I blinked once, trying not to cry; I'd done enough of that for a lifetime.

"Jean, I can read on your face that there are things I don't know. I've known for a while that there's something you've been trying to keep secret. The pain of having to hold back from me and others is very apparent on your face. There's a mystery surrounding you all the time. Since the first day I met you on the plane, I've known."

Mark wasn't stupid. I'd known that for a while now. Of course he'd been starting to get suspicious, but I hadn't known he'd been wondering about the secret that plagued me since the first time we met. Was he capable of making the connection between me and the female monster who'd confronted him on his boat?

"That's part of the reason why I first started hanging out with you," Mark said, looking guilty.

My heart broke for him. I tried to picture myself in his place: just losing a beloved sister, his parents thinking him crazy, friends deserting him. And then I'd come along, tossing everything around and lying to him about the most prominent part of my life. The fact that he hadn't become bitter through all this surprised me.

"And then I started really enjoying being with you," Mark continued. "You never thought I was crazy. You never wanted me for more than just a friend. I could tell you were sort of depressed when you first came here, but you've changed since then. And now things are going insane! Actual monsters appearing...." His voice trailed off, and he ran a hand through my hair. I was aware that he was leaning in, and my body tingled when he kissed my forehead. The warmth of his lips didn't remain long enough. He drew back and said, "You've acted as if it's normal to have monsters haunting lakes. You completely believe everything I've told you."

"Remember, I was visited by the monster as well," I said, covering myself from exposing the monster right then and there.

"Yes, you were. But when I showed you the photograph of the monster, you didn't care." Mark's voice had become so tender that I melted inside. "I know there is something going on inside you, like an internal struggle with yourself, and it's plain to see that it bothers you. I've told you my secrets, Jean; now tell me yours." He fingered my hair and was again so close, I could feel him breathing.

Darkness inside me wanted to laugh at him and myself because, if I told him the truth, what we had would disappear as fast as the fish darted away from me in the depths of Teal Lake. My heartbeat quickened its pace, and my stomach turned, because Mark would find out my dreaded secret. I needed time to think; this was too important to make a rash decision. This wasn't the time to give in to Mark just because I had intense feelings for him.

"Mark," I began. "There isn't a real secret if you think about it hard." My breath left me when I noticed the hurt in his eyes.

"Why are you playing games with me?"

"I'm not," I said. "Please, just give me more time."

"Okay," Mark said smiling at me. "I'm not going to leave you, Jean."

"That's all I need to hear right now, Mark," I whispered into his ear before kissing him. The kiss continued until both of us were breathless and my body felt aflame with desire. My fingers reached for the top button of his shirt, but Mark's hand stilled them.

"Jean, we shouldn't go further than this."

"Huh?"

"We're spending the night together here; maybe we should stop and do something else now."

I understood then why he didn't want to go any farther physically. I hadn't told him my secret, and that in and of itself was enough to make him wonder if hardcore making-out was a good idea. "Okay, Mark," I said, smiling at him, feeling intense respect for him. The lust in Greg's eyes flashed through my mind; he'd been after this one thing that Mark viewed with a reverence. Mark didn't *only* want me for sex.

"First, let me call my parents; I want to know when they're coming back."

"Mark, I don't have cell phone service in my cabin."

"I'll go by my cabin, then. You can figure out a place for me to sleep in the meantime." Mark chuckled. "And don't say *your* room, Jean."

Glad that everything had turned lighthearted again, I giggled. "Aw, come on, Mark. I'm not a blanket hog, and my body is so nice and *warm*...."

Mark raised his brows, frowned, and waggled a finger at me before stepping out of the cabin with his phone.

*

I'd fixed a luxury hotel room for Mark in the cabin's living room. The furniture had been cleared away, and I'd placed a sleeping bag on the floor with a pillow. I'd found the sleeping bag in the cabin's storage closet along with a book filled with pornography. Grandpa was just full of surprises. So many things about him in the past didn't add up anymore. Who had I known then? Who had inspired my love of history?

The squeak of my cabin door sounded, alerting me that Mark was back. His expression seemed strained.

My breath caught in my throat. "What's wrong?"

"There was a brutal murder near where I used to live in New York."

"What?"

"It sounds very close to what happened to Jessie." Mark's face was paler than I'd ever seen it. He sat on my moved couch and shook his head.

"Did your parents say who'd been murdered? Did you know this person?"

Mark shook his head. "I never knew this person. He was some guy named Gregory Peterson."

26

"Greg," I breathed his name. An image of his handsome face swirled into my memory. My loathing for his pathetic shallowness became sadness, followed by surprise.

"You knew him, didn't you?" Mark looked up, suspicion filling his face; it hurt.

"Yes. He was, well….he was the guy who I went out with….very briefly."

"So he just got slaughtered."

Grandpa….I shoved out the thought and asked, "Do they have any suspects? Are there any reasons why someone would target Greg?"

"This Gregory fellow had been claiming something radical about this girl who'd committed suicide—"

"A girl who'd committed suicide…." I didn't want him to say any more. I knew now Mark had found something out that would kill our entire relationship.

The intensity of Mark's gaze on me grew uncomfortable, and a silence followed.
"The girl who'd committed suicide had a name."

"Yeah?" Already, I could feel my face burning with complete shame. I swallowed back the bile, which rose in my throat. "And what was her name?"

"Jeanine….Stafford…." His haunting eyes were filled with so much pain; I couldn't stand it anymore.

"What was he claiming about the girl?"

"That she was some sort of slimy, reptilian monster," Mark murmured softly, looking away from me.

"Mark, I—"

"Don't say it, Jeanine Stafford." The way he said my entire name chilled me to the bone. "Did you think I wouldn't figure out? What the *hell* is going on?" I'd never heard Mark use a swear word. It made me shiver. The word wasn't said in anger, though.

"I'm a monster," I said under my breath. "But I didn't kill Greg; I was here."

"What?" Stepping away from me, Mark's expression held confusion and hurt. "How are you a monster? How?"

"It's a curse."

"A curse?" His eyes narrowed; his jaw clenched. The muscle in his neck twitched.

"I guess it's best explained as a family curse…."

"So your family has the same problem?" Mark continued to back away from me toward the cabin door. "When I'd come in here, I'd hoped you'd explain everything, but this is—this is insane."

"Mark, I'm not lying." Tears began welling up in my eyes.

"Who are you, Jeanine?" Mark's voice had risen almost to a shout. It was a shout of complete frustration that I couldn't blame him for. "Who are *you*?"

"I just said I'm a monster, Mark." I clenched my teeth; in some ways, I wanted to show him right then and there what I was. I wanted to pour water on myself. Water….

"That's impossible; you're a human being," Mark said slowly, as if talking to a crazy person. "It's not true. You can't be that hideous beast. You're beautiful."

"Mark, watch this—"

"What are you going to do? How are you going to show me? Did you kill my sister then? Did you leave me crazy? Are you admitting guilt?"

"No! Shut up! Just hear me out!" I screamed, surprised at the anger that spilled over without warning. "I'll show you just how it happens, but I also want to tell you that I know who killed Jessie. I *know* who killed Jessie," I repeated; the words coming from my mouth sounded harsh and unfeeling. Nothing could pull me from the abyss I was slipping into now. "My own grandpa did it," I stated, tears blurring my vision. "He's a monster just like me; except he became one a long time ago, and he let me become one...."

"What are you talking about? I don't understand. How are you a monster? I know I've never seen you well—"

"You know that creature that hopped up on your boat and, well, licked you?"

"But I never told you that it licked me—" Mark's eyes grew huge, and his brows rose. "Oh."

"Water," I said simply. Saying the word caused me to dwell on the idea.

"What do you mean?"

"Have you noticed anything strange about me ever, Mark?" I took a step toward the sink. Only a drop of it was all it took. "I've tried not to show it, but sometimes it was so glaringly obvious that I was sure you'd figured out I was a freak. Remember how I told you my god was water?"

He nodded.

"Well, whenever water touches my skin, I get this rush at first," I said, swallowing hard before continuing. I felt nauseated. "This brilliant experience turns into the most agonizing pain anyone could experience. My body transforms. It changes shape into a monster." I looked to him to make sure he was following all this; his face had become a stone. "I know you won't believe me unless you actually see me transform." My voice cracked. "But you need to understand something: I didn't kill anyone. My grandpa did, and I've only known for a very short time, so it's really not like I've been holding it from you."

"Why did they claim that you'd committed suicide, then?"

Horror began to fill me as the possibility that Mark might not believe me settled in. It was almost like Grandpa had set me up for all of this. Maybe he'd planned from the beginning that all the blame would go to me. "They were ashamed of me, and my grandpa told them to say I'd committed suicide," I said. My mind began to whirl, but I had to keep explaining, convince him of my innocence. "I didn't know Grandpa also had my same curse when this first happened to me. It wasn't until earlier this week, when he visited, that I found out."

I approached the sink and turned on the faucet. "I'm addicted to the water now," I explained, taking a deep breath. "It's part of the curse."

"So let me get this straight," he said, shaking his head with disbelief. "You are a monster when *water* touches you?"

"Yes, but let me warn you, sometimes I forget who I am. I'll try not to, but even if I do forget, I won't hurt you," I said, feeling as if this entire conversation was a very bad dream, and I was over-explaining myself. I'd dreamed of this happening many times before, and each time it ended the same. Mark left me forever, or worse, assumed I'd killed his sister. Finding myself praying that this would not be the case, I placed a hand under the faucet and fought to keep control of myself, but I realized that when I tried to focus on maintaining my human mind, the pain of the transformation grew almost unbearable. Losing my mind while transforming made it feel like I'd slid into a new skin, but this hurt much like the very first time I'd transformed, shifting and tearing in shots of agony down my spine. As my nails extended into claws, I noticed for the first time that blood oozed from the expansion as my skin changed and peeled.

My eyes went to Mark; he watched without words with an expression on his face that I figured it was similar to the face I'd get if I'd hit him with a baseball bat out of the blue.

"Why did you wait so long in letting me know the truth?" he asked, staring at my reptilian scales, tail, and claws.

"I was afraid to tell you that I'm cursed," I said, biting my lip, or what used to be my lip. "I'm sorry, Mark, but would you have told a stranger that you look like *this* when water touches you?"

No more excuses, Jean, an internal voice seemed to say. You've given more than enough to this man….this man that you love.

No, I couldn't love him; I didn't love him….yet. I—I had to see what the outcome of him knowing would be like first.

Stop lying to yourself; you do love him, and that's why it's going to kill you when he leaves in a few minutes, the voice in my head said again.

"We've been more than strangers to one another for a while, Jean." Mark put a hand to the back of his neck. His eyes were glassy.

Words didn't come from my mouth, as if my tongue were stuck to the roof of it.

Without emotion, Mark's eyes left my revolting, monster form. "I have to go." His voice was barely audible. He turned and started for the door, slumped over just a little.

The fact that he'd not attacked me with words of hatred or anger made revealing the monster to him even worse. Everything inside me raged to follow him, to stop him from leaving me here with nothing. No pride, no dreams, no future. When I'd been exiled to live here, I'd thought nothing could exceed that pain; but this — this was a thousand times worse. The sound of the door shutting behind Mark as he left hit like a slap to my face, and upon hearing his car start up, my mind caged me in, clamping around my skull and encasing my thoughts with bulletproof glass. Emotions welled up inside me, so intense they frightened me. My hand had dried off and my normal human appearance took over. Cold, naked, afraid, and broken, I collapsed on the floor of my cabin, sobbing until my sobs turned to screams of agony. No pain could compare to this rejection.

*

A feeling of betrayal and conditional love from Mark haunted my existence, as I continued to live. My world had slipped away from my grasp after he'd left. Nothing made sense to me. Why had this happened? What had I done to deserve all of this crap being dumped on me? I'd planned on Harvard, planned on making a name for myself. Sure, I could make a name for myself now, but it wouldn't be viewed.

I cried myself to sleep the next two nights after Mark left and woke up on those mornings with my eyes stinging and face red. I couldn't go anywhere anymore. There was no will left in me to live. In less than a month now, Grandpa would be back with his promises of freedom through the destruction of my soul. The curse had taken my life away, but it wasn't going to take my soul. It couldn't take *Jeanine* from me. I wondered at that moment if the reason Grandpa could kill was because of what he'd done to control the curse.

A knock on my door sounded, and I rose from the couch. I'd left the setup for Mark's sleeping quarters, instead of setting up the living room furniture again.

"Jeanine," a man's voice said. "It's me, Charlie."

I walked to the door and opened it, knowing that I looked horrible, but I didn't care. "Hey, Charlie."

"Can I come in?" Charlie asked, his eyes taking in my disheveled, sleep-deprived appearance.

"Sure, why not?" I said, stepping back to allow him in. I felt like crying on his shoulder. Even though I sort of disliked him, I wanted to spill my soul to someone.

"What's going on?" Charlie's voice was filled with concern.

"I'm not sure," I said, trying to hold myself on my feet.

"What did he do?" Charlie's blue eyes had traveled to the sleeping bag on the floor.

"Who?"

"Mark, the idiot."

"Charlie, please don't call him that," I pleaded, taking a deep breath.

"Why not? He's a complete dick to leave you like this." Charlie put an arm on my shoulder. "Jeanine, I'll take his balls off if you want me to."

"Please, Charlie, I just want him to be okay." Rubbing my upper arms, I plopped down on my couch.

"How can you want him to be okay, Jeanine? He broke your heart!" Charlie threw his arms in the air and plopped down next to me. "This is the reason I'm not friends with him anymore; he's a complete hypocrite. He claims all this stuff about God and then—if you ask me, God doesn't want us leaving people like this when they're down."

"Charlie, please." My eyes pleaded with him not say anything more about Mark. I felt tears start to pool in my eyes. I wanted to be alone. I couldn't stand other humans smiling and trying to cheer up my breathing corpse.

"You're going to be okay. There are plenty of other guys who would love to be with you, even if they knew about the curse."

"But Mark was so untouched by the darkness of the world."

"Untouched? His family thought him crazy, his sister thought him crazy, and I—I secretly always thought he was the one that really killed Jessie, not your grandpa."

"That couldn't be true," I murmured.

Grandpa had killed Greg and…. A shot of fear injected itself into me. Grandpa had killed Greg because Greg had known about the curse! He'd killed Jessie because she'd known, too! He would kill Mark because I had just let him know. But would Grandpa ever figure out that Mark knew? I wouldn't tell him. And I'm almost sure Mark would keep his lips sealed. So I didn't have to worry, did I? After all, Mark had left me. He had left me. That alone was enough to prove that he had not murdered his sister. There was something strange about Mark, but it wasn't that he was a murderer, just that he felt as if no one believed him and was out to prove it. It had been his obsession. I loved him. It was true. But now I had to admit that sometimes love isn't enough when it's one-sided. Sadly, I was the side that had loved.

"Jeanine, you need to think for yourself; you can't let anyone tell you what to do anymore," Charlie said, rising from the couch. "I came by here because I saw Mark. He seemed upset about something, and I asked him what was going on."

"Huh?"

"We were at church."

"And what did he say?"

"He said that you turned out to be someone different from who he first thought you were." After searching Charlie's eyes, I knew he was telling the truth.

"But what do I do now? I'd committed myself to finding out who murdered Jessie and to helping and being with Mark." The tears spilled over, trickling down my cheeks.

"Your grandpa called me."

My gaze shot to Charlie again. "Why?"

"He said to keep an eye on you. He told me that you might be upset enough to do something rash."

"How would he know about Mark and me?"

"I told him."

"Oh, how nice," I said, clenching my teeth. "I know for a fact that my grandpa is a murderer, Charlie, so you can put any weird thoughts about Mark out of your head. Why did you tell him about Mark and my affairs?"

"He threatened me!" Charlie's eyes were filled with regret at this point. I could tell he was ready to defend himself to the end, even if he was mad at himself for telling my grandpa something that could get someone else killed. "I know what Jessie looked like after he got to her, and I don't want that to be me."

An image of Jessie from the pictures in her room floated through my mind; I pictured her torn up to pieces, blood covering her broken, decapitated body. Mark had said they'd found her arm in the lake. I shivered.

"Charlie."

"Yeah?"

"Please, promise me something." I swallowed and took his hand in my own. Part of me wanted to bash him across the head, and the other part of me wanted to not let him leave, because Grandpa was right. I knew now that Grandpa knew about Mark discovering I was a monster. I was sure my worst fears would come alive, and there was nothing I could do about it.

"Okay," said Charlie.

"Stay away from my grandpa; you'll be safer," I said.

Charlie nodded. "I will. Can we prove that he murdered those people?"

I shrugged. "Maybe; maybe not. No one would believe us if we said he turns into a monster. He's got a way to control it."

"You're right, and none of the deaths were knife injuries or gunshot wounds, so it looks like it either had to be a man with his bare hands or a large animal, and that's not your grandpa in his old man form."

"It's hopeless, isn't it?"

"Yeah."

I had come to three conclusions though: Mark hated me, I would never be rid of the curse, and the anger burning inside of me was enough to kill my grandpa if I ever saw him again. All these truths terrified me. A rumble of thunder shook the cabin, and I knew an impending rain was on the way. Could I take another rainstorm?

Beep. Beep.

Oh yeah, the message on my phone from my grandpa that I hadn't heard yet.

"Charlie, I'd like to be alone now," I said, holding the phone to my ear.

He smiled at me. "Whatever you want, Jeanine. Remember, I'm always at the next cabin over."

"Okay," I said, but as he began walking away, I followed him and touched his shoulder. "Charlie, do you know why Grandpa killed Jessie? It seems that you knew him better than me."

"I think she saw him as a monster too many times."

"But she wasn't able to prove anything. Why did he kill her?"

"Secretly, I always thought he had sort of a crush on her. But he's an older guy, and she was a teenage girl. Do you have a grandma, Jeanine?"

I blinked once, searching my mind for a memory of a Grandma Stafford to mention. I'd been told that she had died before I'd been born. My dad had never spoken of her, and neither had Grandpa. "I have no idea who she was. Nobody talks about her." For the first time, this struck me. I'd had a Grandpa Stafford for so long that I had never thought of Grandma. "His curse should have ended if he found truest love with her," I murmured, feeling again the tears coming on, but I willed them to stop. There would be no more crying, no more tears. If truest love didn't break the curse then I'd be stuck as a monster forever. Unless, what Grandpa said…. No!

Charlie shrugged, "Personally, I think he killed her himself."

"I can't—yes, I can believe that now." I sighed. Evils that my grandpa had committed knew no bounds anymore. "Thanks for being honest with me, Charlie."

He smiled at me, and for a moment I thought he looked better than average. But Mark's face appeared in my mind at that moment, his haunting eyes staring into my soul as he saw me as a monster.

I turned from Charlie and heard him shut the door of the cabin behind him. A single raindrop fell on the roof of the cabin, but I heard it loud and clear. Pressing the listen-to-messages button on my cell phone, I sat on one of my kitchen chairs.

"Jean, it's me, your grandpa. I don't know why you're not answering your phone. I heard that you were going to that dance, and you should have a connection—"

How had he known?

Drop. Drip.

"I'm just checking to see if you got your Internet yet, and also—"

Drip. Drip. Drip.

"I have to tell you that I might not be back for a while….plans have changed…."

Yes, stay away, I thought.

"I have some unfinished business up there that I still need to attend to." His voice was beginning to fade as the water became louder. A loud hush, as the rain began to pour, overcame me.

"And as you must know already, I *was* cursed just like you. I figure that, since you know, we now can work together. Maybe you could reconsider my offer—"

No, Grandpa, there will be no reconsidering of that offer.

Water.

Rain pattered on the window panes of my cabin. Most would find it soothing, but my breath stuck in my throat as I glared at the tantalizing droplets on the glass. Each glittering splotch tempted me. "We want you," they seemed to call, "and you *know* you want us."

As I gripped the arms of my chair, I pondered my life up to this point and why I wanted to experience the liquid running down my skin.

Hush. Drop. Drip.

The sound of the rain reminded me of seductive whispering, and I longed to close my other senses as well as I could close my eyes. I was cursed.

Splash.

The sound of a disturbance on the lake took away all reflections — I wanted it now! Water. The feeling of it against my skin, so cold and smooth. I lunged out the door, and my heart fluttered with excitement as the rain soaked through my clothes. The taste, smell, and touch of it melded together in a delicious combination of the senses. I stripped my shirt and jeans off and dove into the lake. Water embraced every inch of me, bubbling underneath, tickling my stomach, legs, and tail. Regret set in as I bobbed above the depths of the lake, and I realized what I'd done. The blood in my face grew hot, and I clenched my fists under the light waves. I knew I'd never be returning to shore again. As my mind began to slip away with the pouring rain, I realized that maybe it wasn't so bad not remembering.

27

- 3 months later -

Breaking surface and half leaping out of the water, I took a gasp of autumn-chilled, sweet air. After coming down, the water lapped against the tip of my chin and splashed into my mouth. I was at home here in Teal Lake. Paddling my webbed feet hard, I propelled myself under the water again so nobody would see me.

Once, I'd been human. My short human life was a mist of the past. The only thing that stung my memories now was that the man I'd thought I'd loved had rejected me, and I would be cursed forever to live this life of nothingness under the surface of this secluded lake.

The familiar humming noise of a slow boat, a pontoon boat, irritated my sensitive ears. I growled at the noise under my breath. A disturbance in the water to the right of me indicated it was time for lunch or dinner. I snapped the fish up in my claws and ripped it open. It still jerked about in my mouth as I crunched its bones in my sharp teeth. Something about this fish was different from other fish, though — I was being tugged in the water by an invisible force after biting it! There was extreme pressure on my upper palate, and it hurt. With a roar, I followed whatever was pulling me to the surface and leapt into the air next to a parked pontoon boat. Whatever it was that was causing this pain in the roof of my mouth, I wanted to be rid of it. The pain increased, and I winced, grasping at my mouth, trying to figure out what was going on.

"Holy Mother of—I think I just caught the biggest fish in Teal Lake!" I heard a human voice exclaim, and I wondered if he was alone.

The blood in my veins pumped with anger at the object that

was embedded in my mouth. I snapped, hissed, and leapt out of the water.

"What the hell was that!" the human being shouted. I barely understood the words.

After much struggling, I got the object out of the roof of my mouth, but my palette still stung and tasted of blood. Releasing bubbles from my nostrils, I swam deeper until I reached the bottom of the lake where the silt and clay didn't blur my vision. I nursed the wound in my mouth. My tongue sensed the tangy taste of blood. I had to keep telling myself that I really did like it here, that I wanted to live in this quiet, lonely place. Somewhere in the back of my fuzzy monster head, there was a tiny piece of the human, longing to not be alone, and I had been forcing it away a little bit every day.

Swish.

Something swam past me. Narrowing my eyes, I followed the current and stirred-up silt the thing left behind. Was it a large fish? No, it had been much too big to be a fish. A dark object appeared in front of me. Two red eyes stared back at me from the murkiness that surrounded us. This creature was similar to me, but it was older and male. A human's name formed in my head: Grandpa. I didn't say it aloud. So this was what had killed my love's sister? These were the eyes Jessie had stared into during her last moments? The tiny bit of human mind fought to return to me, but I forced it away. I'd have to think about my problems if it came back, dwell on how the disease of fear and shame that afflicted me every day was because of some stupid mistake I'd made in my basement. The creature studied me, and a wide grin spread across its hideous face.

"I've found you, Jean," Grandpa said, speaking to me through the water. Bubbles rose from his mouth when he spoke.

I didn't say anything. Couldn't.

"Look at you; you are so pathetic. Join me, Jean; you will be able to maintain two lives. Look at how strong and beautiful you are right now. Do you want to give this up? Do you want to give up being human and special at the same time?"

"I don't think you've learned how to control the curse. It controls you," I found myself saying the words and not understanding them at the same time.

"Very well. I will just force you to see reason." Grandpa darted away, and I watched him disappear as fast as he'd come. Whatever. I didn't want to leave this life of nothingness. I knew what was going on above the surface, and I wanted nothing to do with it. Sinking again to the bottom of the lake, I gave myself back to my monster mind.

The hollow sound of a loud, agonizing howl occurred above the surface; something horrible was happening to someone. Darting in the direction of the noise, I found that I recognized the voice that came after the howl.

"I don't know where she is! No one has seen her in months!" I couldn't place a face to the voice, but I knew it all the same.

A loud roar from a creature echoed. I could decode from the tone that it meant to kill.

"No, Fred! I just want to be like you. I swear I didn't tell a soul!"

I rose with just my eyes above the surface and noticed that a young-looking, human man stood facing Grandpa.

Grandpa lunged at the small human that he towered over, swiping his claws into the other man and cracking his arm in half with one blow.

Screams of agony hit my sensitive ears. Diving under once again, I torpedoed myself in the direction of the fight. The smell of blood brought me in to observe it.

"Where is the other one?" the deep monster words boomed under the water.

"Mark? He lives next door to you? Don't you remember? You murdered his sister after all."

Mark…. No, I didn't want to think about Mark. I didn't want to remember him. But Mark—my entire body awakened with remembering and wanting.

"Is he there right now?"

"No, no….he's out….looking for her." The human was hurt bad. He spoke as if his insides were spilling out.

"I'm going to put you in this lake to drown now, just like I did to the little thing," Grandpa growled. Whatever the human had done had displeased him.

"Don't, please!" the voice pleaded through the pain.

Falling rain began tapping against the surface of the water above me. I wasn't able to hear the conversation going on anymore. The sound and wave effect of something large falling into the water rippled against me. Grandpa had dumped the human in the water right in front of me. Unable to see through the water because the splash had stirred up the silt on the bottom, I felt around and grasped hold of the human. It struggled against me, but I realized that one of its arms and both legs were broken or missing. Nausea flickered in the pit of my stomach. Grandpa had done his work. After all, he'd killed others before.

Dragging the struggling, bleeding form out of the water, I set it on the bank. It stopped struggling the second it saw me. "Jeanine?" The human's blue eyes were wide. "You—you've come back." He began coughing, and I touched his face.

"Who are you?" I asked. "Why was my grandpa angry with you?"

"Don't you recognize me? I'm Charlie." He put his one good arm on my shoulder. "See, look at my face. Who am I? I was the last person who ever talked to you."

Charlie….Charlie! I knew his face, knew his smell, and knew his voice.

223

Don't remember. Don't remember.

But I had to! I couldn't forget the world when someone I cared about was dying. "Charlie, you need help," I said. My eyes widened as I became conscious of his bleeding, knowing that his life source was seeping out as he tried to bring me out of my insanity.

"I'm going to die, Jeanine," Charlie said, with a hint of remorse in his tone.

"Why did Grandpa do this to you?"

"Because he thinks I've been telling people about the monster curse. He thinks Mark will do the same. You need to save Mark, Jeanine. It's too late for me." Even though Charlie's words were choked, he had determination. Signs of oncoming death filled his eyes. "I've always been too late."

"What do you mean?"

"I fell in love with you, Jeanine." Charlie grasped my hand with his good limb. Dark red liquid seeped from the corners of his mouth. He coughed again. "Mark loves you, Jeanine. I-I lied to you the last day I saw you. I thought that maybe i-if I told you Mark was upset, you'd fall into my arms. I'm sorry."

Mark hadn't been angry with me? That fact hit me like a slap across the face. If he wasn't angry with me, then why had I ever jumped in this stupid lake? Charlie had lied to me....but I couldn't blame him. Maybe I had wanted to think that Mark had left me because he had hated me, because I myself couldn't believe someone could love someone cursed to be a monster. "Charlie." I held his hand up to my lips and kissed it. "Thank you for telling me."

"Please, please tell my family that I love them when you see them."

"I can't let go of the past. I can't escape this, Charlie; I'm stuck."

"Jeanine, the reason you jumped in this lake and forgot

everything is because you gave up. Don't give up anymore. Please, save Mark." Charlie became urgent and he pushed me away. "Save Mark! For God's sake, go!"

I backed away from Charlie's fallen, mangled form. Memories began tumbling back into the thick, scaly head that had tried to keep any recollection of land-dwelling days out. In my mind, an image of Grandpa as a monster flared up. An image of him attacking Charlie appeared without my assent: defenseless Charlie, who had only wanted to be extraordinary, who had wanted a chance at being with me; he had thought me beautiful even as a monster.

Clenching my fists, I let out an earth-shattering screech. I hoped everyone in the state of Wisconsin heard me. I hoped everyone in the United States of America heard it. Most of all, I hoped that Grandpa had heard it. Trembling, I brought myself to stand on two legs for the first time in months and screeched again.

Tearing at my insides were a million voices. I dropped back to my knees next to him and let my voice become soft. "I'm sorry, Charlie." My eyes watered, and I wiped the tears away with my hand. "I wish I could have stopped this from happening."

"Don't blame yourself; it's my fault. But you can prevent this from happening to Mark," Charlie urged, although his words were barely audible. The rain drenched us and washed most of the blood from his face.

"But I don't know where he is."

"He's probably out by one of those islands looking for you." Charlie squeezed my hand.

A cold air prickled against me; its chill went right through my scales.

"There is nothing you can do for me, Jeanine," Charlie said when he saw the look in my eyes. I stared down at his pitiful situation, willing him to tell me he would live. "Please, go to Mark." His teeth were clenched now.

"I will. Goodbye, Charlie."

"Goodbye, Jeanine. I pray that you reach him in time. You are perfect for each other." Charlie closed his eyes, a look of regret on his face.

Going against all instinct to stay with Charlie until his last breath, I turned from him and ran for the lake.

28

Hoping my grandpa somehow didn't figure out where Mark was before me, I swam like a bullet through the water of Teal Lake. I was familiar with every rock on its bottom. My memories from the months of living, eating, and sleeping here were clearer than I'd ever experienced. When I was almost to the north islands, I felt my heart rate rising, not only because I was afraid for Mark, but I also was afraid for myself. How would it feel to see him again? I had left him and given up on life, and I'd thought the worst of him.

Rising to the surface upon arriving at the island, I scanned the area for a parked pontoon boat. Relieved when I saw the familiar white boat, I crawled through the muddy shallows toward the island. Covered in the icky mud, I shook the pieces off before rising to stand upright. The rain continued to fall without ceasing for a moment. It washed the rest of the grime off me. In my monster form, I stood a chance against Grandpa, and that thought kept me from despairing.

Twitching my nostrils, I caught the familiar smell of Mark's cologne. He couldn't be far away. On all fours, I zipped in the direction of his scent. My sensitive ears detected nearby footsteps and a man breathing. Finally, I saw him: He wore jeans, a rain-soaked T-shirt that hugged the muscles and scars on his back, and his black hair was slicked back against his scalp. He knelt on the ground as if studying something.

"Mark," I said.

He wiped his brow. He was searching for me out in this cold rain because he loved me. "Oh, Mark," I said louder, near tears again. Emotions that I'd deprived myself of during my time in the lake welled up inside me.

Mark froze and then turned until he faced me, his wonderful

blue eyes wide.

It hit me that I was wasting time by just staring at him; both of us might have only minutes to live. "We have to get out of here."

"Jean," Mark said, taking a step closer to me. He blinked, and his eyes were glassy. "Jean, you're alive."

"We have to leave now," I said, feeling unworthy of his love. I couldn't bear to even bring myself closer to him.

He was running toward me. He took me in his arms and pressed his lips hard against my *monster* mouth as if he couldn't see the pointy teeth or scales.

I must be dead. He's kissing me while I'm a monster, I thought. Warmth enveloped me, and I felt safer than I'd ever been before.

Mark drew back, looking into my eyes without flinching. "I'm sorry about everything."

He was sorry? What did he have to be sorry about? I'd been the one who'd left him without a hope and thought the worst of him. When he leaned in to kiss me again, I remembered why I'd come, and that doused my sense of safety like an icy bucket of water. I pushed him back.

"Mark, you're in danger!" I exclaimed. "You need to get out of here now!"

"Why?"

"My grandpa wants to kill you." I closed my eyes and kissed him again; I couldn't help it. I'd forgotten how wonderful the taste of his mouth and the feel of his lips were. My entire body was alive with a frightening desire, and I found every part of me longed to embrace him. "Let's go," I told him, breaking myself free from our embrace but still gripping his hand in my own, unable to let go.

Mark looked dazed. I couldn't blame him; I felt dizzy.

A roar shook the island trees. Grandpa had found us.

"He's here?" Mark's dazed expression left.

"Yes," I said. "He's going to kill you. I heard him say so."

"We need to bring your grandpa to justice, Jeanine. I know he's your grandpa and all, but—"

"I agree with you," I interrupted. "I know that he's my grandpa, but he's no longer a human being." We began jogging together toward the pontoon boat.

"Where have you been?" Mark asked.

"In the lake."

"That's what Charlie said….he said that you didn't want to see me again."

"Yeah, he would." I tried not to choke. "He told me to look for you. He's dead now, probably. Grandpa killed him the same way he did Jessie, and he'll do the same to you if we don't figure out something quick."

"What does he want?"

"He knows that you know about us, about the monster curse."

Mark's eyes widened. "I haven't told anyone since learning that you were, um, cursed."

When I looked at Mark, something behind him caught my eye, and then a dark monstrous thing stood next to him without warning. Its claws wrapped around his neck.

"No!" I screamed.

The creature jumped as if surprised, and its gaze traveled to me. "Jeanine?" a deep voice rumbled. "What are you doing here?"

"I saw you kill Charlie, Grandpa," I said, a chill rushing through my being. "Please, stop!"

"What are you talking about?" Grandpa threw Mark to the ground. "This boy, this sniveling rat, has told the entire lake about your existence!" He gazed at Mark, hissing.

"No, he didn't, Grandpa. No one knows!"

"No, he did. Mark, go ahead and tell Jeanine about the recent tourists who flock here because of this poor, innocent girl and a picture you took. They hunt you, Jeanine, because of *him*!"

I searched Mark's face. What was Grandpa talking about?

"Jeanine, I never told anyone anything. He's lying!" Mark stood strong, although his shoulders bled from Grandpa's savage throw.

"He wanted revenge, Jeanine, for the scars I put on him," Grandpa growled, bringing himself next to me and putting his arm around my shoulder. He hugged me close. His tail flicked as a cat's would.

"You know me, Jean. You know that's not true!" Mark exclaimed.

"Look at him, Jean; he's been looking for you not because he loves you, but because he's been trying to hunt you down. He knows one of our kind killed his sister," Grandpa whispered in my ear.

"I can't believe that, Grandpa," I said, shaking my head, pulling away from him and backing toward Mark.

"I'm your grandpa!" Grandpa narrowed his serpent-like eyes. "How can you not trust me?"

"You're a liar! I saw you kill someone minutes ago; I can never believe anything you say again."

"If that's how you want it to be," Grandpa growled, rushing at me with such force that as his body collided with mine, all the air was knocked from me. His horrid scaled face leered at me. Like a viper, he bit into the flesh of my neck, sending shots of pain through me.

My breath returned to me, and I shrieked in his sensitive ears, jolting his head away from my neck. "You'll have to kill me if you want to kill Mark."

"All right then," Grandpa said, grinning. "I'm stronger than you; just give up and join me."

"Never," I said. I freed my tail from his grasp, swung it around, and whacked it against Grandpa's back like a whip.

With a roar, he again bit into my neck, but I dug my claws in his face before he could get a good hold. "Get off!" I screeched. His heavy body pressed against mine with suffocating weight, but using all my strength, my long, webbed feet kicked him off just enough that I could roll out from under him and dart away.

"I'm impressed, Jean; you're fast," Grandpa said with a laugh. He brushed himself off. "But this is like a lion against a mouse; you won't win. I've spent years perfecting the best way to kill."

"But you've never fought against one of our kind," I taunted, crouching low. Noticing Mark in the corner of my eye making a run for the pontoon boat, I decided to buy him time and lunged at Grandpa. My claws extended outward and dug hard into his sides. This blow was met by Grandpa ripping himself free. His claws dug into my shoulders, and the world blackened for a moment as my head was knocked against a tree. He had me pinned.

Whack! Smack! Whack!

His claws swiped and hit my hard, scaly skin with a force I hadn't expected from him. Pain shot through my entire being as my body was battered again and again by his sharp claws. I shrieked and fought back, my own smaller claws causing less damage but still injuring him.

"You're pathetic," Grandpa sneered, pinning my arms against the tree so I couldn't scratch him anymore. "You're like a pesky mosquito. Just give up and help me eliminate these rumors."

Biting my lip, I kicked against his lower torso and then

dragged my sharp nails across it. I could feel flesh peeling back under my toes. I'd done damage that mattered.

Grandpa gave a groan, which turned to a growl. He grasped me by the neck and slammed me against a tree again, knocking the wind out of me.

Hardly able to breathe and unable to move, the adrenaline rush I'd been on began to fade, and the pain that I hadn't felt before became more than apparent; it tore through me worse than any transformation I'd suffered because I knew my body had begun to give up in this fight. Blow after blow from Grandpa's claws hit. I felt my life disappearing in a cloud, and I couldn't fight back.

A loud noise went off, nearly deafening me. Grandpa let go of me so that I dropped to the ground in a broken mess. He backed away with a look of wonder on his gruesome, frightening face. Another loud noise went off, and I realized that what I'd heard had been a gun.

Something began oozing from dark holes in Grandpa's scales. It was then I realized he'd been shot. Collapsing to the ground, he stared at me, his eyes huge.

My broken body began shaking. My breath returned to me. Crawling toward where Grandpa lay, I grasped his clawed hand as his eyes rolled back. "Grandpa," I murmured. He didn't return to human form; instead, he remained in his ugly monster form forever, never to return to humanity.

I had no idea who had saved me, nor did I know why I shivered. All I knew was that Mark wasn't dead and wasn't going to be murdered by Grandpa. The brutal killings had ended. Moving a hand to my face, I realized that the skin was different. Pale pink, covered in droplets of rain, which trickled down its smooth surface, it was a skin that I'd once known in another life: beautiful, soft, wet, human skin.

"Jean!" A familiar voice called my name. "Jean!" I heard the sound of footsteps crunching and squishing dead leaves. Shivering, my body felt completely spent, as if I'd just run for miles without stopping.

"You saved me," I choked to owner of the voice. It was Mark.

"Please, we need to get you to a doctor." Mark was next to me, and he lifted me in his arms.

"I'm human," I said.

"Shh, hold on," Mark said, stroking my hair away from my face. "You're going to be fine."

The rain had slowed to a drizzle, but it did not call to me as it had in the past. "You saved me."

"I shot the monster because I was afraid it would kill you." Mark's eyes were watering.

Shaking my head, I put a human hand against his cheek. "No, I mean, you. You saved me...." My voice trailed off.

Mark's face became puzzled. "Huh?"

Although pains and aches clung to almost every part of my body, I knew I would never again become a monster. I was filled with a happiness that blurred out the hurt. I was free. I'd die free.

"Only truest love shall unbind, this curse to which thee shall be tied," I mustered out those words as my surroundings faded into a black mist.

29

A stark-white world greeted me as my eyes fluttered open. Perhaps I was in heaven. But no, heaven wouldn't have the sterile smell of a hospital room. Gross.

"She's awake!" a happy young girl's voice exclaimed. "Mom, Dad, she opened her eyes!"

A girl's face loomed over my own, and it had to be Corrine's. An older Corrine than I remembered, but she had the same golden curls and round little face.

"Jeanine!" Dad grasped my hand. It was the most sincere gesture I'd ever experienced from him.

"Oh, thank God!" I heard Mom say from behind him.

"Mark," I said. I was unable to think of anyone else. "Mark?"

"Who is Mark?" Corrine asked.

"You mean the boy who called us?" Mom asked. Her hair wasn't up in a bun as I'd remembered, and she put an arm around Dad. What had caused this change?

"Why are you so—" I almost asked the question but couldn't, so instead I asked the other that remained on my mind. "Where is Mark?"

"He's at his home." Mom came forward and put a hand on my face. "How are you feeling?"

I shifted in the bed. My head spun, and the bed seemed to move in waves like the ocean. "I don't know….I feel dizzy and numb."

"It's the pain killers they have you on, baby," Dad assured.

"Grandpa's gone missing, Jeanine!" Corrine exclaimed. "They can't find him."

I closed my eyes. Would it ever be right to tell them that I'd assisted in his death or that he'd almost brought about mine? No. Maybe it was best that they didn't know….ever. "What do you mean?" I decided to play dumb.

"He went to the cabin to go see you," Mom explained, "and he never came back."

"That's horrible!" I tried to look worried but realized I couldn't; acting is impossible when you're drugged.

"It's okay. I'm sure they'll find him." Dad hadn't caught the fake surprise in my voice.

Grandpa had been a lie; a stupid part of me mourned him, but it was more like the past idea of him. "People get lost in the woods all the time. Who knows? That place is pretty remote." I shrugged. Mark's face appeared in my mind. "When will I see Mark again?" I asked myself more than them.

"Don't worry, I'm sure you'll see him again. He said he was coming to visit you after he took care of some business. We told him that we'd reward him for what he did, but he refused," Mom said.

"What did he do?" I asked, blinking.

"He saved you from the bear that attacked you, shot at it before it ran away." Mom patted my hand.

"A bear?"

Mom shot a worried look to Dad. "She doesn't remember," Mom whispered.

"The doctor said she'd hit her head." Dad took Mom's hand. What was with my parents acting so happy around each other? What had changed them? "Don't worry, dear, everything will go back to normal. You can even go to Harvard this coming semester. We've called the board and…."

Normal. The word resonated in my mind, so I couldn't process whatever Dad said after it. My mind traveled back to the day that I stood in my bathroom screaming at the mirror about how much I hated myself.

"I'm not normal," I said.

Dad stopped talking about Harvard and furrowed his brow. "What?"

"I'm not normal anymore, Mom and Dad. I'll never go back to being who I was before I'd been cursed."

"What do you mean?" Mom asked.

"You sent me away because I wasn't normal, but I'm still not normal."

"Jeanine, what are you talking about? We sent you to Wisconsin to protect you." Dad laughed, took a glass of water from the hospital tray, and sprinkled some on my skin. Nothing happened. "See? The curse is broken!" Dad smiled.

It was useless. They would never understand, even if I tried to explain.

*

Snowflakes whirled in the northern Wisconsin air as I stepped outside of my truck and walked up to Mark's front door. Knocking on the door once, I waited, wondering what it would be like to meet his parents. A dark-haired woman opened the door for me. She gave me a big smile. "So, you're the famous Jeanine Stafford."

"Yeah, that's me," I said, putting out a hand.

"It's great to finally meet you." The woman took my hand and shook it. "I'm Amelia Calvin. You can call me Amelia." She motioned for me to follow her inside the house. The sound of drums beating and guitar music playing blared in my ears. "I'd say make yourself at home, but I learned from Mark that you both lived here at one time."

"Did Mark tell you the whole story?" I asked as my face heated.

"Of course he did, Jeanine, but don't worry, the secret is safe with us. I must tell you, though, it was a little relieving to know that my son hadn't gone insane," Amelia said. She called up the stairs, "Mark, Jeanine is here!"

The music stopped, and I held my breath as I heard his footsteps on the stairs. I felt self-conscious about the bruises that covered my face, the blackened right eye, and the stitches above my right eyebrow. Mark appeared in the hallway and rushed to me, scooped me up in his arms, and gave me a long kiss.

"I'll leave you two alone," Amelia said, giving us a smile. Already I liked Mark's mom.

"I've missed seeing your beautiful face," Mark said, smiling at me. "How are you feeling?"

"I was feeling better until you crushed me in your arms," I muttered, trying to remain serious and contain the giggle that wanted to emerge from my throat.

"Oh, I forgot. Sorry." Mark gave me a sheepish grin. "I hope any damage I've done isn't permanent."

"I don't know. I might never recover now." Our eyes connected, and I flung myself again into his arms and kissed him. "You can crush me all you want," I whispered in his ear.

"Let's go for a walk," Mark said, pulling his coat from the closet. "Come on."

*

"How is Charlie's family doing?" I asked. The question had been on my mind since getting out of the hospital.

"They're recovering; he's getting out of intensive care, last I heard."

"What?" I stopped mid-step and whirled to face Mark; my throat tightened.

"You didn't know?" Mark blinked.

"He's alive?" My eyes widened. "How is that possible?"

"They found him after you left; he'll never be able to walk again." Mark put an arm around me when he realized that I was crying. "Are you okay?"

"I thought he was dead." I sniffed. "Poor Charlie."

Mark smiled at me. "You're such a sweetheart. Do you realize how much I love you, Jean?"

"I love you, too," I said between tears and gave him a quick peck on the cheek. "I'm afraid that this all will go away, and I'll be cursed again."

"Don't you dare think that way," Mark said, flicking my hair away from my face. "This snow is made of water, right? Well, I don't see you sprouting a tail or scales."

"You're right," I said. We continued walking until we reached the lake.

Mark skipped a rock across its surface. "I've been meaning to tell you something. I'm sort of famous now because of you."

"What do you mean?" I blinked.

"My songwriting has taken off; I have bands playing my music now."

"How is this because of me?" Giggling, I threw a rock after his. It didn't skip and plunked to the bottom of the lake.

"Most of the songs are about falling in love with a monster." Mark threw another rock, and it again skimmed across the surface three times before dropping.

My face grew warm. "Falling in love with a monster?" I blinked, then shoved him. "You're sick, you know that?"

"Thanks." He dropped the rock he had been about to throw and wrapped his arms around my waist. "I *did* fall in love with a monster."

"So glad that phase is over," I said, loving how it felt to be so close to him without any secrets and without feeling like a part of me belonged to something else. My eyes traveled to the waves washing up against the shore.

"How is your family?" Mark asked.

"They're fine; don't think I'm ever going to tell them the truth about Grandpa, though."

"Are you going to school next spring?"

"I might. I'm still trying to figure everything out. I'm not into history anymore, though." I cast my face downward.

"Whatever you decide to do for a career, just make sure you're passionate about it." Mark rubbed my back, relaxing my nerves.

I turned in his arms to gaze up at his beautiful eyes. "Well, I do know one thing I'm passionate about."

"I'm not going anywhere," Mark said, bending to kiss me.

The snow changed into rain, and splotches of it hit the bare skin on our faces as we continued to kiss, but I didn't care. After all, a little water never hurt anyone.

ABOUT CHRISTINA J. REYENGA

Christina enjoys writing on paranormal and fantasy romance novels, creating artwork, and enjoying her growing family (now including a baby and a standard poodle). Christina lives with her husband near Chicago, Illinois.

Facebook
http://www.facebook.com/christina.reyenga

Twitter
https://twitter.com/#!/search/realtime/cjreyenga

Author Website
http://www.reyenga.net